Cloning
Galinda

Cloning
Galinda

A Novel

JAN SMOLDERS

CLONING GALINDA
A NOVEL

iUniverse books may be ordered through booksellers or by contacting:

iUniverse
1663 Liberty Drive
Bloomington, IN 47403
www.iuniverse.com
1-800-Authors (1-800-288-4677)

Because of the dynamic nature of the Internet, any web addresses or links contained in this book may have changed since publication and may no longer be valid. The views expressed in this work are solely those of the author and do not necessarily reflect the views of the publisher, and the publisher hereby disclaims any responsibility for them.

Any people depicted in stock imagery provided by Thinkstock are models, and such images are being used for illustrative purposes only. Certain stock imagery © Thinkstock.

ISBN: 978-1-5320-2194-7 (sc)
ISBN: 978-1-5320-2195-4 (e)

Library of Congress Control Number: 2017907714

Print information available on the last page.

iUniverse rev. date: 05/15/2017

Acknowledgements

For their contribution to this manuscript, I express my gratitude to my spouse, Lut; my daughter, Helena, and her husband, Peter Fellows; my sons, Willem and Tom; Krista Hill of L. Talbott Editorial, Matt Schwartz and Jeff Stewart.

Chapter

7:30 p.m.
Friday, February 17, 2012
The City of Noredge, Ohio

"**I** don't buy it," Mary Jenkins muttered quietly to Joe, her hand covering her right cheek. She had been standing with him at a community meeting for the last twenty minutes, nervously shifting her weight back and forth. Arms firmly crossed, lips pursed, she listened and frowned. "Those suits are too smooth— feel too superior—the mayor and the ministers already in their pockets."

"*Shh!*" Joe whispered, hands behind back, chest protruding, a hint of a kind smile.

"Not on my land! Jenkins land. Over my dead body."

He sighed audibly. "Quiet." He threw quick glances left and right.

Mary nodded.

The "suits" were three officials of the Doornaert Oil

and Gas Company headquartered in nearby Canton, Ohio. One had said he was a lawyer, and his two companions spoke polished marketing and vague public relations lingo. It had rubbed Mary the wrong way from the moment they'd uttered their first words.

This was serious business, a community matter, the issue of bringing fracking, hydraulic fracturing, to the fourteen thousand citizens of Noredge. The elderly, bald Mayor Sanders, all of his two hundred pounds on his short-ish frame, had opened the meeting. "Community Outreach," the announcement had said.

Mary knew a thing or two about fracking. Amidst kids' soccer games and homework, the kitchen, house cleaning and her fifth-grade teaching job at the Deep Creek Public School on Main Street she had read up for more than a year on the good and bad of the oil and gas industry's recent technology. She knew the history of a good number of fracking wells in Ohio—and that more than one hundred of them were being drilled every day in the USA.

In her mid-thirties, divorced for five years, Mary lived with her boys Andy and Jimmy, ages nine and six, and her "refrigerator" boyfriend, Joe. She and Joe had been together for eighteen months. He worked for Doornaert, employed there since 2009. When she first met Joe Bertolo she had fallen head over heels in love with the uncomplicated, former high school linebacker. His straightforward talk, his voice, his rugged looks, his folksy humor—she adored all of it. But she had raised her eyebrows when he explained that he hauled "dirty water" from Doornaert wells in the region to special injection wells near Youngstown. Every day, with his huge tanker trailer. He was specialized in this work, which was, he said, much more complicated and important than he described it. He argued with conviction that he was involved in a business—fracking—that did a lot of good, but also had some problems. "Me, I don't do any harm. I clean up. I help Doornaert be a good citizen. The company has a good reputation." His face had radiated pride and Mary was shocked when he went on to reveal his weekly pay was fifteen hundred dollars.

The Doornaert marketing man stood at the end of the oval table, its fifteen seats filled by elderly folks and persons of authority; he looked too refined and sounded too cocky for Mary's taste. But his story apparently impressed the standing crowd of about sixty that had filled to capacity the Noredge Chamber of Commerce's conference room.

The place was spartanly decorated, with just a black and white historic picture of downtown, a framed photo of the then youthful mayor and one wide, aging bookcase sporting, besides books, a flat TV screen and piles of magazines. The heating was overdoing it. The coffee- and teapots on the table had their screw stoppers removed, signaling to the empty cups spread out over the table that they were all done for the day.

The company's pitch, complete with a flashy, six-minute video and patriotic music, had seemed overwhelming for many of the folks in the room. Noredge would take "the Great Leap Forward." The Doornaert folks hadn't credited Mao Tse-tung. *Shock and awe,* Mary thought, a little disdain slipping in.

"Utica!" the Doornaert man shouted, hands up high. "Let that Utica shale under your land work for you! Make Noredge rich!"

"That shale, the 'source rock,' sits a few thousand feet under your city," the lawyer added, his tone overly friendly. "Its oil and gas have been waiting there for us for more than four hundred million years. Haven't we tested their patience long enough?" He welcomed nods and shouts with open hands. "A good leasing fee can mean three thousand per acre or more, depending, of course, on your location and topography. That's money in the bank. And if we can get a well or wells drilled and working on your property, you're also looking at a minimum, *mi-ni-mum,* of twenty thousand dollars in royalties, per well, *per well,* over a period of a few years."

"Wow! Guaranteed?" a woman asked, sounding skeptical over the soft murmur that floated through the room.

The lawyer nodded. "These are ballpark figures, of course, ma'am. I can't guarantee you that the sun will come up tomorrow, but it would be a pretty good bet, right? Nothing's guaranteed in life, but we're not kidding. This is real. And once the well's done producing we'll lock it all up with cement and you'll have your acres back unscathed." He paused. His big smile mixed confidence and condescension.

The woman turned to the man standing next to her, wide-eyed with both disbelief and enthusiasm.

The murmur got louder.

The PR man added suggestively, "And how would you like to pay two bucks at the pump? For Premium?"

"Yeah! We won't have to import dirty oil from dictators! We're paying the tyrants and ayatollahs through the nose!" a young adult hollered. "USA! USA!"

Some chimed in. "USA! USA!"

"Quiet!" It was Phil Jones, the stocky nonagenarian in the room.

Joe smiled at Mary.

"How about all those accidents? That gas in the water in Pennsylvania?" The gray-haired lady's question was barely audible.

"The gas? The gas! Yes. Of course! The gas and all these accidents on TV! How about them?" the lawyer repeated loudly, sounding pleased with the question.

"That faked tone," Mary whispered.

"Just listen." Joe sounded a bit irritated.

The PR man coughed and took a few seconds to formulate his answer. "Well, ma'am, like everything else in life fracking isn't perfect all the time. But it's damn…it's pretty close. And we're getting better every day. We all love clean water and air, and we'll do our damndest, uh…our very best to keep it all clean. We Doornaert people breathe and drink too, you know."

For the past three or four years Mary had paid her seventy-dollar dues to the Sierra Club and devoured their literature. The Doornaert people were speaking the truth, more or less, as far as she could tell. Bloggers' gossip and YouTube often blew accidents, failures and misery out of proportion.

It had taken Mary many hours of late-night browsing fueled by gallons of black coffee to learn some of the intricacies of the rather new technology known as "hydraulic fracturing." It introduced "horizontal drilling." Vertical drilling still came first, down to the shale rock, a mile or more below the surface, but at that point it gradually went horizontal. The pipe then ran horizontally more than half a mile far inside the shale rock. One well pad could be used to drill several horizontal wells. A cement coating was always forced into the gaps left between soil and both vertical and horizontal pipes. That process was called "cementing."

Various fracking companies produced excellent videos about the technology. They showed how, once all pipes were in place and cemented, a number of small holes were shot through the horizontal pipe walls and cement over their entire length. In a next step the drillers pumped a secret mixture of water, sand and chemicals through the holes into the surrounding shale rock under extremely high pressure—so high that it created cracks in the rock.

This was "hydraulically fracturing," or "fracking." Oil and methane, natural gas, thus got freed from the rock and flowed through the holes into the horizontal pipes and up to the surface through the vertical pipe.

Applying the new technology, the drillers captured oil and gas in greater quantities from far larger areas than was possible with vertical drilling only.

From the back of the room Mary heard a voice. "France is going to ban fracking!"

"Oh, really?" The marketing man's surprise was clearly feigned. He sounded amused. "You all heard that? France? The French? Our 'friends?'" He rolled his eyes and snickered. "That must mean that fracking is a good thing, right? France? Freedom fries anybody?" His subtle finger movements invited applause.

It came. Even Mayor Sanders, seated at the table, seemed to smile knowingly, both from his portrait on the wall and in person. It was difficult to tell whether the latter was clapping his hands or folding them.

Mary noticed who applauded the hardest. One of them was the Methodist minister, Reverend Douglas. He stood up and, waving his Bible, declared, "Here's what God wants, Genesis one verse twenty-six. He said, 'Let us make man in our image, in our likeness, and let him rule over the fish of the sea and the birds of the air, over the livestock, over all the earth, and over all the creatures that move along the ground.'" He looked up. "Good enough for me. And I have another—"

7

"So do I!" The Catholic priest, Father Bianchi, smiled confidently as he interrupted his fellow pastor and unfolded a sheet of paper.

Pockets of conversation took a few moments to die out. The father waited.

"No offense, Reverend, but it doesn't look so clear cut to me. Just read Leviticus, Jeremiah, Revelation, and the terrible judgment in Isaiah: 'They will neither harm nor destroy on all my holy mountain, for the earth will be full of the knowledge of the Lord as the waters cover the sea.'" He slid his hand in his coat pocket. "I've printed some out—"

"I hadn't finished, Father," Reverend Douglas retorted. "I have Genesis—"

"I guess it's all a matter of interpretation." Mayor Sanders's tone was appeasing.

Joe gently elbowed Mary and whispered, "That Isaiah must have been quite a tree-hugger."

The woman in front of them shot them an indignant look. Joe put up his palms and gave her a smile.

Mary chuckled but showed her rascal a frown. She wanted to say, "Yep, Isaiah, prophet and Sierra Club founder," but she bit her tongue.

"The European Union will soon issue its general approval of fracking, with conditions which, honestly, we should welcome," the lawyer went on, making it sound like the conclusion of his presentation. He pointed at a hand that had been raised. "Let's answer some more questions, address your concerns. I've seen some on your faces."

A long back-and-forth ensued. Many of the queries resembled those of politicians who make statements to show off their "deep" knowledge, or that of their staff. Some of the attendees even forgot to finish with a question.

Concerns crowded the room. Thousands of tons of sand, chemicals with secret names and millions of gallons of water would have to be supplied, day in, day out; noise and traffic might grow out of proportion; fumes would foul the air; dangerous explosions, prostitution and other problems would follow.

On the other hand, many workers would find new jobs paying twelve hundred to two thousand dollars a week. New businesses would pop up.

A boom, good and bad.

Joanie, a mother of five, drove home her worries. "Sir, my apologies, but what if I wake up one morning, check the weather from my kitchen and see a bunch of service vehicles in my neighbor's backyard, a hundred feet away from my window? What about that, sir?"

The lawyer shook his head and put up his hand. "Won't happen, ma'am. I swear."

"On paper?"

"Yes, ma'am. And on the honor of my company. The State prohibits drilling within one hundred fifty feet from a dwelling. And what's more, you may know we're a family-owned business, from Canton. Jules Doornaert, our founder and owner, is a first-generation pioneer who takes care of his people and their community. He values humans and humanity. Listen carefully: we will discuss well ahead of time placement of any rig with the owner who signed the lease, and we'll be very conscious of our impact on people's lives and the environment."

"Sure?" Joanie leaned her head.

"I know it's asking a lot to take a lawyer at his word, but you can believe me. Mr. Doornaert is a neighbor. I'm a neighbor. A close one. And we do want to make many of you richer and happier, including the city, the community."

"And Doornaert," Mary muttered.

"Good, sir." Joanie wrinkled her graying brow. "But what if Mr. Doornaert dies? Or sells the company? Will the next—"

"Mr. Doornaert's not going to sell, ma'am, and he's in excellent health. So are, I'm sure, his finances. And he has two very capable sons."

A few slow nods and headshakes, along with eye-rolls in the crowd.

"Next question?"

Mary looked at her watch. "The sitter, Joe. We must go. We're late already."

On their way back to Mary's single-story house on Maple Road, Mary looked straight ahead and murmured, her voice monotone, "Doornaert has two sons. Do-nothings, losers on drugs."

Joe's head veered to the right. "Hmm. Why didn't you say that?"

"I thought I'd better keep my mouth shut. The rumor mill already whispers that I'm a Sierra person—a Sierra plant."

"You ain't."

"Right. But I do pay my fee and go to their website for information. I have to."

Joe remained silent for a while as he nervously tapped the steering wheel. Then he sought Mary's hand and squeezed it. "If you lease and they drill on your acres, it'll pay your mortgage for how many years?" His tone was pleading.

"Could be many. A big 'could,' though. For starters, the lease must be negotiated." She was skeptical and abhorred any kind of haggling.

"Of course. So what? Come on! It's cash in hand."

"You want it to ruin our place, our life?" Mary felt weak and scared.

"Doornaert's honest. The company treats me fairly. Those folks seemed sincere. 'Neighbors,' they said. And twenty grand per well. Maybe thirty."

"That's what they tell folks."

"If you sign the lease and they decide not to drill on your acres, you wouldn't have any problem: no drilling, no harm. And you'd have the fees in your pocket."

"Joe...." *He knows better.* "No harm?" She raised her voice as he made the left turn onto Maple Road. "You know damn well they might drill on Harriet's acres, feet away from us! We'd have to 'savor' her mess, whether I sign or not. We must keep fracking out of Noredge! Nobody should sign."

"Harriet's mess. Hmm. I guess you're right. Shit, if she signs they might even suck the oil and gas out from under our feet."

"No. That's illegal."

"Oh. Yeah, right again. And Doornaert's honest. But many of my friends think—"

"Illegal!"

He glanced at her, clearly surprised by her abruptness. "Okay. Okay. So, no leasing, but…."

"But what?"

"If Doornaert comes knocking on our door, they won't forget to mention that I have a good job with them."

"Right. They won't. And yes, you've got that job. Good money. Great money. With work night and day, and not without danger. And your health…." She had read stories about accidents, hoses bursting under terrifyingly high pressure, and explosions. She worried constantly about him.

Mary put her left hand on Joe's leg, felt his warm quad muscles, and sighed. In an hour or so they would make love. Great love. The tall man sitting next to her, a former elementary school football coach with a receding hairline, sturdy and kind, straight and upbeat, not prone to overly sophisticated considerations, was a safe refuge for her after a painful divorce from a cheating, abusive husband. Joe's down-to-earth humor brightened her life. He compensated for his limited education—he'd dropped out of college after six months—with his readiness to take on unglamorous work with a smile. She loved him, the good ol' boy who loved to live.

Her own life had been tumultuous. With a bachelor's degree in anthropology and a minor in Spanish from the University of Cincinnati, she went into teaching. One year later she bolted for a two-year stint in the Doctors Without Borders organization, which led her to a remote jungle area in the Cajamarca province of Peru. There she had met and married Bill, a Lumberton, Texas native. After Peru she joined him in his hometown of about twelve thousand. When they divorced four years later, she moved back north, to Noredge, where she had deep roots.

Of average height, her skin fair, her brownish locks not quite reaching her shoulders, Mary had lost six pounds in Texas. It accentuated her sharp facial features. "Yes, for now," she would say with a wry giggle, nervous as she always was about almost everything, including her waistline. Shopping for clothes was a breeze for her, and she wanted to keep it that way: blouses, slacks and skirts straight off the rack looked tailor-made on her tight, fit body. "You stride like a twenty-year-old." That was Joe's expert opinion.

She softly rubbed his leg and murmured, "We must stop him, Joe."

"Huh? Doornaert?"

"Doornaert."

"But he's a good man. Means well."

"He may, but he's seventy-two. We don't need this fracking and it may ruin our lives, our family." She longed for the day Joe would agree to get married. Her kids called him "Daddy."

"You really want to throw all that money away? The lease money, the royalties? *Your* royalties?"

Mary's house sat on thirty-five acres and the Chamber had hinted that Doornaert was eyeing them and the surrounding area. The land had been in her family for generations. It was part of her.

"We…. I'll stop him. For us. For our family." She squeezed his quad.

"Come on, Mary. The State will shield us from abuse by Doornaert."

He hasn't heard me. She would have to rephrase her 'family' hint—later, when they were in bed.

She sighed. "Politicians? Shielding us? I don't know how much, how honestly, Joe. Politicians can be bought."

"Doornaert wouldn't," Joe affirmed.

Pure Joe can't even imagine that. She chuckled inside. The thought made her happy. "Maybe not him, but the good old chap won't be around forever. I'm not signing any lease, and I'm going to move heaven and earth so that they don't move one rig into Noredge. I'll start a campaign. I don't want an Avella in Noredge."

Avella Township, thirty-five miles southwest of Pittsburgh, had seen a dramatic well explosion in February 2011. Joe's cousin lived twenty miles from the place, and had told them about the horrors that ensued there. Weeks earlier, five workers had been killed in similar circumstances in Allentown.

"I see. So, what are you planning?"

"A quiet campaign. My way." Mary was determined. "It may get unpleasant."

He put his hand on hers. "You're scaring me, baby, the way you talk. Don't forget I work—"

"You did mention that, Joe. And I heard it." She looked straight ahead, nodding slowly. "But I have to protect my kids, you and myself. Do you know what that means? My kids?" She regretted her last two words the moment she spoke them; Joe, basically single for over twenty years, had no children.

He sighed. "What it means? No. I guess I don't, Mary."

They kept silent until they arrived home.

Joe parked the car in the driveway.

She felt his hand on her waist as they walked to the side entrance.

"Are you serious? A 'campaign?'" He sounded nervous.

He thinks I'm going to say, "Oh, no. Not really." She was going to leave no doubt in his mind. "I must. I know too much. It's not just the Avella disaster. I must, whatever it takes," she repeated.

"Whatever…. Are you thinking about speaking with… the Sierra Club?"

She knew he had mustered all his courage to ask her the question. "Whatever it takes. Because I love you, Joe, and our Andy and Jimmy. You have the key?"

Chapter 2

Three weeks after the community meeting the city of Noredge agreed with the Doornaert organization on terms for drilling. Mary was furious, although she had seen it coming. She had to be fair in her assumptions, but felt she could make reasonable guesses about the maneuvering that had led to the decision and the names of the players behind the scenes. Pouring breakfast milk for Andy she looked at Joe and grumbled. "I bet we'll see a doubling of the size of the library, that new meeting hall at the Chamber, a new track for the high school—"

"A new track? Hurrah!" the boy exclaimed. "When?" He swung his little head to throw back his blond locks.

Mary turned to Jimmy, gesturing with her free hand that he should reach out to her with his glass.

Joe didn't look up from the giant bacon and cheese omelet that smiled at him from his plate, but said, "When, Andy? Hmm. I don't know, but I think Mommy does." He winked at her and forked a load of egg into his mouth.

"Soon, Andy," Mary said, her tone motherly. She turned to Joe, rolled her eyes and muttered in a hushed voice, "I can guess whose sons or daughters will have three or four of the new big jobs with Doornaert; and we'll see a few more Cadillacs and Lincolns, driven by 'people' who think we're naïve idiots."

"We're idiots? Why do they think so, Mommy?" Jimmy sounded indignant, showing a frown too deep for his age.

Mary chuckled. Jimmy was a scaled-down version of his brother. "Because they're wrong of course. That's why."

"Mommy's right, Jimmy," Joe added. He hadn't bothered to clear his mouth.

"I am," Mary said curtly.

Jimmy stared at her, taking his time before lowering his gaze to his toast.

Joe concentrated on his fork as he spoke to Mary. "Sound a little bitter."

"Surprised?" she whispered, frustrated.

The kids had turned their attention to their bacon.

"No, sweetie. But you can't do much about it. Might be better to get over it."

She was ready to explode, but just closed her eyes; the shrapnel would hit innocents.

Her quiet "whatever" plan to stop Doornaert had not been effective.

She hadn't told Joe how she might react to a pro-fracking decision by the city. She couldn't do anything official—she had no function in the city's management—but had been meeting with a couple of like-minded friends, Sierra Club sympathizers but not real activists. One was Dan Clark, a tall, bearded high school science teacher of Hartville, father of five grown children. The other one, a single, middle-aged, plump pediatric nurse named Jill Smith who worked at Timken Mercy Hospital in Canton. Both lived less than ten miles from Mary's place.

The trio's plans for flyers and radio ads had taken too long to materialize but they had spent a good deal of time and effort on them. Mary always made sure not to miss a minute of work and to never leave the kids at home by themselves. When Joe came home, she would be there on the days he had his regular day shift. He didn't question her, and she thought it was better not to bother him with tales about her discussions or actions. He was too honest, though she questioned whether she was not equally so.

"I can declare that we have a real victory, Joe," she said scornfully, sighing. "Doornaert has kindly agreed not to drill less than two miles south of McKinley. How generous!"

McKinley Avenue, running east to west, intersected with Main Street in the center of Noredge. The villa of John Livingston, Jules Doornaert's brother-in law, was the pearl of McKinley Street. It flaunted its tree-lined driveway a quarter mile east of the city center.

Joe raised his eyebrows. "Yeah? So you're still not going to sign the lease when Doornaert's landman knocks on your door? Harriet says she will."

Mary shot him an angry glance. "You know damn well I won't."

"You also said it won't be just Harriet who'll suffer. We'll have to enjoy the noise just as much as our friendly neighbor, and the congestion, the fumes, the invasion of strangers. All of that. Without a penny for you...."

"It's only money, Joe." She dropped into her chair and smiled weakly at the boys, whose expressions were all puzzlement.

Chapter 3

On a Thursday afternoon, about a month after Doornaert and the city of Noredge signed their fracking agreement, Mary arrived home from school with Andy and Jimmy. The kids jumped out of the car, Andy holding the door key. "My turn!" he shouted, fighting off Jimmy as they raced to the door.

Mary savored the burst of young energy and the smell of early daffodils.

As she dropped her bag on a chair in the kitchen, she noticed drops of spilled morning coffee on the table. She opened the refrigerator and took out a bag of bread and a jar of peanut butter to prepare a snack for the boys. The electronic clock on the wall next to the defunct, dust-covered, cuckoo-clock said 4:20. The smell of bacon still hung in the air. She felt happy, relieved that Joe didn't smoke any longer. She exhaled profoundly.

She was half way through her snack duty when the bell rang.

Jimmy ran to the front door, exclaiming, "It's Seth!

With his new ball!" A moment later he returned to the kitchen, pouting and dragging his feet. "It's Mrs. Woods."

"Oh." Mary rushed to adjust the big map of South America that hung askew against the wall opposite the refrigerator—next to a much smaller framed copy of the Declaration of Independence. Andy had taped his signature next to John Hancock's. She hurried to clean the Formica table top with a paper towel. "Tell her to come in and don't worry—I'll make your sandwich first."

Harriet Woods walked in, a smile covering the matron's face framed in an abundance of bleached curls. She wore a light-beige pantsuit that looked a size too small. "Hello, Mary! How tall the boys have grown! Lovely."

"Thank you, Harriet. Please come in. Take a seat. They eat like wolves." Mary puffed, handing the boys their snacks. She wiped the seat of one of the metal chairs and smoothed her gray skirt.

"They're playing hard, those champions. I see them kicking the ball in the yard," Harriet commented, her tone jovial, as she carefully sat down, overstretching her pants in the process.

Mary joined her.

Harriet, a sixtyish widow of five years, lived right across Maple Road, to the north, in a single-story house. It was almost a copy of Mary's, but with its forty years it was about fifteen older. Harriet's had greenish aluminum siding; Mary's was off-white. Mary had two half-size soccer goals without nets; Harriet had a garden shed in the far back.

Both had three bedrooms. Harriet's two-car garage was spic-and-span, always; Mary's was a chaotic refuge for too much. A John Deere riding mower dominated its left side, sharing authority with Mary's Corolla on the right. The vehicles had to tolerate the company of discarded toys, four bicycles, numerous soccer balls, a roll of leftover carpet and a half-finished wooden cabinet—a project abandoned by Joe long ago.

The Jenkins and Woods driveways, both one hundred feet long, were almost perfect extensions of each other across Maple Road. Both front yards were impeccably manicured from early May on: Mary and grudging Joe had to keep up with Harriet and her gardener. Much of Mary's backyard showed the wear and tear from mini-soccer matches the boys played with friends, and sometimes with parents. Harriet's was strictly off-limits for kids and adults alike. The rescue of wild soccer balls from her yard required diplomacy.

"Oh yes. Joe kicks balls with them too. And eats just as much," Mary quipped. Her usual "and it shows" lay on her tongue. She kept it there. Rotund Harriet might not have appreciated that kind of humor.

"Well, Mary, I apologize for dropping in without notice, but I thought I should bring you some good news."

Not about another perfect boyfriend. Mary noticed the piece of paper her neighbor had taken out of her pocket. "Great! I can use some."

"Yes, great indeed, for the two of us. That's why I came.

I just made myself forty-eight thousand four hundred dollars! Can you believe it? I signed a lease on my forty-four acres, forty-three and a half actually, but the gentleman was kind enough to round it up to forty-four because I was the first one on our road who signed." She leaned forward and lowered her voice. "I think you should hurry. He said that he would sign only six leases this year on Maple. I thought he was speaking the truth. I brought you his telephone number. You weren't back yet at three o'clock, when he left my house. Take this little—"

"You just signed? Just like that? No lawyer?" Mary blurted out, disregarding the sheet her neighbor tried to hand her.

Harriet recoiled. She briefly closed her eyes.

Mary quickly added, "Sorry. None of my business, of course." She realized the kids were still in the sitting room, watching TV. "Andy, Jimmy, why don't you get the ball and play some. Okay?" She noticed Harriet's two or three slow nods.

The kids looked at their mother askance, switched off the TV and sauntered to the back door.

After a short, silent intermezzo, Harriet coughed and smiled. "I'll get the dollars, Mary, no question about that, and my son in Youngstown said he signed two years ago but they never came to his place to drill. Same for his neighbor. See? It's gravy, that signing money, and no harm done." She looked at the back door—the boys had left it ajar—and went on, "If they would drill, I'd be really rich.

Thirty thousand dollars in royalties over a couple of years. Thirty thousand at least, the man assured me, maybe much more. An honest man. I'd be richer than I ever could've dreamt and after a few years I'd have my land back the way it is now." Her enthusiasm had made her last sentence one too many for her pulmonary capacity. Panting, she placed the paper on the table. "The Watsons will sign too," she managed to add.

Bill and Dorothy Watson had forty or fifty acres bordering Harriet's to the north.

Mary raised her voice. "Thank you, but I won't sign, Harriet. I don't want any fracking mess on Maple. If it were up to me, I'd ban the damn thing in all of Noredge." She got up and closed the back door. Angry. She had no position of authority in the city. And she heard rumors that the State was mulling prohibition of fracking bans by cities and counties. Oil companies were making huge donations to judges up for election or re-election to the Ohio Supreme Court.

"Well, I have my paper for the forty-eight thousand anyway." Harriet frowned. "A mess, you said?"

As if she doesn't know. "Of course! Take a little trip to Pennsylvania. Bradford County. You can get a taste of what *we* can expect when the Doornaert folks set foot on your land."

Harriet sounded undeterred. "Oh. I'll have to talk about that with my son. He knows what he's doing. I'm by myself now, of course. I thought Ed would have done what I did, if he were still with us."

Mary wrinkled her nose.

"Okay. Got to go now, Mary. Take care." Harriet pointed at the sheet. "Don't wait too long!"

Mary walked her neighbor and her penetrating perfume to the front door.

A few feet out, Harriet turned to Mary and pointed at a Buick parked in her driveway. "Marvin," she half-giggled. "He's early. We love Happy Hour at Daddy's Bar."

"Daddy's?"

"In Canton. Very thin pizza snacks. Out of this world. I must tell him about my acres!"

"Yes. You must. I'm sure Marvin will be happy for you. Bye now." Exuberant Harriet had to notice the sarcasm in her tone, but Mary didn't care. Her neighbor's case was very different from hers: the Woods land was not a cherished inheritance in the family for ages. Mary felt privileged, a willing and trusted custodian of her Jenkins acres in a line that stretched over generations.

Around eight-thirty Mary and the kids heard the loud horn of Joe's Highlander. Andy and Jimmy ran outside. "Daddy! Daddy!" Mary stayed behind on the threshold, drying her hands on her apron.

Joe slammed the door of his vehicle, high-fived the boys, and walked past them toward the house. His step lacked the usual bounce.

"Are you tired, Daddy? Can we play?" Andy sounded worried.

"Later," Joe said without looking at him. "Just kick penalties. Give me a few minutes." He seemed low on energy.

"It's late, boys. Getting dark. Daddy must be tired after such a long day," Mary tried to explain. She welcomed Joe with a kiss. "What's the matter?"

Once inside, he let out a sigh.

"Tired, right?"

"I don't feel well, Mary."

"Oh?" She took his arm. "Sit down. You must be hungry. It's late."

"No. Not hungry." He plopped down in a chair at the kitchen table and started coughing. "My throat. Burning. I need a shot of Jim Beam. Damn!"

"Jim Beam?"

"Best you can do for a sore throat."

"Says who? I have your chili on the stove—"

"I said I'm not hungry," he shot back.

Mary disregarded his tone. "Okay, sweetie. Okay. Bourbon. I'm so happy to have you home. Maybe you worked too late," she said softly, hiding her skepticism while taking the bottle and a glass out of the wall cabinet. She poured his drink and reached across the table to put it in front of him.

He took it without saying a word and gulped it down. His trembling fingers dropped the empty glass on the table, where it landed with a slight bang. "Sorry. I didn't mean to, Mary."

"No problem, Joe," she said tenderly. "Does it make you feel better? The drink?"

"Damn cough. So bad I had trouble driving. Couldn't breathe." He leaned his head back, mouth open.

The door swung open and Andy's head popped in. "Ready, Daddy? Jimmy's hands hurt. He doesn't want to play goalie anymore. Are you having dinner?"

Joe showed a weak smile. "Just a minute. Tell him I'll take over." He turned to Mary and said, "One more, Mary. This stuff helps."

She doubted the wisdom of his request but she complied.

He took his second drink and stood up, unsteady. "Jimmy needs me," he said.

Mary wasn't sure he was swaying because of the bourbon. He wasn't a drinker. She embraced him and held him, resting her head against his sturdy chest. Heat radiated from his body. He might be running a low fever. "You'd better go to bed," she whispered.

"No, the boys—"

"I'll get them to bed, too. And I'll join you soon. You need rest and water. And a little coddling."

Joe rubbed his eyes. "Itching," he said.

"Don't rub. Not too hard," Mary warned as she walked her linebacker to the bedroom.

Later, as she lay awake, Joe snoring and coughing, she

told herself her long-held fear was coming true: his job was hurting him, and it might kill him.

On the memorable, cherished day of their love at first sight, their "*flechazo*," as more than one Peruvian young man had taught her in Cajamarca, a spark had ignited her concerns when Joe proudly described his job. That night, when she got home, she dived into the books and jumped onto the web.

She recalled reading then about health issues, possibly but rarely fatal, with the kind of work Joe was doing: hauling dirty water from wells to special "injection wells." Later, she often dropped subtle hints to him, suggesting he take precautions: ask Doornaert for installation of gas monitors; be religious and precise in following instructions. She had watched him unobtrusively, trying to detect signs of trouble. But sturdy Joe, appetite and sex drive unassailably robust, hadn't faltered in any way. Not until now.

Today she couldn't be certain he wasn't suffering from the flu or another bug that might be making the rounds, but her intuition overrode her doubts. She knew her man carried a special virus: his job.

The "dirty water" Joe transported was a mixture of very salty water, up to ten times saltier than ocean water, and many special chemicals. It could not be treated adequately. It was either "flowback," the waste water that came back up to the surface through the wellbore during fracking, or its cousin "production water," the fluid that came up later, during the years of exploration.

Ohio had a good number of "sour" wells. They produced methane gas that carried, among other things, hydrogen sulfide, the "rotten egg" gas. That's why the "dirty water" temporarily stored in stories high tanks or in pits near the wells often had the putrid odor. Hydrogen sulfide gas could be poisonous, even deadly if present in high concentrations. A shiver had run over Mary's spine the day she discovered that it could deaden Joe's sense of smell, even at rather low concentrations. His "do-good" job might hurt him even if he didn't detect anything.

Maybe Joe had forgotten or neglected to put on that cumbersome gas mask? His detector might have failed a few times. Or was it just the flu?

She said her second good night to her man, but he didn't hear it. She told herself he'd awaken in the morning alive and kicking. And that Jim Beam would get the credit.

Chapter 4

In early May Noredge experienced an invasion.

After Doornaert and the Chamber published a cryptic "Fracking comes to Noredge!" three paragraph press release, a torrent of opinions and comments engulfed the city. Bona fide journalists, pundits, preachers, schoolteachers, sedate as well as foxy TV anchors, talk radio barkers, and the occasional regular citizen calling in to a show or penning a few lines for the Noredge Sentinel, all scrambled for their share of the news bonanza. They dusted off old clichés and fought fiery opinion battles. Scenarios ranged from doomsday to utopia. Exhortations and predictions ran the gamut: "Utica gold for Noredge!" "We'll never be the same!" "Jobs, Jobs, Jobs!" "Noredge into the Modern Age!" "Traffic Jams ahead!" "Test your Water! Get your Gas Masks!" The title of the Seniors' Association's one-page special edition said it all: "Change! Change! Noredge Will Never Be Good Old Noredge Again."

The first physical agents of that change now descended upon the little city.

Around 9 a.m., Mary and her colleagues were alarmed by earsplitting sounds of engines and horns. "Doornaert!" one of her colleagues had yelled into her classroom. "Let's get on the sidewalks! Control the kids!" The principal couldn't curb the excitement.

Students and teachers all ran out onto Main Street. The ground was shaking under their feet, the exhaust fumes suffocating, the noise deafening. The teachers shouted their instructions to the kids as best they could over the rumblings of a giant metal snake, a massive convoy: two SUV's flashing their lights; tanker trucks, some marked "flammable," big letters on their bellies; huge oversize trucks carrying bulldozers; and more trucks carrying heavy equipment. The serpent crawled north on Main Street and then, about hundred feet past the school, crept left, northwest, onto Maple Road. Mary tried to hold on to Jimmy's hand as he jumped up and down. "The ground makes me dance, Mommy!" The asphalt at the intersection of Main and Maple was being slowly ground to pieces by the reptile worming its way through the turn. Clouds of dust, noxious fumes, eardrum-busting decibels and excited, uncontrollable schoolchildren.

"They're going to clear a big site near Rutgers Lake!" Sonya, a colleague, hollered at Mary. "My brother should already be up there! Frank!"

Rutgers Lake was about two miles from the center, northwest, about a mile from Mary's house.

"Your brother?"

"I never told you? He's been an engineer with Doornaert for five years."

"Oh."

"Let's hope this kind of spectacle isn't going to be daily fare," a young teacher shouted.

"Don't get your hopes up too high, Judy," Mary responded. "They'll drill many wells, and each of them will require massive amounts of water, sand and chemicals. I already can picture those trucks coming. Hundreds of them. Every day. And we haven't even seen one of those huge rigs making its way through the city."

"I don't think it'll be that bad," Sonya said. "Maybe they'll build a road that spares downtown. Half a loop. Frank mentioned that to me."

"Oh. That's interesting." Mary was unable to keep the scorn out of her smile. She assumed that Frank Anderson had spoken as a loyal Doornaert soldier to his sister. "Okay," she said, "I'll get my kids and my class back inside." She cupped her hands around her mouth and shouted, "Children! Children! We're done! Just a few more trucks! Math time!"

Chapter 5

A few days later Mary felt a sudden urge she couldn't resist: she had to set foot onto the Rutgers site—see the action near the lake with her own eyes. She took the bull by the horns and drove out there.

As she stepped out of her car she noticed that bulldozers had already flattened a fifth of the terrain and that the Doornaert folks sure knew how to erect threatening signs. The fine-print under the giant "no-access" letters left no doubt. Loud, awe-inspiring vehicles and machinery crawled over the site. She felt dwarfed. She hesitated. *I'd better turn back.* Being caught trespassing wasn't the best idea for a person trying to talk sense into the heads of her fellow citizens. Disappointed, but still determined, she decided she would solicit Sonya's help.

She called her colleague on the way home. "Would your brother mind if you and I would drop in at Rutgers for a brief visit? Just a few minutes?"

"Oh? The site? Well…."

"Do you think he'd mind?"

"I'm sure he'd spare us a few minutes. Show us around. I know you're concerned."

Mary adopted her trademark sarcasm. "And he wouldn't mind a wiseacre, a know-it-all like me?"

"Oh no. Let's try for tomorrow."

When she arrived at home Mary spoke with Joe about the planned site visit.

He warned her. "Bite your tongue. Please don't do or say anything rash. We do have the mortgage."

She put her hand up. "We're a team, Joe. You and me. Good enough? You have the early shift tomorrow, right?"

After school the next day Mary and Sonya dropped Jimmy and Andy off at home with Joe and made their way to the drill site. Mary parked in the street.

Sonya pointed at a huge white and blue van. "Frank's place. Sometimes I think he even sleeps in it—bachelor forever," she joked.

In her low thirties, svelte and athletic, not an ounce over her perfect runner's weight, Sonya was a petite blonde with a boyish haircut who taught math and physical education. No children yet, but she was married. Once they had saved the down payment for their dream house, she and her marathoner Jack would think about producing babies. "A boy and a girl," she would confide in Mary, not a trace of doubt in her voice.

She phoned her brother, nodding slowly while she waited. Then she put up her index, winked and said, "Hi. It's us, little dude. The two intruders ready to take over your place, remember? Tree-huggers. Barbarians at the gate. Got our machine guns!" She listened and laughed. "No! Not kidding! Not at all! Can you let us in? Yes, my friend Mary and me." Another wink. "Yes, the one I told you about. Okay?" Slipping her phone into her purse, she explained, "I'd mentioned your concern to him after we talked. He's a guy who wants to do good. Really."

They neared a no-trespassing sign and stopped and waited.

Mary heard a whistle. From a distance, two young, bearded roughnecks shot big smiles from under their hard hats, thumbs up. She turned her head the other way.

Frank arrived, thin and tall, wearing loose coveralls free of grease spots, his clean boots too heavy for his ascetic appearance. Smiling down at the two women in running shoes, he shook hands. "Welcome!" He towered over his sister and Mary. He handed them hardhats and helped struggling Sonya adjust the strap. "Let's go."

He didn't walk like an oilman. He didn't look like one except for his attire. He hastened to apologize for the mess they would find at his "office" and for the limited time he would have to spend with them. "It's a race against the clock," he said as he motioned them up the four mud-covered aluminum steps and into the van.

Inside, an array of electronic equipment and monitors greeted them, hanging down from the ceiling. They covered the entire length of the vehicle on one side.

Frank started rattling off a list, pointing, "Geological

stuff, chemical analysis tools, satellite communication. Computers and headphones. Soon we'll start logging pressures, volumes, speeds, chemical analyses, temperatures—"

"Too much for me already, Frankie!" Sonya had her hand up. "Give us a minute. You'll have to use simple words, slowly, to tell us ignoramuses what's going on here and what's going to happen." She glanced at Mary, turned 180 degrees and asked, looking intrigued, "What about that piece of art, that labyrinth?" She was pointing at a huge chart taped to the wall.

He looked at his sister askance. "You're asking me? Read the title. Flow Chart Alpha Ritgers." He smiled down again; he had pronounced it as it was written.

A youngster on a swivel chair nearby snickered.

"Yes," Frank said, sounding dismissive, "some secretary misspelled it but who cares? This isn't Princeton."

Mary chuckled. *Princeton.* She thought Frank might fit in there.

"Labyrinth! Yeah. It's our plan for the next five months and two weeks. Alpha. Our first well in our Noredge alphabet. One hundred sixty-eight days from today we start producing. Not one day later, hopefully earlier." He made the money gesture, both hands. "Every day costs me or makes me more."

"You?" Sonya raised her eyebrows.

"Yes. Ditto for accidents. Safety first. Can make a big difference in my bank account."

"Are you in charge of this? All of this?" Mary asked in awe.

"This? You ain't seen nothing yet, Miss."

"Mrs."

Sonya hushed her giggle.

Frank tapped his forehead. "I'm sorry. Mrs."

"That's okay." Mary felt she had sounded both peevish and flattered.

Frank leaned his head in the direction of the site, pride in his gaze. "Right now you see just bulldozers doing their thing: digging, cleaning, flattening and packing the land for the well pad. Heavy trucks hauling earth, bushes, tree trunks; four tanker trucks, compressors and pumps and their backups. Everything here is backed up. And just a few people—for now."

The two women had their noses inches from the window. It needed washing. Mary already knew, more or less, from literature and from her uncle in Youngstown what it was like when a drill crew arrived near your place. This was the real thing, but just the first stage of it.

"In a week, fifty-sixty workers, maybe more, will move in and so will the rig," Frank went on. "The rig!" he exclaimed. "It'll be treated like a queen bee: a tall, petulant, fickle girl eighty-ninety feet tall, an army of trucks and tankers dutifully swarming around her, unquestioning. Their buzz will be quasi-monotonous, nonstop day and night, but it will be mercilessly violated by the queen bee's screams, her clanging sounds."

He paused, his eyes radiating pride.

The women chuckled.

Mary wondered what made him more proud, his poetic detour or the power of the scene he had painted for them.

He suggested they take a seat. "Now, all those crazy queen bee-loving trucks, they'll keep moving in and out twenty-four seven. They'll carry tons of steel, pipes and all kinds of shapes and forms and parts; valves and pumps, fuel and chemicals, tons of them; and heavy lifting and drilling tools. When the queen finishes and leaves, a few weeks later, other vehicles and tankers will arrive and line up—just imagine a feeding line for a giant hog trough—and start spewing, feeding tons and tons of sand, water, cement, and chemicals, many chemicals, all of it into steel pipes lined up one next to another. Each pipe in the line will ultimately lead into the big pipe that'll go down into the rock deep below. It's a hell of a maze of pipes and valves. I'd like to use the word 'amazing' if you don't mind."

"Wow." Mary was impressed.

"We'll have to come back in a couple of weeks," Sonya said.

"Yes. And you should write poems, Frank," Mary the teacher suggested. "Or write books for our kids. You have a talent." The inveterate bachelor seemed so out of place.

He showed a friendly frown. "Thanks for the suggestion, Mary, and no, Sonya, in a few days visitors will be turned back. You understand we have to guarantee safety for our workers and of course for the community, as well as protect our technology."

Mary hesitated but asked anyway, "Between us here, Frank, may I ask you how you feel about the impact all of this will have on our daily lives in Noredge? This is just Doornaert's first well here—"

"Of course you may." He paused briefly. "Let's get you back to your car," he said with a brief glance at the youngster glued to a computer screen.

Mary and Sonya waved a quick goodbye to the young man and the threesome left for the parking area. Once there, the women removed their hardhats and returned them to Frank. He took his off as well.

"Don't tell anybody," he half-joked.

Not one single hair was out of place. Rimless glasses with thin, gray temples and top bar complemented almost too perfectly his orderly hairdo, which was graying although he couldn't be much older than forty-five.

As Mary unlocked the car, Frank said, "About the impact, I don't mind discussing it here." He seemed to take the question seriously, rubbing his forehead, pondering his answer as he surveyed the area. "Sonya knows I'm neither a 'drill, baby, drill' nor a 'frac no' guy. Fracking is saving our country from the whims of the Arabs and the Venezuelans and so on. I don't have to explain that or throw figures at you. And soon you'll know where your cheap gasoline and heating oil and gas comes from." He pointed down at the ground.

"I love those low prices. I guess we all do."

He smiled at Mary.

She felt her intervention might have sounded like a platitude.

He went on, "At Doornaert we do a lot of good but, I'll be honest, we're not yet able to do everything one hundred percent perfectly at all well sites one hundred percent of the time. Neither is anybody else. But we all get better at it every day. That's it. Sh—er, stuff happens now and then. Will happen. Okay?"

Okay. Mary didn't think he had sounded condescending or defensive, but the tone of his "okay" said he wasn't keen to expand either. She knew he had to wear his company hat. "Yes, Frank. Thank you," she said. For a moment, he had reminded her of politicians reciting talking points, but his pure facial expression had told her the thought was probably unfair.

In the car on their way back Sonya asked, "How did you like my 'little' brother? And what he said?"

Mary adjusted her rearview mirror. "A great guy," was the best she could come up with.

"And an even better piano player."

"Piano?" Mary had trouble picturing a piano player on a drill site.

"He loves his job. Makes eighteen thousand dollars a month. College loans paid off, I think."

Mary was making less than a tenth of that. "Wow. Good for him."

Chapter 6

It was only mid-June, but unexpectedly early oppressive heat was taking its toll on Mary and her restless kids.

Already she had moments when she missed the relative quiet and tight organization of school life. Her living room, facing south and west, became an inferno in the afternoons. The noisy air conditioner, running full blast, complained of the overload even though she kept the drapes closed from noon on. Whatever she touched felt sticky and then teasingly showed her fingerprints. On the maple dresser Joe's huge high school wrestling trophy, a nickel-coated figure of a muscled, tough-faced youth, seemed to perspire, having lost its gloss. The six Peruvian Karajia statues lined up next to it—souvenirs of Cajamarca—looked homesick. Her two, towel-wrapped armchairs facing the dresser across a low coffee table stared reproachfully at her, their arms hanging listless and tired, unhappy oldies forced into oversized, baggy clothes.

She sighed. How many times had she unsuccessfully argued with Joe for the installation of an awning over the terrace behind the house, the south side? It always got postponed and soon the hottest days would be gone. It was going to be "next year" again.

This summer was even a bit worse than usual: Joe hadn't been in the best of moods lately. His limp, compliments of a badly twisted football knee, had worsened. Considerate and kind, Mary patiently absorbed his complaints and suggested braces, creams, massages, but Joe wasn't interested. "Sissy stuff," he would say, shrugging. The bright side of the football knee situation was that it had enabled Mary to talk him into soccer for the kids. And goals in the backyard. He had taken to the sport, even kicked balls with the boys and watched an occasional Major League Soccer game with them. They taught their daddy some of the rules and fine points of the game and she never heard them comment on the latecomer's lack of soccer skills or knowledge, although some of their friends had.

His cough and irritability now kept coming back in ever more frequent flurries. Those were days when Mary would get fever blisters and stomach cramps, and tried to hide them. She could handle his outbursts, understood them, but not so well her concerns about his slowly deteriorating health.

She knew that a job change was not in the cards and off limits for discussion. Andy and Jimmy loved his stories about huge tire blowouts, traffic congestion, his tanker truck stalled on a big, busy highway, a heated argument with police about a silly turning light, and mountains of snow blocking the roads. She knew that Joe's job and salary were his indispensable sources of pride. He didn't just *have* a job, he *was* his job. "You have a degree, Mary," he would say at times, feeling, she thought, a bit out of her league, and sounding defensive. "I screwed up in school but I've fought my way up to a good living."

"You have, Joe. I admire that," she would respond soothingly. "My parents basically carried me to Cincinnati. Yours had their hands full just to scrape by. And they did. I love you just the way you are. I'm proud of my man!"

She meant it all.

Joe would stare briefly at her and occasionally tear up.

She knew that he was grateful to her for lifting him up. She also realized that she would have to keep worrying about his health and maybe start talking to the Chamber folks or the mayor about working conditions at Doornaert—or to the weasels at the Noredge Sentinel if they would dare to even listen to her.

Another worry suddenly arose when, on a lazy afternoon, she went shopping with the kids at Walmart and ran into Sonya. Her friend pulled her aside into a quiet corner. "Doornaert's going to be sold," she whispered into Mary's ear.

"Huh?"

"Yep. Two big companies are competing for the prize. My friend Joan at the Chamber told me."

"Good companies?"

"Hope so." She raised her shoulders, her eyes wide.

"Hmm. What about Frank and Joe?" Mary turned away briefly to check on the kids.

"Frank's worried. One never knows. He told me the names of the two Texan companies. I never heard of them. He said that one of them has the best technology in the country. Of course, everything is biggest and best in Texas. But it might be an improvement for Noredge."

"Could be. It's one way to look at it." Mary's thoughts flashed to Joe. Might the new company with all that super technology be able to install equipment to capture the gases that escaped when he had to open the valves of the dirty water storage tanks?

"I think 'fingers crossed' is about right, Mary. I hope that Joe and Frank can hang on to their jobs. It would—"

"Jimmy!" Mary shouted. "Stop!"

The boy was loading a huge bag of apples onto the scale. The poor thing seemed to groan under the weight.

"Hold on, Sonya. Sorry." Mary rushed to grab the bag. She emptied it furiously back onto the shelf.

An elderly lady looked confused but kept moving, using her shopping cart as a walker.

Jimmy, his face signaling disappointment as the apples tumbled, argued, "But they're good for us, Mommy. You always say that."

"Stop it. Quiet." She had lowered her voice.

"They looked healthy and shiny," Andy said.

"Don't touch anything. Stay with me or I'll—" She didn't know how to go on and shook her head.

"They're kids, Mary. No harm done." Sonya smiled and caressed Andy's locks.

Mary checked around. "I hope nobody else noticed. Cameras everywhere…. So, your brother knows? Is he worried?"

"A bit. But he's got a good track record. He's working his butt off to make the deadline at Rutgers Lake. He should look good, not only in the eyes of Doornaert. Should be okay."

Mary had to suppress a little jealousy. "I'm sure he will," she said, and sighed. "Joe loves his job."

"I heard he does good work. But don't worry too much. Let's say a good prayer."

Mary stayed silent, concerned about Joe's health: the new owners might not have any use for a "weakling."

Two days later Joe arrived home early from work. Visibly upset, he threw his car keys on the counter top. "You were right, Mary. Damn! Two giant sharks from Houston fighting over Doornaert. Heard it on WHBC. Texas will ruin Noredge."

Mary looked up from her knitting, put it carefully down on the little table next to her and said calmly, "But nothing's official yet. Right? The sharks still may have to swim back home hungry." She had no grounds for her soothing language. It was just her feeble attempt to calm Joe.

He grumbled, "Not what they said. The reporters were already discussing what was going to happen to Doornaert.

How many millions the old man could make on the deal. I was so damn mad that I did a one-eighty and came home. To hell with Doornaert. A traitor. Another one." He coughed, spat into the sink and turned the faucet on.

Mary frowned. "Don't shout, Joe. The kids could hear you outside. I told you that Jules Doornaert's getting up there in years, and that his sons aren't up to speed, never will be. They can't take over the reins of the company. He must know that. Maybe the old man means well: he may be trying to assure the survival of his life's work and his people's jobs."

"Not a word about that stuff on News Talk," he said, holding the refrigerator door. "It sounded like it was all done. I's dotted and t's crossed. Done. Big money at its best again." He slammed the door of the fridge shut and poured himself a glass of juice.

She tried to sound more upbeat. "Even if Doornaert's taken over, it doesn't mean you'd lose your job. The new guys need you. Go kick some balls with the kids and their friends."

He took a couple of quick sips and walked out, muttering.

Mary didn't understand what he said, but she could intuit it. She felt for her man.

She called Sonya—Frank might have told his sister more about the names and maybe the reputations of the companies—but had to leave a message and raise her voice to talk over the suddenly heavy hum of the air conditioner. It badly needed maintenance.

Irritated, she opened the back door and stood on the terrace, hot, humid air hitting her in the face and on her bare legs. Seven or eight boys romped and hollered, over-enthused, running up and down the field. Andy and Jimmy's daddy didn't often make it home so early, in time for playing in their late afternoon game. Joe showed poor soccer technique and style, but still had speed. And enthusiasm. The players barely acknowledged Mary's presence on the terrace.

Her mind had drifted elsewhere anyway. She couldn't imagine that this yard and her way of life would be sacrificed for more unneeded oil dollars into Doornaert's full coffers. Much of her grass field was worn out and abused by the soccer players, but it was her land—Jenkins land.

She went back inside, turned on the radio and aimlessly surfed channels, faintly hoping for tidbits of news. Her search was unsuccessful. Even her favorite WKSU, Public Radio, the "boring" channel as Joe put it, didn't mention Doornaert in their five o'clock newscast. She took a Budweiser out of the fridge, kicked off her flip-flops, plopped down on the couch and put her legs up on an armrest.

She hadn't heard from Sonya at six-thirty, when her three boys came in, the young ones shirtless and the older one breathing heavily. She smiled as they gulped down cold water, argued about missed shots and complained of bruises and unfair tackles.

"It's true, Mommy. Look." Jimmy showed her his shin.

Joe winked. "Sorry again, Jimmy. You deserved that penalty," he snickered and bent down to put his arm around the boy's shoulders. "He'll be a Messi soon, Mommy. FC Barcelona will make us all rich!"

"Yeah!" Mary exclaimed. "Richer than oil can. She took a look at the boy's leg. "Peroxide," she said, using a serious tone. "Lots of peroxide. And a big dinner."

"I know where Barcelona is, Mommy," Jimmy said.

She noticed Joe's smile, the first one since he had come home. She decided that after dinner she would take a trip to the bedroom, drop her tee-shirt and worn shorts and put on something a little more alluring.

Chapter 7

Sonya's panting was audible and her distress palpable when she called Mary the next morning around nine. "They fired him," she said, her voice low.

"Frank?"

"Of course! Who else?" Sonya snapped back, sounding scornful.

"Of course, of course." Mary put her towel down. Dishes could wait.

"They have no shame. He worked day and night, but the Gods from Houston decided."

"Out immediately? So suddenly? I'm so sorry."

"Two weeks' notice. They have their own man ready, Frank says. He has to get him up to speed on the Rutgers well. Now. How nice." Her tone was pure bitterness.

"I'm so sorry to hear that." Mary knew an endless litany was headed her way, of recriminations addressed to Doornaert and the new company, of praise for Frank and of laments about injustice in the world. She picked up her cleaning cloth with her free hand and started pacing the kitchen, noiselessly rearranging dried cups and glasses, wiping away crumbs, cleaning up little spills.

"They just booted him rudely over the phone. A recorded call. He had to submit his resignation. Immediately. A big personnel guy in Houston. Registered letter to follow. No courtesy. No recourse. Higher ups had made the decision. He was 'just HR,' couldn't comment, just communicating arrangements, severance, etc."

Mary stared at the phone in her hand. She saw her friend's indignation streaming out, thin, endless, transparent strands that were impossible to catch or control or stop.

"Frank deserved better," Sonya said.

"If those Houston guys had any smarts they would keep him." It was the best Mary could come up with; her mind had wandered to Joe the moment Sonya had blurted out the word "fired."

"My poor brother already started cleaning out his drawers at the site. He's got a good severance. He seemed less upset than me last night when he came to see Jack and me, and told us the news. 'Things were going so well at Rutgers,' he said. 'At least I can say I'll be leaving with a clean slate. I have proof. Alpha.' He looked proud. We decided to have a few drinks for consolation. Actually not a few. So, I didn't return your call last night. I'm afraid I wouldn't have made much sense anyway. You might have smelled my breath over the phone."

Mary was surprised to hear a weak laugh when Sonya

finished. "I might have. And who did this to him? What's the name of the new company? Who are they?"

"Some Houston outfit by the name of Supren. Beats me, Mary. I never heard of them but Frank had. He picked up through the grapevine that they'd had a bloody fight with another Houston company over Doornaert. The name escapes me. No—Viola. That was it. They and Supren were literally at each other's throats, he'd been told. Frank said Viola would've been better for him and for most of the Doornaert people. He knows Viola. Smart management and very good technology."

"Too bad they lost. But who knows how these deals get worked out, what exactly counts for how much? Who has the nicer yacht? Who has the lower handicap? Who all had a thumb on the scales? Politicians?" Mary knew she sounded sarcastic. She had quietly taken a cup and poured herself some more coffee.

"The scales? We'll never know. Maybe we'd better not."

"I'm thinking…Joe…."

"Frank thinks that he's not in danger because—"

"He's not important enough!" Mary instantaneously regretted her words and tone.

It took a couple of seconds before Sonya went on, sounding calm and subdued, "My brother feels that he alone was targeted. That they wanted him out because he has a critical job and maybe knows too much. I told you they have their man ready. They must want to bring in their own secret know-how, run their own show, these 'big Texans with their unbearable swagger.' Frank's words."

"Hmm. And what's Frank going to do now? 'Spending more time with my family' doesn't work for a bachelor, I guess. Take a well-deserved vacation?"

Sonya giggled. "As well he might, with that severance in his pocket."

"Maybe the busy bee can spend some time looking for a girlfriend or a wife. Not just playing the piano," Mary joked.

"I wish he would."

"Oh? If I were him, Sonya—" Mary broke off and changed her tone, concerned. "I must talk to Joe now. He'll be...I don't know what he'll say."

"It's hard."

"I should go now. The kids need me," Mary sighed. "Vacation isn't 'vacation' for me. Stay in touch."

They hung up.

Mary noticed she was still in her pajama shorts. Joe's favorite. *I must call him.* She dreaded the thought.

"I know!" he shouted over the traffic when Mary reached him.

"Oh. Where are you, Joe?"

"Interstate 76 near Youngstown. You sound worried. Relax!"

"Huh? How can I—?"

"I'll keep on trucking. Got no time for politics. Somebody will sign my paycheck. Texas dollars are fine for me."

She knew he meant confederate dollars. She smiled, surprised. "No worries, Joe?" Actually, she had mixed feelings herself: getting fired could be a lifesaver for him, but the job also meant good money and self-respect.

Andy came in looking concerned. "Are you worried, Mommy?"

She waved "no problem" with her palm and gestured he should go outside.

Joe roared again, "Worries? Me? I'm doing my part here. More than I have to. I know it. They won't find a big fat Texan to replace me!"

"They fired Frank."

"Frank? Anderson?"

"Anderson."

"Well, yeah, not surprised. He's high up there. Company man. The boss on the site. No simple roughneck like me. Tall trees catch much wind. Strange, though. I hear he's really good."

Mary pictured her partner, two hands on the wheel, eyes staring into the distance. She counted the wrinkles he had to have on his forehead now. He couldn't be as unconcerned as he sounded. He wasn't leveling with her.

She heard a loud horn. "Careful, Joe!"

"Some kid cutting me off. Probably on something," he grumbled. "Idiot."

She pictured him making a fist. "Relax, Joe. Back to Frank, the Texans want control, I think. Isn't that normal? It's their money."

"Sure. Let them come. We'll teach them how to shovel snow." Now she detected bitterness in his voice.

"And to say 'pop' instead of 'coke,'" Mary played along; she didn't want Joe to come home like a beaten dog tonight. She had to be his crutch, whether he realized it or not.

"Coke?"

"That's Texan for pop. Kind of." Mary reminded herself of her four years in Lumberton, Texas, married to Bill.

"Shit!" He laughed again. "I knew they weren't very— never mind. They'll have to drink pop! Plain old Ohio pop!"

Mary spoke seriously. "Too bad you're losing Frank."

"No problem. He's not my boss. Jeffrey is, my coordinator in Canton. He's a good guy."

"I hope Jeffrey survives."

"He will. He's a bit of a snake," Joe snickered. "Politician. I bet he'll save his ass in the deal. He's got Jules Doornaert's ear."

"Good for him." She sighed. "Be safe now, Joe. Love you."

"Love you too. See you tonight. Can't wait for you-know-what."

"Your hot chili," she teased.

"You know me better than that, sweetie!"

"I do?"

"Something much hotter!" he roared.

As she put down the phone she had a warm, fuzzy feeling. She pictured her strong guy high up in his tanker truck and looking down on little ladies coiffed and painted for their lunch appointments. Enthroned over them, commanding his monster vehicle, humming along defiantly with Johnny Paycheck, "Take this job and shove it."

She smiled.

***

Robotically chugging along on the interstate, Joe felt strange after his conversation with Mary. He was confused, lost in a labyrinth.

A shiver had run down his spine the moment Mary had spoken about Frank's firing. *If Supren fires me, I'll be a loser, a nothing.* He'd never forget the wide eyes she had shown him when he told her about his salary the first time they met. *But hey, that wasn't the only way I impressed her that evening.* His confidence returned. He had to rub his crotch.

Hadn't she laughed spontaneously, not just politely giggled when he joked? She had reached for his hand when she half-whispered to him about issues with her kids. And she had said, quietly, checking around in the bar, that he was doing good work, good for Mother Earth. That it had to be done with care and skill, and that she thought he had all of that and more. That he was valuable to Doornaert and could be for many companies in the field.

She hadn't told him right off the bat that she had a college degree, taught school and spoke a foreign language, although he assumed it as he observed her and listened to her sweet voice. When he had asked her about college she had said, "Oh, college. Yes, I went to college, but how about these tanker trucks? They must be awfully hard to drive? I'd think so." He'd never forget that. And in the weeks and months and years that followed Mary had seldom hinted at her superior education, not intentionally anyway—except for the few times when she slipped, in some of their rare angry discussions. She always apologized soon afterwards.

Mary told him she loved him. Often. And that she worried about him. She made him feel it. He couldn't blame her for her concern; he had bad days, and today wasn't a very good one. His rotten egg disease, whatever it was, made him nervous, irritated. Headaches kept haunting him, his chest hurt. On and off today he had feared he was getting sicker again, gliding a few more feet closer to the point where his body would tell him to quit his job. Mary had a point. She had her way of hinting without hurting too much.

Of course, she liked the good salary he made too, but that was only money. If that were what she wanted she would've signed a lease with Doornaert the day Harriet showed up with her little sheet, or even before. He knew she didn't ever want to lose him. He hadn't doubted it since the day he had met her. He loved her kids and Mary didn't show a trace of jealousy when, on and off, in trouble or hurting, they would ask him for help and not her. He was their daddy. Maybe he should ask Mary to marry him. No doubt she would accept. But his first marriage, at age twenty, had gone sour in just a few months. Brief relationships in between hadn't worked out. And Mary was so much smarter than he. Marriage scared him. His thoughts drifted back to work.

What should he do now, after the takeover? He wouldn't be touched by corporate reforms. He was small fry. He could sit back and stick to his job, not ask questions or volunteer comments. Nobody would want to hear them anyway. He was safe. The new bosses wouldn't fire him. The question he was asking himself was whether he should quit and save his health. Only he could answer that one.

He just hoped he wouldn't be at home the day that Supren would show up at Mary's doorstep and offer her a big, fat check for a lease because their clever geologists had discovered that her acres were an ideal spot for a spectacularly promising well. He knew she would flatly refuse to sign a lease. She, their employee's common-law wife, or whatever they would call her. That day Supren might answer his big question, the one he struggled with. He didn't know whether he feared or hoped they would.

Chapter 8

On June 25th the Noredge Sentinel published a brief article regarding Michael (Mike) Doyle. He had been appointed ten days before to manage the activities of the Supren Company in three counties. One of them was Stark County, which included Noredge. The Sentinel said that he was an experienced Texan oil man but it didn't provide specifics about Mr. Doyle's credentials. He and his spouse Edith had rented a residence on McKinley. The article also listed the address of a temporary office Supren had set up in Noredge: 23 Main Street.

Frank Anderson immediately went to Google and LinkedIn to check into Mr. Doyle's background but came up empty-handed: he had found many Mikes and Michael Doyles but none who could possibly be the man appointed to the important position in Noredge.

He knew the old house on Main, now Supren's office, a two-storied rental property of Mayor Sanders. A consultant who on and off provided monitoring services to Doornaert had lived in it and moved on to North Dakota, where the pastures were even greener and the Bakken oil money even more abundant than Utica's. Frank himself had a few years of Bakken work under his belt.

The next day he got up early and drove his Explorer to Main Street, hoping to see the new boss before the man would get swamped by conference calls and SMSes and, more importantly, before the arrival of any curious or nosey assistant or secretary.

He noted two cars in the driveway. He rang the bell at seven forty and waited. He had to hit the button a second time. Traffic was building up on Main. A friend driving by looked at him twice, frowned, and then smiled, his hand up.

Nobody answered the bell.

He turned the door knob and found the office unlocked: the entrance hall and the adjoining room were eerily empty—no sound, no humans, no furniture, just a big, coverless plastic trash can. A "Doyle" card taped on a door stared at him. He walked up to it and knocked, two polite knocks in quick succession.

"Yes!" It was an impatient bark. The man inside clearly didn't want to be disturbed early in the morning. The rudeness didn't come as a surprise; Mr. Doyle probably didn't know where to turn first. If he would agree to see him, Frank would make sure he made his points concisely, his questions and requests straight to the point, and the entire conversation as effective, efficient and brief as possible.

He opened the door and popped his head in. "Mr. Doyle?"

The person behind the worn, wooden desk in the barren room looked up. Thick, gleaming hair, brown but graying and impeccably groomed framed his deeply tanned face. A thin mustache trimmed to perfection accentuated his sharp features.

"Huh? Yes. Mike Doyle. You are?" The preoccupied-looking man didn't drop the sheet he was holding and seemed irritated.

"Frank Anderson. Maybe you—"

"Anderson? Aha, yes. I know who you are. Why aren't you at the lake? With the guys? I'm still paying you."

Frank walked in. "Right. Two weeks, sir. I've got everything covered at the site. If you don't mind, I'll be just a minute. I worked until nine last night."

"Just a second. Hold on. Have a seat there." Doyle pointed at a crooked metal table, repositioned a heavy file folder, finished his coffee, took his phone and stood up. A tall man. His white, long-sleeved, expertly ironed shirt wore its starch proudly but combined uncomfortably with his casual jeans and western belt buckle as they tried to tame a bulging belly. He shook hands with a firm grip and shouted, "Vince!"

"Yes, sir!"

Within seconds a door opened to the right of Doyle and a short, heavyset man in his mid-thirties appeared sporting a raven crew cut and a ready smile. He was clutching a note pad and his phone.

"Here." Doyle waved the man over to the table. "He joined us yesterday, Vince Davis," he said to Frank and sat down.

Vince glanced inquisitively at Frank while he carefully lowered his sizeable bottom into a chair.

Frank had hoped to have a one-on-one discussion with Doyle, but didn't feel it was smart to object to Vince's presence. He showed him a friendly smile. "Hi Vince, I'm Frank Anderson." He liked the young man right away.

"Oh. Frank Anderson. Your name's all over the Doornaert files."

"Hopefully nothing bad," Frank said jovially.

Doyle rushed to intervene, obviously busy and eager to get the visit over with. He said to Frank, "This young man's taking over for you. He's our new company man for Rutgers. My plate's more than full so I wanted him here right away. Vince is getting up to speed, finding his way around Doornaert documents and Supren systems, bugging me with questions I don't know the answer to, and burning the midnight oil—or so he tells me."

Vince wiggled a bit uncomfortably in his chair.

The boss winked. "Just kidding. He's a top graduate of the University of Akron. I hear a lot of good about that place, even in Houston. He's a chemical engineer. Great background and reputation at Chesapeake Energy."

Frank nodded a few times while Doyle spoke. "Engineering at Akron U is strong, I know." He showed Vince a brief smile.

"So, I already asked you, why are you here? What can I do for you?" Doyle looked at Frank and then his watch.

"Actually, I have a personal request for help, one that I hoped to discuss with you."

Doyle frowned.

Vince moved his chair back, with difficulty. "I'll be back," he said and got up.

The Texan looked irritated. "No. Stay," he said curtly. He turned to Frank. "It's not about money, I hope, or state secrets."

"No, no," Frank said.

Doyle picked up his phone from the table and glanced at the screen.

Young Vince sat down, smiling at Frank.

Doyle started tapping his pen on the table with his free hand. Sounding impatient, he said "Okay, Mr. Anderson. 'Help,' you said. What help?"

Frank's voice was grave. "I'm worried. Being laid off—"

"Hold on. You resigned." The boss had raised his hand and pointed his pen at Frank.

"Correct. Because you…sorry…because your HR people told me to. But that's not the point."

"Right. The point is that a man with your experience understands that Supren wants to implement its own technology and knowhow in sizable projects. Not just wants to, *has* to. Vince is a sharp man and young enough to be molded the way we want our people. We're just starting our involvement in this region and we want to do it right."

"I get that, but—"

"I'm not saying you're old or unqualified. I hear you're an established value in the industry, Frank. But you have your Doornaert way of drilling wells. You've been at it for many years. Always that same technology. We gave you a good severance arrangement. And you know damn well that some of our competitors are fighting for people like you. Even here in Ohio. You may get more money than at Doornaert."

Frank hadn't heard anything new or surprising. "Thank you, Mr. Doyle. And I hope you're right about my prospects. The really bad thing for me is that I had to resign during the drilling—close to the end of it, a very critical phase of an important project." He paused. "I see you nodding. Employers frown on that kind of unusual move. You know that. I'm here to offer my help to Vince anytime, not just during these two weeks you gave me but also afterwards."

"Hmm. Well, go on."

"Not just because Vince looks like a good guy, but because it's of great personal importance to me that Rutgers be and remain a success. It's on my sheet. I feel I've done a good job at Rutgers, that all's in good shape there. I'm sure Vince can keep it that way."

"That's very kind," Vince said. He stared at his boss, who still frowned, apparently not too pleased with Vince's spontaneity.

"And that help you wanted? Tell me." Doyle didn't sound unfriendly but kept nervously tapping his poor pen on the table.

"No money, but a pledge from you that you will speak highly of me when an employer calls you for a reference; tell them I made Rutgers Alpha a success. Me. I'm damn proud of it. Proud to have…." Frank became emotional.

Doyle briefly stared at the ceiling. Then he threw a quizzical look at Frank. "Okay," he said, "if that's all, no sweat. You have my word. Anything else?" He put his pen and phone in his shirt pocket, and got up.

Frank feared for the snow-white shirt. "That's it. *No más.* I wish you success, Texans in Noredge," he said as he got up too. "And I'm sure Vince has found my phone number in the files. Thank you for your time."

"No problem, and thanks for the good wishes, Frank," Doyle said and shook his hand.

"Let me know if I can be of any further assistance, anytime."

"Oh? Right. Okay." The boss was already halfway to his desk, his back to Frank and Vince.

On his way out, Frank bumped into a thirtyish woman when he entered the front room. She was finishing a donut and offered him an embarrassed yet friendly smile. She looked Hispanic.

"My apologies," she said, smoothing her light-blue cotton blouse with her free hand. She carefully positioned her sizable handbag on the windowsill. "I'm a little late today. Mr. Doyle's a very early riser." She looked at the trash can. "Our furniture should arrive in two days, maybe. They promised, anyway." She sighed.

"Never mind. Good morning. Frank Anderson." He looked approvingly at her, noticing her dimpled cheeks as she smiled at him, her head tilted up.

"Joanna Tavares. Nice to meet you."

"Joanna." He tried to imitate her guttural j. "You're not late, are you?"

"One minute."

"Yeah. Did you move here from Houston?"

"Do I sound like it?" she giggled, her dimples deep. "Cleveland. And Puerto Rico."

Frank was charmed. Her English was perfect and he loved her two r's in Puerto Rico.

She kept adjusting the tiny, intricately crafted silvery earring on her left lobe. "They're so delicate," she said but sounded proud.

"They look very special. May I ask you where you found them? Not in Cleveland."

"They're my grandma's. She's seventy-two and didn't like the way they started pinching her as she got older. So, lucky me!" She showed him a pair of wide, dark eyes, two open palms and a big smile.

Frank chuckled inside. "They're exquisite. I hope they don't pinch too much."

She shrugged. "Just a little bit. Thank you."

"Good luck here, Joanna."

"Thanks, Mr. Anderson."

"It's Frank. Take care now."

Chapter 9

One late afternoon near the end of June, on her way to Walmart with the kids, Mary received a call from Harriet. Her neighbor sounded all excited. "A drilling crew will be on its way to my place soon! It could be any day this week, even tomorrow."

Shit. Damn D-day's near, Mary cursed inside. *For Harriet and for her hapless, defenseless neighbors like me.*

"They told me the noise will be like a big hum, not much more, and only at the worst moments. I'm so happy. You should sign, too! We do have oil here. Thirty thousand a well," Harriet cackled.

Mary had always thought the royalty figure was inflated, just part of the sales pitch to credulous landowners. She rolled her eyes in the rearview mirror and mumbled, "If they say so...."

"It's true, Mary."

"Maybe. Have a good evening. Entering Walmart's parking lot, see you later."

"Mommy, you made a mistake!" Jimmy shouted. "We're not yet in the parking lot."

"Almost, Jimmy," she shot back. "I must be careful, all these cars."

That evening, the bloody Supren Company was all she could think about. She was a royal pain and got on the nerves of whoever called her or got within ten feet of her, including Joe and the kids.

The next morning around nine she decided to get Andy and Jimmy in the car and go shopping for clothes in Akron: breathe some different air and forget Supren.

The cool and spaciousness of the mall early in the day, the excitement of the kids trying out new toys and the discovery of summer clothing bargains were a welcome relief.

By three p.m. fatigue had set in.

"Damn you, Supren!" she muttered inaudibly on her way home. She felt nervous again.

As she made the left turn onto Maple, Andy asked from the back seat, "Does your stomach hurt, Mommy?"

"No, Andy. Not at all. Don't worry."

"But why do you make ugly faces?"

"She's angry," Jimmy advised.

Mary reassured her boys. "No, I'm not. Do I make ugly faces? I'm sorry. It's nothing. Just a little toothache. And I'm a bit tired. Are you guys ready for some good kicking? How's the new ball?"

"It's not that new," Andy said with little enthusiasm. Mommy had refused to buy one in Akron.

About half a mile from her home, Mary noticed her first Supren truck. It moved slowly. *My God. It's today.* She sighed.

"S-u-p-r-e-n," Jimmy spelled.

"Supren. What's Supren, Mommy?" Andy asked.

"I'll tell you later. Too much traffic here. All that dirt."

Nearing her house, Mary noticed trucks moving on and off Harriet's grass, leaving clumps of mud on the road, which had been reduced to a narrow, single lane. Parked vehicles and a huge van occupying three quarters of the road width stated categorically that they were in control of traffic.

Mary wormed her way into her driveway. She stopped to let Andy pick up the mail. A wave of dust-laden fumes swept into the car when he opened the door and ran out to the mailbox.

"Hurry!" Mary shouted over the noise of the engines.

Jimmy had his eyes and mouth open wide. "They're so big, so big, Mommy!" he exclaimed. "Wow, those trucks! They—"

"Shut the door!" Mary hollered as Andy returned, his back still to the car, eyes glued on the huge vehicles.

As soon as she parked in front of their garage door the boys jumped out. "Race you, Andy!" Jimmy sprinted toward the road, looking back at his competitor.

"Wait!" Mary yelled. She ran after them, concerned,

although she knew they wouldn't get far: security would be tight at Harriet's. The ubiquitous no-trespassing signs were already up. "Let's go back now. Maybe we can come back later. With Daddy."

"Yeah, when they stop working and the noise is less," Jimmy said.

"But before dark." Andy insisted, sounding disappointed.

"Right." Mary grabbed Jimmy's arm. "Let's go, Andy," she said.

She would have to explain that this was going to be a twenty-four seven operation. The noise, fumes, dust and eardrum-rupturing clanging wouldn't stop; they would get much worse. Supren's oppressive, sleep-robbing lights wouldn't let darkness set in for months.

The boys went to play in the garden.

She entered the kitchen and dropped down in the nearest chair. She sighed, elbows on the table, head in hands. She needed a shower—a long, hot shower with lots of steam. A little pampering. She got up.

As she stared at her body in the mirror, she stood on her tiptoes to inspect her thighs. Always those thighs, although Joe assured her often—and not just before sex— that they were just right, divine. So were her firm breasts. She wanted to believe him. She heard him tell her that she was his leggy brunette. She smiled and stepped into the shower.

The soft caress of the moving water curtain teasing her skin felt like Joe's fingernails eagerly running their course as they explored her body. She visualized her bloodstream slowly picking up speed. *To hell with Supren.*

She toweled off and worked herself into her brand-new, vivid blue jeans. She pulled a flashy, tight fitting yellow blouse from her wardrobe: a special welcome for Joe on this dreadful day. She reached for her perfume.

At seven-thirty, watching cartoons with the boys in the sitting room, she heard two very loud honks.

"Daddy! Yippee! We can go now! See the trucks!" Jimmy jubilated. He jumped off the worn-out couch. "Come on, Andy!"

Mary heard two more loud, long honks. She checked her hair one more time, kicked off her flip-flops and picked a pair of shiny high heels.

Jimmy and Andy had already reached the car when she made it out the door.

As she paraded over to meet Joe, she noticed that the Highlander's doors were still closed. The boys had their noses pressed against the passenger door. Jimmy, standing on his toes, stretched his little body. "Look Mommy! Daddy found a dog! Can we keep it?" he begged.

Joe, smiling in the driver's seat, pointed at his companion. When Mary reached the Highlander he rolled down his window. "Sorry I'm late. Look who I found. His name's Jake."

The dog barked.

Mary stared at an adorable, black and white Collie, not quite a puppy anymore. Jake kept barking. She thought of the countless walks, rain or shine, the cleaning, the food, the vet, the shots, the neutering. All coming her way. *Just what I need on my thin schedule. Joe will take the relaxing evening walks and the rest will land on my list.*

"You *found* him?"

"Kind of!" Joe laughed. He threw a quick glance at the kids and stepped out of his vehicle. "I'll tell you later, Mary. Grab the leash. Jake's still a youngster." He whispered, his eyes lighting up, "Wow, you look great! Those jeans…."

"Okay." She stepped gracefully to the passenger side, feeling Joe's eyes glued to her back.

"I get the leash! I get it!" Andy shouted. "Let me!"

"Watch it!" Mary screamed and kept the door closed.

Andy looked up, surprise in his eyes.

"Sorry, Andy." She knew it had been the unreasonably sharp tone of her cry.

As a kid, she had been bitten by a dog. That was, she had to admit, the real reason why they didn't have one, although they lived in this rural section of Noredge. Joe had often expressed his worries about her and the kids' safety and suggested a dog. But she'd always categorically said no.

"Okay, no dog, but you need a gun," had been his repeated retort.

She had shot back that a gun didn't make a home safer. The contrary was true, she had argued, citing statistics. Joe had told her they were put together by sissies. And now, here was "her" dog. She knew she would be outvoted by a coalition of three. She decided to concede silently, hoping that the boys would help her overcome her fear of Jake.

Joe opened the passenger door, took the leash and handed it to Andy. "Hold on now. He can pull hard and run fast."

Seconds later, Andy and Jimmy sprinted away, romping and hollering.

"See, Mary. They have no fear. Jake's no problem." He put his hand on her lower back and raised his eyebrows.

"So, you did find him," she said matter-of-factly, moving closer.

"Of course, sweetie." He winked, towering over her. "I got him for hundred twenty bucks. Cecil's a friend."

"Cecil?"

"The pit watcher at the Devil well in Alliance."

Amused by Joe's little maneuver, but also resenting it, and still dreading the work Jake would add to her heavy load, Mary stared at her beaming man, then at Jake and the kids frolicking in the distance, and finally at a *fait accompli*. "I love him already, Joe," she said softly and kissed him welcome home.

"I knew you would, Mary. I'm glad you do." He squeezed her tight, one hand on her bosom. "Jake's going to take care of you. Jake and me. And the kids and me will help you make friends with him."

"Enough about that dog." She had turned her gaze toward the road and reluctantly freed herself from Joe's warm grip. "They're watching. Across the road." She heard no whistles. *Not yet*, she groused inside.

"Across the road, yeah, across the road. Has Harriet from 'across the road' come to see you?"

Mary shook her head, lips pursed.

"I knew this would be a tough day for you, Mary. Cecil had those two puppies for a while. He let me choose. Jake will help you, sweetie.'

"Hmm."

"We're going to see lots of people running around here, some of them we've never expected to even know where our town is. Good ones and bad ones. Not just the people on the site but many who're drafting off this…this fracking business. People will be making lots of money, some clean, some dirty. Drug pushers won't be far behind. Jake will be here for you when I'm not around."

"I assume Jake promised," she said with a straight face.

"Huh?"

"Thank you, Joe. Andy, Jimmy and I, we're in good hands." They embraced again. This time she didn't turn her head to the road.

"Look at the little rascals," Joe said, chuckling as he pointed at the boys.

Mary checked her watch. It was getting dark. "Andy! Jimmy! Time to pack it in, boys!" She waved them back.

Andy put his hand up, obviously without enthusiasm or commitment.

Half a minute later three tired buddies walked up to

Joe and Mary. Saliva dripped from Jake's tongue as he panted.

Mary kept her distance.

"Now we can go to see Mrs. Woods, right? Daddy's back. You said so, Mommy," Jimmy reminded her.

She turned to Joe. "Can dinner wait a minute?"

Joe waved her question off, put his arm around Jimmy's shoulder, took over the leash and headed toward the road with him. "Come on. Jake wants to meet our neighbor, I bet."

Mary and Andy followed.

"My friends say Mrs. Woods is scared of dogs, Daddy. Her too."

"That's true, Jimmy," Mary interjected and looked at Joe, who rolled his eyes and shook his head.

He smiled. "Jake will be very kind to her."

"You know, Daddy?"

"I do, but let's watch out now," Joe said, taking the boy's hand as they reached Maple Road.

Bulldozers already were busily preparing the well site: leveling, digging, hauling dirt, bushes and tree trunks. Signs and markers had been placed. Heavy lights mounted on top of SUV's, temporarily according to Joe, provided an eerie, unreal spectacle. Two tanker trailers were on the spot and a third crawled over the grass toward the back of the house. Another truck sat next to the driveway, loaded with heavy equipment. "Generators, pumps, compressors...." Joe knew it all.

They crossed the road with Jake and headed for Harriet's front door, up her asphalt driveway featuring a wall of no-trespassing signs on both left and right sides. They reminded Mary of the walls of snow that used to build up day by day on both sides of their driveway as they dug out after those drifts from the west.

Harriet appeared at the front door.

Joe whispered to Mary, "She looks scared of Jake, eh? Maybe we should put a lion's wig on him."

Her elbow hit his ribs.

He handed the leash to Andy and quietly told him to stay back with Jimmy and Jake.

"Well, the show is on!" Harriet exclaimed, hands up in the air. She looked at Jake for a moment but didn't comment.

"It looks like. Moving along," Joe said.

"Honestly, the people, the Supren guys and one girl, they couldn't be nicer. So considerate." Her voice turned fluttery. "Three of them came to see me last week to do measurements, for two days. They were so—"

"So nice. I'm sure they were," Mary interjected dryly and looked for a smile on Joe's face. She was amused by the quick, puzzled glance Harriet threw at her high heels. "I've noticed Doornaert crews months ago on your land, Harriet. Yours. Measuring. They too seemed 'nice.'"

"Oh. Anyway, it looks like they'll be able to save most of my pine trees in the far back and my rhododendrons to my east side. They told me today. I'm so grateful to these strong guys. Big guys." She looked approvingly at Joe, who quickly turned away toward the kids twenty feet behind him.

Mary knew he had to be rolling his eyes. "Well, Harriet, good earplugs and heavy nightshades should help a lot. Maybe enough," she observed, trying to sound no worse than neutral.

"Oh, they said that the noise—"

"You told me about the humming. When you came with that phone number."

Joe looked away again. "Excuse me, Harriet. My cough."

Harriet seemed unperturbed. She went down to whispering, as if telling a secret. "They say we may see more than one well. You see, the Watsons signed too. Fifty acres, I believe. Together, the Watsons and me, we'll have a big spread for Supren. The guys tell me that changes the picture a lot. Twice the site but much more than twice the oil and gas. You could throw your acres in, too. We might all benefit together with an even bigger spread. I don't think it's any problem that we have Maple Road running between your and my land. They'll be digging a mile deep, they said." She stared at Mary.

"I have Supren's number. I know whom to call there," Mary said brusquely.

Joe frowned. "You do? Supren's contact number? The landman's?"

"It came in our mailbox a few days ago, with a letter. Up to sixteen hundred per acre, negotiable, whatever that means." She enjoyed throwing that tidbit of venom at Harriet, but it was the truth.

Joe frowned.

"Really? I got only eleven," Harriet complained.

"I know. And I got nothing," Mary snapped back. "I think it's bedtime for the boys. And dinner time for Joe." She took his hand and squeezed it.

"Well...." Harriet seemed ready to continue but held back. "Yes, time for the boys. Good night," was all she said.

On the way home, Joe seemed happy to focus on Jake but he held on to Mary's hand. She wondered out loud how her kids would sleep during the night. Joe's coughing was bad enough already, but it was nothing compared to the racket created by the Supren crew today. "And this is just the beginning."

"Yeah. Harriet's queen bee hasn't arrived yet, Mary."

"Who cares? Your queen's right here, with you. Let's walk a little faster."

Chapter 10

That night, after the lovemaking, Joe heard Mary sigh and sigh as she tossed and turned in bed. *Jake,* he figured. The dog would be one more burden on her. He felt guilty. He should have asked her—at least informed her. No, she would have refused; she would have said she was scared. He had tricked his Mary. For himself, but also for her own good. In any case, it was his fault that she couldn't sleep.

Caressing the inside of her right leg, he asked her quietly, "It's Jake, right?" He thought he knew the answer.

Mary turned toward him. Her perfume came with her. As his fingers softly touched her cheek he felt tears. "I know it's an additional load, sweetie," he said. "You're so busy already. I'm sorry. But I'm sure our Jake will be good support for you. He'll get bigger and stronger. He'll protect and—"

"It's not Jake." She sounded weak and not angry at all.

"Oh? What is it?"

"You. I don't want to lose you." She sobbed.

He was taken aback. "Lose me, Mary?" He pulled her over into his arms. "I'm yours, Mary. I'm yours."

"I know. Thank you. I love you too. But Supren may kill you. Doornaert already did great damage to your beautiful body." She ran her hand over his back. "Your coughing...." Her voice broke. "It...it scares me Joe. It may...you may get very sick. Jimmy and Andy and I, we may have to go on without you." He felt her grip tighten.

He had shared her fear many times, but had always said, "It's not that bad. Even less than last week." He rocked her softly.

She sighed.

She already made me give up smoking. And now my job? He couldn't handle the silence. "Okay," he said. "I'll speak with Doyle. Wherever I have to go to find him." He couldn't deny he was scared too; his life could be shorter than it had to be.

"You will? He has an office on Main." She still sounded feeble and sighed, as if she didn't really believe him.

"I know. Good. I might be lucky; he may be one of those rare bosses who're at least willing to hear what their people have to say." He coughed and turned briefly away. He took a tissue from the box on the nightstand for Mary's tears and raised his voice. "Whatever kind this Doyle is, he'll have to listen to me. I'll demand that he put those monitoring devices and warning signals on the dirty water tanks and pits and pumps. On all of them. The systems you've read about for sour wells. Or that the company capture these gases before they can hurt anybody."

"You will? Thank you. Thank you."

"I will."

"But he'll say it's too much money."

He knew she didn't mean it: her joyful, teasing tone told him she was celebrating the success she had pursued for so long. "Whatever he wants to say. I'll tell him it's only fair to me. Don't I have the right to be warned if I'm about to be gassed?"

"You'll need to make an appointment—then he'll dig up some excuse not to see you."

Egging me on. "What? Refuse me? Me?"

"Yes."

"Yeah. You may be right. Okay, I'll surprise him. Catch him on his nest. He'll have to listen or he can do his dirty work himself," he joked and softly poked her belly button.

"Sure!" She laughed.

"See? I made you happy."

"You did, Joe. Surprise him." She kissed him good night and whispered, "You must stay with us."

"I'm not going anywhere, sweetie. You'll be stuck with me for a very long time. Sleep well." He knew she was thinking marriage.

When Joe opened his eyes in the morning and faced reality he was a pack of nerves; he feared he had stuck his neck out an inch too far when he promised Mary he would confront Doyle. He felt pangs in his stomach and it wasn't because of hunger.

At her insistence, he forced himself out of bed at five. He would have a normal breakfast and then drive to the Alpha site near Rutgers Lake to pay an early visit to his friend Al, who worked the five to one shift in the chemicals lab. Next on his list was the Supren office on Main Street, where he would knock on the door no later than seven thirty to see the big boss. He figured he could be on the job by eight fifteen, driving his tanker trailer that sat at Rutgers Lake waiting for him. *If by then Mike Doyle hasn't killed or fired me.*

Shortly after six-thirty, he parked his Highlander at the entrance of the Alpha site, took in the cool morning air, donned his hardhat and headed for Al's lab, an oversized van.

Al Morton worked the chemicals. He was the man who cooked up and tested the various brews that, once blended, became a heavy mush. Supren pumped it down the pipes a mile or more deep at pressures two-hundred times as high as that in a car's tires to do the fracking there. Joe was convinced Al had to know, more or less, what that gelatinous mixture was. Water and sand, of course, and what else? Joe didn't want to look like a fool or ignoramus when he faced Doyle. He had to sound a little smarter than an idiot complaining about rotten eggs. Mary had read and heard about so many chemicals being mixed into that viscous stream. "I worry about much more than bad odors," she had told Joe repeatedly with an eye roll. "Those chemicals and those dangerous pressures."

He knocked on the door of the lab van around six and entered.

Al, a grumpy-looking man around fifty, heavyset and puffing, looked up from his screen with a surprised expression. But he produced a big smile as soon as he recognized his unusual visitor so early in the morning.

"What the hell! Joe! You must need something *real* bad!" he joked as he looked at his watch. "Or did Mary kick you out of bed?"

In a way, that was what Mary had done. With gentle persuasion and good reason. "You guessed it, man. Want to see the bruises?"

Al snickered. "What's up, buddy?"

While they traded jabs, Joe stared at a collection of strangely marked plastic containers surrounding Al's barren work area. "It's my cough, man. Getting worse. Mary's getting very concerned. Me too. The kids are bugging me. Hell, I don't need any damn doctor. I know it's that rotten egg stuff that's killing me. I'm going to talk to the new guy and—"

"Good luck, bud. I hear...well, I haven't talked to him myself. Change, new bosses—it's always hard and dangerous for us peons. But...." Al didn't go on. His eyes showed concern and doubt. His raised, open palms told Joe that he wasn't going to get involved in that delicate discussion with the new chief.

Joe nodded and raised his own hand. "I get it, don't worry," he said. "I came very early. Few people around. My lips will be sealed, but, well, you're adding all kinds of chemical stuff. We all know you do. Much of that it is secret. Know that too. I don't want to get you into any trouble, but could you just tell me the names of the chemicals that are really bad for me?"

"For all of us." Al wrinkled his nose and showed big eyes.

"Of course, but I'm the one snuffing more of them than anybody else."

"I know you are. I get my share too. Okay, names." Al sighed. "If I knew."

"You don't? I hear some are regularly used by other industries, even the food—"

"See all those bloody markings on the plastic?"

"I do."

"Code. All code. Chinese for me. All that crap here is code, man. I could give you the names of a few run of the mill chemicals we use, but they won't harm you, and you probably would forget them anyway. What I do know is that some of the shit we pump down is used in cars. Diesel. Some you can eat, I'm told; some are used by dry cleaners and painters or in camping stoves; some of them carry the fancy name of 'inorganic salt,' whatever that is. I can go on but I can't make you any wiser, because dumb Al simply doesn't know. This roughneck just follows the manuals, or else." He threw up his hands and stared at his early visitor.

Joe pursed his lips. He might as well have slept an hour longer, but Al was an honest person and a friend. "I'd better get out of here," he said. "Thank you and sorry for bothering."

"Anytime, buddy. Give my regards to Mary and don't talk to anybody here. Just walk away like you're in a big hurry. I know you're not. I wouldn't if I were on my way to that Doyle!" Al laughed.

When Joe arrived at 23 Main Street, he noticed a black BMW sitting in the driveway. His watch said seven twenty. He stepped out, stretched his arms, suppressed a yawn, kicked his heels up and proceeded to the front door.

He rang the bell and adjusted his belt while waiting. The door remained closed. Also after his second try.

A car arrived in the driveway. A young woman emerged in a hurry. She waved briefly at Joe, but turned away from him and the house and looked around, up and down Main Street. Then she retrieved a set of keys from her bulging purse and turned to him.

"Sorry for being so rude, sir," she said. "I was looking for a delivery truck. They promised our furniture for yesterday. At four p.m. I called them for the third time and they told me it would be *mañana*.'"

"*Mañana?*"

"Yes. It must have been my accent. From Puerto Rico. Does Mr. Doyle expect you, Mister…?

"Bertolo. Joe Bertolo. I'd like to speak with Mr. Doyle, if he's in today."

"His car's here. He's an early bird. He has a lot of catching up to do, so new on the job. I'm his administrative assistant, Joanna." She extended her hand.

He held it for a second. "Nice to meet you, Joanna. I understand. I won't be long. A few minutes, but it's really urgent."

"Oh?" She seemed to wait for details.

"Urgent and personal."

"Okay. Normally I must tell Mr. Doyle what the visitor wants to discuss." She made wide eyes and softly rocked her head, looking concerned.

"Of course. But this is very personal," he managed to blurt out between coughs.

"I see, Mr. Bertolo," she said hesitantly.

They had drifted toward the front door.

She turned the key and eased Joe in.

A near-empty room stared at him. Binders and loose files were stacked on window sills and covered the floor in a far corner. There was a row of empty picture hooks on the wall to his left. Below them, one lonely-looking metal beach chair sat against the wall, a few feet from a plastic trash container.

Joanna lowered her voice to a whisper as she pointed at a door left slightly ajar, with a "Doyle" card on it.

They heard loud conversation.

"Let me take a look. He must be in the midst of something," she said, tiptoeing toward the door.

He followed her.

"This one? Linda...Yep. Linda! Big...What? Galinda? Oh, that Galinda?" A man inside the room shouted with too much enthusiasm. It had to be Doyle. "Do I remember? Of course. That beauty! Do I remember! Galinda! What? You still there, Jim?"

Joanna frowned. A moment of silence ensued. She motioned Joe away from her.

He moved back just a couple of feet.

She eased closer to the door, until her ear touched it.

The man inside started roaring again. "Yes! Another Galinda! A clone, Jim! A clone! Right! A clone...Agree... Funny! Absolutely. Just as cute! Just as much fun! A clone of Galinda! Wow!"

Joe looked at Joanna in amusement.

She briefly returned his gaze, put her hand up and, looking embarrassed, turned away from him and knocked gingerly.

Saving her boss's ass.

The loud banter stopped.

The door flew open.

A man faced Joanna. In his mid-forties, brown hair, very little gray, tall, average built, he had all the features of a fitness fanatic, despite the evident stubborn little belly under his Polo shirt. Hands on narrow hips, panting, mouth inches away from her he hissed, "What the hell! Don't you see I'm busy? You didn't announce anybody!"

"My apologies, Mr. Doyle. I—"

"Great start, girl," he mocked scornfully. "One more of those and you're out the door, get it?"

"Very sorry, Mr. Doyle. I had no idea—" She shrank as she spoke.

"Who's that?" He had lowered his voice as he pointed at Joe. The anger had faded somewhat from his face.

She looked back at Joe. "It's Mr. Bertolo. He has an urgent personal problem he needs to discuss."

"Bertolo?"

"I'm an employee, Mr. Doyle. Supren employee," Joe said, stepping forward.

"Doing what?"

"Hauling the company's dirty water. To the waste-disposal, the injection facilities in Youngstown. Joe Bertolo."

Doyle sized him up. He offered Joe a handshake and his tone changed to almost jovial and sympathetic. "A personal matter?"

Joe admired the man's capability to make a perfect U-turn without a trace of embarrassment. "Yes, sir." He briefly closed his eyes, folded his hands as if in prayer and nervously pressed his finger tips hard onto his dorsals.

"To be discussed before we're even awake?" Doyle seemed to deliberate internally but then he gestured to Joanna that she could leave. He leaned his head to wave Joe in and closed the door, still grumbling something undecipherable to Joanna. Then, walking to his desk, he said, "Take a seat."

"Thanks," Joe said while taking the metal chair facing Doyle's across his desk. He searched nervously for the best position for his legs and arms.

The impeccably combed man with the detailed mustache kept reshuffling papers. Still standing, he asked, "So, what's up?" He sat down with a slight, tired groan.

"It's my cough. My job. The gas. I catch fumes twice: when I collect the dirty water out of the tanks and pits into my truck, and when I pump it out in Youngstown." He put up his index and middle finger. "Twice."

"No need to teach me the job." Doyle smiled. "You don't pay attention to your detector. Do you wear your gas mask?"

Joe jerked his head back. "I do both. I do. But—"

"You don't bother to put it on correctly." It was an accusation but Doyle's empathetic tone somehow made it sound soothing.

"I've forgotten a few times. Right. It's cumbersome. It's necessary, I agree. But cumbersome. I'm pressed for time. Often. And my detection device," he rolled his eyes, "it doesn't always work. Sorry to be so direct."

"If it doesn't work you have to turn it in." It felt like a suggestion.

Joe knew that. But turning it in wasn't that simple for him, just a roughneck. He shook his head, trying to smile. "It does work, but not really well. Not always." He paused, gathered up his courage and said, almost murmuring, "If we'd have permanent monitoring devices and signalization, or gas capturing devices—"

"And all the money in the world…." Doyle smiled and slowly rocked his head from left to right.

Money. Seething anger rushed through Joe's entire body. "I don't know, sir, Mr. Doyle. But I can tell you that my terrible coughing bouts, the irritation in my eyes, my moments of near-fainting are enough to worry the hell out of my kids and my wife. I believe she's right. She thinks that my grumpiness and the cough that keeps her up at night…. She blames my work at the company for it." He quickly added, "Most of my years were at Doornaert, of course."

"The company? The company. I assume your wife is no doctor. Well, Supren's new here, so she can be forgiven for not knowing what the organization is and stands for."

Joe nodded. "She reads a lot, sir. She says that companies like yours, ours, don't like to spend money." He didn't know how he had spat that out.

Doyle didn't seem offended. "I'm sure Mrs. Bertolo will get to know us better." His eyes solicited agreement.

"We're not married. But we're a steady couple, a family. She's got two children. They need me. They're all afraid that someday…they could have to go on without me." Joe had to fight tears.

"I understand."

Joe now looked at an emotionless face. "I'm not

dramatizing, sir. Not making this up. I'm not." Powerless, he felt like jumping up and screaming.

Doyle coughed softly and said, "Listen. We do take care of our people. We have our procedures for serious accidents, spills, etcetera. Just like Doornaert. We're continuing their excellent program of updating rules on a rolling basis. And I can assure you that Supren is first class in investing in safety and protection equipment." He stared at Joe, stood up and checked his watch.

"I see." Joe realized he had heard corporate lines delivered by a well-practiced messenger. He half-lamented, "All I can do is work more carefully. That's what you're saying. I had hoped for a little more." He trembled.

The Texan shook Joe's hand. "We're unfortunately not in the charity business. We have rules and competitors. I do hope you understand. Thank you for your visit," he said, sighing, and walked toward his desk.

"I think I do." Joe threw a last glance at Doyle's back and strode to the door.

When he entered the front room, dejected, he got an inquisitive stare from Joanna. She had her shoulders hunched, as if expecting bad news or an outburst of disappointment. He wasn't sure whether or not she had overheard part of his plea for help.

"On to work now, Joanna," he said, trying to sound upbeat and jovial. He knew she was having a bad day herself so far. "My truck's waiting for me. My best friend, after my family." He winked.

"And the Lord, maybe?" she asked, her tone signaling she hoped for a positive answer.

"The Lord? Yes, Him too. I should go to church more. Mary's right."

"Your wife?"

"Yes. My dear wife."

"Oh." Joanna looked up, at the ceiling, her hands clasped. "It's all in His hands." She turned to Joe, compassion filling her eyes.

She must have overheard us. "Yeah. Probably. So, you're from Puerto Rico. Catholic, I suppose?"

"Yes I am." Her face was one smile. "I went to see Father Bianchi after Mass on Sunday. At Saint Agnes."

"My wife's a regular there. Rather regular. With the kids. Maybe I should join them more. Talk more to the Big Friend." He laughed, then doubted she appreciated his tone and choice of words.

"One more thing." Joanna kept her voice hushed and her eyes on the "Doyle" door as she gestured Joe away from it. "I think we should keep it between us, what we heard Mr. Doyle discuss so loudly. I might get fired if he'd hear we—"

"Don't you worry. I would get booted myself. Loose lips sink ships, right?"

"Thank you, Mr. Bertolo. I need my job. I'm on my own now." She sounded a bit sad.

He nodded kindly. "I see. And I'm Joe. Very sorry for the trouble I got you into."

"Maybe I'll see you at church?"

"If the Lord lets me." He laughed knowing it wouldn't be the Lord but Father Bianchi who would remonstrate with him if he showed up to mass. It had been months, and Mary wasn't his wife. The father had wagged his index at him more than once.

"Hasta pronto, Joanna," he said and walked to the front door. Holding the knob, he turned his head to offer her a final smile.

She waved, her hand low.

Chapter *11*

By early July Noredge was bursting at the seams, confronting sea-changes as best it could, like a teenager struggling clumsily to control limbs that suddenly felt too long. Supren had injected a hefty dose of growth hormone into the small town as well as the region. The company was speeding along on the alphabet route: in addition to Alpha at Rutgers and Beta at Harriet's, Supren crews had popped up at two more sites, the future homes of Gamma and Delta. Both were located a bit more than two miles northwest of Rutgers.

Smartly using the same syringe, Supren's HR department had pretty much silently complemented the growth hormone with a hefty dose of organizational antibiotics: they had eliminated many non-crucial employees and replaced some of them with independent contractors.

So far, Joe had escaped the ax, but a couple of his friends hadn't. Mary worried when, from the kitchen, she would watch her man pacing the porch, hunched and mumbling, unresponsive to the shouts of the kids. Since his discussion with Mike Doyle, he had turned inward. Brooding.

When she would ask him to see a doctor he would fire back, "That damn doctor again?" He'd just purse his lips and shake his head. "I've got plenty of syrups and pills. And enough other poison in the air."

Across the street, at Harriet's, the site preparation crew was doing its job with its entourage of trucks, vans, trailers, pumps, compressors, generators, lifting devices, piping, tanks and a crowd of workmen and technicians, their blue hardhats and bright yellow clothing adding color to the noisy, fume-laden dustbowl that her neighbor's backyard had become.

The new Noredge made Mary's head spin.

Endless lines of trucks and tankers, fumes fouling and coloring the air, lights shooting their rays all night long, torturing Mary and her family, transforming the sky over Harriet's land into a whitish onyx globe. Earplugs, loud television or music unable to match the banging and clanging, louder than a pile driver. Telephone conversations morphed into shouting matches, except when sporadically a brief, mysterious decibel drop created shocking silence. Dust permeated Mary's entire house, every nook and cranny, and exacerbated Joe's pitiful, cruel coughing. Roughnecks brawled and shouted near every corner tavern and a herd of fortune hunters toiled long hours for big salaries. A porn shop opened and there were more arrests involving drugs and prostitution.

New barber shops popped up, grocery stores, medical offices, accounting firms, clothing stores, bars, restaurants, rental agencies, temporary housing, garages…. Tsunamis of new dollars magically splashed broad smiles on the faces of Mayor Sanders and his Chamber friends. Mary hated the eternal traffic jams and the long lines at the bank and the post office.

She started meticulously locking the doors and shutting the windows when leaving the house for school or shopping. Jake had become her loyal friend, but she had a hard time controlling him since the moment the first crew of Doornaert had set foot on Harriet's land. One day he had crossed Maple Road unsupervised. When Mary caught up with him he was feasting on a piece of sausage. "Eating my lunch!" a jovial worker joked as he measured her longer than he should have.

Once Harriet had come to the house to complain, panting as she pleaded for a chain or at least a reliable leash for Jake. "That animal's paralyzing me, Mary. I hope I won't have to call the police," she said, her stare ominous.

"I'll make sure Jake's no problem for you," Mary had assured her. "Much less of a problem than the one my family and I must face." She had leaned her head in the direction of the drill site.

"It's all for the good of the community," Harriet had

retorted, her tone indignant. "Mayor Sanders appreciates the sacrifice I make, giving up my backyard and privacy."

"And our privacy, and our health, our—"

Harriet already had done an abrupt one-eighty and was headed for home. She briefly looked back and shouted, "You'd better keep that dog away from my yard. Somebody might poison him!"

Andy and Jimmy understood the new "Jake rules" Mary established for them. They just nodded. These already were sad days for them.

One morning they were kicking balls with two other boys. Mary, on her knees, was pulling weeds on a nearby flower bed. She heard a car door slam and looked up.

A woman standing next to an old station wagon in the driveway shouted, hands cupped around her mouth, "Bobby! Over here! Hurry. You're late for your reading!" Her hair curlers and scary heavy glasses complemented the shrillness of her voice. She disappeared into her car.

Mary stood up and walked in the direction of the boys, cleaning her hands on a rag.

Bobby rolled his eyes and grumbled, his back to the vehicle, "My mom again. I finished my book last night. She doesn't want me to play here. 'Your yard's too dangerous,' she says. 'Bad air, crazy people around.' I like it here, but her...." He tilted his head toward the driveway. He dragged his feet as he left. He briefly looked back at his friends. "Bye."

Nathan, the other friend in the game, shrugged. "Mothers."

Jimmy and Andy kept quiet and looked at Mary.

"I'll take Bobby's place." She was ready to go. "Goalie?"

Mary worried constantly about Joe, her rock, who stoically assured her it would all pass. She had thought of moving, temporarily, but rents in the region had skyrocketed, while property values in drilling areas had plunged. Joe pointed out that it wouldn't look too good in Supren's eyes if one of its employees moved out because of the company.

Now and then the boys would ask, beg, "Why can't we go and watch, Mommy? All those trucks and huge pipes and the crazy men shouting? It's fun!"

"No," Mary would tell them.

"We'll watch less TV," Andy would bargain.

"No is no."

Occasionally Mary would drive the kids to her friend Dan Clark's place in Hartville. The Sierra guy had a swimming pool and loved to talk to her about anything environmental. But she worried about wearing out her welcome.

Often on these hot summer days Mary sought solace in work and caring for her family as best she could. Air conditioner set at sixty-seven, Jake stretched out right in front of it, she cleaned and scrubbed and vacuumed, ears plugged and nose and mouth covered, her mind with Joe and the kids, her anger directed at multiple targets.

Chapter *12*

The drilling rig, the queen bee, arrived at Harriet's with much fanfare and a huge entourage in mid-July. It was an impressive, ten-story high structure. A week later it embarked on its newest expedition: a deep dive, Joe had said, through sand, water, clay and rock to about a mile below Harriet's pasture, now transformed into a grimy drill pad. Almost overnight, traffic on Maple Road and even downtown Noredge became unbearable: dust, fumes, and decibels; constant irritants for eyes, ears and nostrils; nerves strained. Bike rides became suicide missions.

A few days after the queen's arrival, Mary drove back home from grocery shopping with the kids at Lou's Market; she had to battle trucks, shouting, eardrum-piercing clanging, dust, mud and fumes.

About a quarter mile from home the rig came into view, a majestic presence towering a hundred feet high. Andy and Jimmy started shouting and oohing again, still excited and in awe over the huge structure. Unlike Mary and Joe, the boys hadn't lost a minute of sleep yet because of the ceaseless clanging and banging and the harsh, eye-torturing lights across the road. They had begged Mary to let them invite friends so they could show them "their" rig and all those huge vehicles. "After dark, Mommy. With the lights!"

Mary had turned them down. The last thing she wanted was a bunch of kids cheering on Supren's brutal attack on Mother Nature. She smiled when Joe explained with great authority and big gestures, "Some of those pipes can explode any minute, pieces flying all over the place, even across the road. Haven't you seen that they all wear hardhats over there? Even those big, strong men?" The kids had stared at him, their faces showing resignation mixed with puzzlement. Mary had winked at him.

Nearing home, she had to shout, "Quiet!" more than a couple of times as Andy and Jimmy competed for the best observation spot on the back seats, wrestling and crawling over each other.

"He's kicking me, Mommy! It hurts," Jimmy complained.

"Ouch!" Andy screamed. "He punched me, Mom!"

"Jimmy! Your seat belt!" She felt small and vulnerable, a dwarf in the threatening crowd of fume-spewing mastodons.

Finally she could make the left turn into her driveway. She noticed a small red car, older model, its trunk seriously dented, right in front of her garage door. As soon as she turned off the ignition and the kids tumbled out of her

Corolla, the driver's door of the red vehicle opened. A young, dark-haired woman emerged, neatly dressed, holding a thin briefcase and, strangely, staring at the grass in the side yard.

Mary stepped out. She didn't recognize the visitor. *I'm wearing my worst jeans,* she worried as she walked up to her.

The lady seemed distressed. She didn't greet the kids but went straight to Mary, lips quivering. "Mrs. Bertolo?" she said

Mary nodded, her heart pounding.

"So sorry. We couldn't...we didn't have your cell number. I've been waiting—"

"Excuse me. Who are you?" Mary trembled. *Joe.* "What's wrong?" She knew it: the woman's tone and faltering delivery had told her this wasn't going to be good news.

"I'm Mr. Doyle's assistant. I—"

"Joanna?" Mary froze. "Is it Joe?" she shouted.

Joanna nodded. Her free palm down she whispered, after a quick glance at the kids in the yard, "He's in good hands. His truck—"

"No! No!" Mary's cry tore the heavy air.

The kids turned their heads toward her and looked at each other. Jake began to bark from inside the house.

Joanna grabbed her arm and held it. "He's going to be okay, ma'am."

"What happened? Okay? Okay you said? You're sure?" Mary begged for a yes. She checked on the kids.

"Mr. Doyle told me so. From Cleveland. He sent

me. Your husband had an accident. He's in the Akron City Hospital." Joanna took a sheet of paper out of her briefcase. "I wrote the directions down from my iPhone while I waited. Almost entirely Interstate 77."

Of course. "Thanks. Thank you...." Mary tried to collect herself. "What happened? Andy, Jimmy, over here! We must go to Akron, see Daddy in the hospital!"

Joanna put her hand up. "I think they'd better wait to see him until he's a bit better."

"Huh? Is it that bad?"

"I don't know any details. Mr. Doyle wasn't entire clear. But he gave me permission to stay here with the children until you get back from Akron."

"Oh, no. No. I want to take my kids with me."

A Nissan Altima appeared in the driveway and out stepped Frank Anderson. He greeted the women from a distance with a half-wave, looking subdued and in a hurry. He shook hands with Mary and nodded kindly at Joanna. "So, you already know. So sorry," he said softly. "I came to help."

"Help? I don't know how." Mary sighed, feeling lost, incoherent. "Joanna...Joanna, right? Joanna says she's going to stay here with the kids. It's not that I don't trust her, but Andy and Jimmy *must* go with me. I know where the hospital is."

Frank shook his head, looking in command. "You shouldn't drive. And the kids had better stay here. We'll take my car. You and me. The kids will be okay. I know Joanna." He gestured he was ready to go.

"You know her?" Mary's gaze drifted toward her kids. *The kids.* Jake kept barking. She lingered.

Frank seemed to grow nervous.

"Is Joe dying?" Mary asked, her eyes wide.

"No, no. I don't think so. But we have no time to waste. It's more than half an hour's drive. You'd better be around when treatment decisions must be made." He raised his eyebrows.

"Joe can't…?" A shockwave shot up her spine.

Frank stared down as he shook his head, lips pursed. Then he said, "I heard he was unconscious."

"What happened? When? Why?" She stared at him. Her plaintive tone made her sound reproachful. He had to be withholding the worst about Joe.

He nodded briefly at Joanna.

She stood with the kids, apparently explaining how she was going to take care of them. The boys listened, looking concerned but staring at her with eyes full of confidence.

Frank turned to Mary. "You've got your driver's license, right?"

"Yes." She ran to Andy and Jimmy and pulled them against her. She had to swallow before she managed to say, sobbing, "My darlings, I must go help Daddy. He's not feeling well and needs me. He'll come home soon."

"How soon?"

"Very soon, Andy. I know he will. This kind gentleman

here is Mr. Anderson. I'm going with him to see Daddy in Akron," she said soothingly.

"Where's Akron, Mommy?" Jimmy asked, measuring Frank.

"Andy, can you tell Jimmy about Akron? I must go now."

The elder boy nodded. "How ill is Daddy?" he asked, sounding fearful.

"I'll have to ask the doctor there. But he'll get better quickly. We must go now. Be good with Miss Joanna. She's a nice lady. I'll be back as soon as…." She had to turn her head away from her boys and started searching in her purse.

Joanna accepted the house key from Mary and put her arms over Jimmy's and Andy's shoulders. "Come with me big guys. I'll make dinner for you. What would you like to eat?" They headed toward the house. Jimmy was crying softly.

Mary was heartbroken.

"They'll be fine, Mary," Frank said calmly as he watched the threesome. "I've met Joanna. A very good person. Let's get in the car. Joe needs you."

Mary felt her world had collapsed as she struggled to the car. Her pent-up emotion opened the flood gates for her tears as Frank sat down next to her and took the wheel.

"Maybe you should take one of these," he said, showing her a little bottle. "The doctor prescribed this for me. I'm going through a rough patch myself."

She frowned. "What is it?"

"Just Valium. Take one. You'll be able to help Joe better. You're not driving." He opened the bottle and handed her a pill.

"You—?"

"Yes. I took one last night. Here's water. Unopened."

"For me?"

"You should take it. Go ahead."

She gave Frank a good stare. She knew what this Valium meant. She said, her voice weak, "Okay, thank you. But you must tell me the truth about Joe. All of it." She swallowed the yellow pill.

"What I know is this: his truck must have veered off the road on Route 39 close to the intersection with Route 43, just before entering Carrollton from the west. I hear 39 is pretty curvy there. His vehicle rolled over and hit a tree. I don't know exactly how." He shook his head, staring straight ahead.

"Oh, no! No!" She buried her head in her hands, sobbing. "Just what I've always worried about."

"Locals tried to pull him out but had to call the fire department, with their cutting equipment. Then an ambulance. He was losing blood from the head. His right leg—I don't—I only know it was in rather bad shape."

"Bad shape? What do you mean?" She wanted to pull his arm.

"The folks in Akron should be able to tell us soon." He kept looking straight ahead.

"Akron. Let's hurry, Frank. But what happened?"

"Nobody seems to know. No witnesses yet, I heard. But his tanker is leaking. Spilling the dirty water. When I left for your place it had reached the intersection with Route 43. By now—"

"By now Joe may be dead," she cried. "I'm calling the hospital."

"I already did. Twenty minutes ago. I thought you were there. They were tight-lipped. I'm not a relative. 'No information.' Everything I told you I heard from Vince Davis. Mike Doyle had spoken with him."

"Davis?"

"The guy who took my job. Not a bad guy. He was very concerned. Have some more water."

"I'll call. They'll talk to me. I'm his wife, his—"

"Wait." He handed her his iPhone. "Here's the number I dialed. Emergency."

She was too nervous. "I can't."

He took the phone back and dialed. "Here you go. Lots of traffic."

The phone rang forever at Akron City Hospital. When Mary finally got through she screamed Joe's name into the phone. "Bertolo! B-e-r-t-o-l-o...Yes! Jenkins...Not his wife...What?...Oh, no!" She slammed the phone into her lap, dejected. "They won't give me information over the phone. Shit!"

"We'll be there soon. Try to rest. The Valium—"

"So you want to really shut me up with Valium? I'm mad as hell!"

Frank jerked his head in her direction. "Are you okay, Mary?"

She covered her mouth. "I'm sorry, Frank. Very sorry. I should be very grateful to you. I am."

"No problem. A few more minutes and then you can explain to them who you are. I'll vouch for you."

She didn't answer but lowered her head.

Chapter  13

The elderly receptionist at the hospital dragged her considerable weight from behind her desk to greet a teary-eyed Mary, who felt lost and helpless in the busy lobby. It smelled like a pharmacy. Frank had quickly dropped Mary off and gone to park his car. "Can I help you, ma'am?" the lady asked, puffing but sounding sympathetic and concerned.

"Joseph Bertolo," Mary blurted out, her voice quavering. She trembled on her legs, staring through the glass entrance door, wondering what was taking Frank so long. She felt embarrassed about her faded jeans. Two younger receptionists looked up and then at each other.

The lady nodded. "And you are?"

"Mary Jenkins."

"Jenkins...."

"Mr. Bertolo's partner...girlfriend. We've lived together for years. Almost two years."

The lady limped back to her seat, sighing as she sat down. "Your address?"

"1034 Maple Road, Noredge." It took Mary quite an effort, her memory blurred. "I can't remember the zip code. Close to Canton."

"Can I see your driver's license?"

Mary felt a tap on her shoulder. Frank. She acknowledged her panting savior with a heartfelt nod and handed the receptionist her identification.

The lady frowned briefly but then said jovially, "Good that you have a friend to drive you. Stress causes accidents." She kept shaking her head; her search for Joe in the computer system seemed to take forever. Then she said, "He's in surgery."

"How much longer?" Frank asked, adding, "I'm a friend of the family."

The receptionist smiled. "I'd gathered that. Take a seat." She pointed at a row of metal chairs near a hallway entrance. "An assistant will come and brief you."

Mary stared helplessly at Frank.

He walked Mary to the chairs.

As she waited she kept her gaze trained on the elevators across the spacious lobby, silent, unable to find adequate words to thank Frank. He had rushed to her assistance although she barely knew the man. *It must be Sonya. Or that Joanna?*

Frank's phone rang. "It's Vince, my successor. Back in a minute." He went to the glass door and exited the building.

Mary hoped and prayed that Frank would be back when the assistant would arrive. Shaken and afraid, she wasn't confident she would understand and remember correctly what she might hear about Joe. She felt lost, vulnerable in the immense space of the lobby with its cacophony of nervous voices and hurried pedestrian traffic. She got up and stepped to the glass door to check on Frank. He was only twenty feet away. She returned to her seat, calmer.

Two minutes later he rejoined her. "Vince told me—oh. This must be the assistant." They stood up.

The young female doctor wore heavy glasses. Her face exuded kindness and empathy as she walked up to Mary and Frank from the reception desk. She looked at Frank, who pointed at Mary. "Miss Jenkins, I'm Doctor Lima."

Mary nodded, her eyes fearfully questioning the diminutive woman.

"Doctor Toro's surgery is progressing well but will take some more time, and it looks like we'll keep your partner in an induced coma for at least a day. He has suffered a serious concussion. The accident has damaged internal organs. And his knee and foot...we're still evaluating. We have no full diagnosis yet but—"

"Oh! Oh! The surgeon will save him, right?" Mary wanted to embrace Doctor Lima. Until this young woman walked up to her, she had feared that Joe's condition was hopeless. That the no-information responses from Joanna and Frank were only part of a well-intended charade to soften the blow. But now she felt relieved: surgeons were devoting their energy to saving Joe. He could be saved! *Will be*, she told herself inside.

Doctor Lima had her hand up. "As I said, we have no full diagnosis, Miss Jenkins, and of course no prognosis so far. We're always optimistic, but also careful. Doctor Toro is excellent. You can contact me anytime, but wait another three hours before you do so. Surgery should be finished by then." She offered Mary her card.

"I don't know how to thank you and Doctor Toro and all the people here." Mary half-sobbed. She looked at the receptionist, who seemed busy.

"Where do you live?" the doctor asked.

"In Noredge. Near Canton."

"Maybe you should wait until tomorrow to visit. Your husband—your partner— he'll be unresponsive for the next twenty-four hours."

Mary looked down to hide her tears. She handed Doctor Lima's card to Frank. "I may lose it."

On the way home, she had trouble staying awake. The Valium. She never took pills of any kind. "Thank you so much, Frank," she said, her voice low and her words slightly slurred. "What would I've done without you?"

"Don't mention it, Mary. It'll be at least fifty minutes in the car. Rush hour on I-77. Try to get some rest. Joe's in good hands and the kids will have a lot of concerns and questions for you when you get home."

***

A soon as Mary had dozed off Frank called Vince back. He felt badly about having cut off his successor so brusquely when he had seen Mary's panicked expression through the glass door at the hospital.

He was anxious to know why Vince had called him. To inquire about Joe? Unlikely. He assumed the two men didn't know each other. But Vince had sounded quite excited about something. What was it? Had he run into a problem at Beta, and did he want Frank's help?

When Vince picked up he said he knew Joe and asked about his condition.

Frank briefed him.

Vince said, "Please tell his wife my thoughts are with her and her family, and with Joe of course. Now, Frank," he went on, changing the subject, "you and I, we've known each other for a just short time but I trust you, and I must talk to somebody. You're my victim if you don't mind." He laughed nervously. "I'm pissed off. Almost ready to throw in the towel. Mad as hell."

Frank had helped Vince during his first two weeks at Supren, as agreed.

"Huh?"

"With that damn Mike Doyle. Here I'm working my butt off to do a decent drilling job at Beta, things going so well, and an hour ago the idiot grabs me for the clean-up at the accident area in Carrollton. As if I'm the company maid. Looks almost like it's all my fault, dammit. No chance to object. 'Right now! Drop everything and get your ass over there! Supren's name is at stake, get it?' As if Beta doesn't count. Couldn't get a word in." Vince paused and added, his tone calmer, "This is between you and me, okay? I thought we got along well those two weeks."

"Wow. How long will you be gone from the drill site?"

Vince sighed. "Who knows? It may take months, from what I hear. We all know about those spills in Pennsylvania."

"Buzz off, you!"

"Huh? Frank?"

"Sorry, Vince. I'm in traffic. Some asshole gave me the finger. Back to Carrollton. Mike should call in specialists. If the job's not done expertly Ohio may shut Supren down all over the state."

"Of course. Well, I know zilch about politics. Anyway, I asked him who would take responsibility for the Beta job. What about that poor orphan?"

"Yeah! And good old Harriet will miss you." Frank had heard stories from Mary about Harriet and her mid-morning cookies.

Vince snickered but got serious again. "Mike shut me up. 'You heard me and don't you try to do my job. I'll face the music for everything, Carrollton, Alpha, Beta, the entire alphabet, got it?' So what could I say? Do you understand how this man's brain functions?"

"Mike will oversee Beta? Him? Mike Doyle?" Frank was more than surprised. He took a look at Mary, who leaned against the passenger door, curled up like a baby, knees pulled up.

"Guess so. But I hear he hasn't drilled a well for at least four years. Maybe he'll call you back."

Frank chuckled. The thought had entered his mind, but he had discarded it. "I wouldn't bet on that. He wanted his own man for Beta, remember?"

"I do."

"He had one."

"Yeah. Me. Vince Davis. Doormat Davis. But Doyle, that idiot— no, I should stop using that word. Love my job." He laughed but sounded concerned.

"Any idea what happened in Carrollton? Joe's tanker just jumped off the road? Just like that?" Frank thought about the concerns Mary had voiced about Joe's health. Had he had a sudden, violent coughing spell?

"When I asked him that question, and about witnesses, Doyle simply said, 'Just stay out of it, young man. Okay? I'll handle those kinds of matters. You understand personal issues may be involved.'"

Personal issues. Frank looked at Mary, who was snoring lightly, and whispered, "You mean he's kind of blaming Joe? Joe asleep at the wheel? Joe on something? No mechanical malfunction or anything?"

"Sounded like he did. Not clear. Anyway, I dropped everything and rushed to Carrollton. The leaked stuff wasn't contained yet but flowed very slowly, movement barely noticeable. Route 39 will be closed off for a long time, the center of town as well, county and state officials hinted. We'll have to find out exactly what was leaked. How dangerous that stuff is. You know more or less what shit we're pumping down the pipes and what comes back up. Looks like Joe Bertolo picked up most of his load in Zanesville. We'll have to talk to the folks there."

"Good luck, man. You'll be in the papers tomorrow. And not because you hit a triple."

"Are you kidding? I'm already on TV."

"Carry your shaver in your pocket," Frank chortled. He wondered why Doyle was acting so strangely with Vince. It had to be nerves: Supren Headquarters had to be all over him. Noredge and surroundings, or the entire state of Ohio might at least disqualify the company for future permits.

"TV. Yeah." Vince's dismissive tone made it clear he had bigger fish to fry.

Frank heard Mary groan. She turned restlessly, shifting left and right in her seat. "Got to go now, Vince. Take care and stay in touch." He clicked off.

"Where are we?" Mary mumbled as she opened her eyes, hand on forehead.

"Close. Less than five minutes. The boys will be happy to see you."

***

As she stepped out in her driveway, feeling drowsy, Mary said, "I can't thank you enough, Frank. You want to come in for a cup of coffee or tea?" She reflexively looked for her key in her purse but then remembered that she had given it to Joanna.

He shook his head. "You need to be with your kids and

tell them the good news about their daddy. I should be heading home."

"Okay." She actually wanted him to join her: he would be so much better than she right now at answering the kids' questions and allaying their concerns. But she didn't insist.

Andy opened the front door before she could knock.

Five minutes later, when she stood again on her threshold saying goodbye to Joanna, Mary spotted Frank's car still in the driveway, a few feet behind Joanna's vehicle.

Jimmy pulled her shirt, "Mommy...."

"*Ssh*, Jimmy!" She quietly closed the door when Joanna was half-way to her car.

Chapter 14

The evening was pure hell for Mary. Her first two calls to the hospital went unanswered. When she got through around nine, a male nurse with an incomprehensible name and heavy accent told her that surgery had finished only half an hour ago, and that Joe was being transferred into the intensive care unit. She checked on the kids one more time and went to bed.

Tossing and turning as she longed for the morning and news about Joe, she kept checking her cell phone.

As she lay half-awake, an army of sadistic torturers kept taking turns on her. Cruel lights and drum-piercing sounds emanated non-stop from Harriet's yard; the short hand and even the long one on Mary's clock irritatingly crawled; painful scenes featuring her suffering Joe evoked cutting bursts of self-recrimination at shorter and shorter intervals, their bile ever more caustic. Why hadn't she forced Joe to quit that damn job? Spoken louder? Threatened to break up? It was all her fault. She had gone along, for the money. That dirty money. Joe had to have lost control of his tanker.

The poison he had been inhaling had caused dizziness or confusion, a headache, or maybe a brief black-out. Had he had a violent coughing spasm? Poor Joe, trying to make a decent living for himself and his family.

It was a night of sighs.

She had concluded that at seven she would call the hospital, no matter what. Then she made it six.

At five she went to the living room and checked the TV news. WKSU first, NPR. Classical music. Fox. Leisure discussion. WEWS, NBC next. Infomercial. CNN. Political discussion, a rerun. She puffed and gave up. She dialed the hospital, Jake devotedly watching her. Did he feel what was going on?

A cold-hearted machine greeted her. "If this is not an emergency we cannot connect you to the department you are requesting at this time. Please call back later."

Cruel. She flung her body onto the couch and curled up.

Jimmy appeared, dazed, rubbing his eyes. "I thought Mrs. Harriet had come."

"Oh no, Jimmy. You've been dreaming."

"I heard her voice, Mommy." The boy sounded upset that his mother didn't believe him.

"No you didn't, baby. It was a lady reporter on TV."

"Baby?"

She pulled him close to her and felt his warm little body soothe her. She needed him. He fell asleep.

She didn't.

At six she carried Jimmy to his bed, called Akron

and got through to Joe's floor. She nervously waited. An eternity.

The nurse advised Joe was resting in intensive care. The details would have to come from Doctor Toro, but right now he was preparing for surgery. An assistant would call Mary within two or three hours.

Mary sighed, disappointed but relieved: Joe lived. *Resting.* She smiled. She had nobody to share the good news with at this hour.

The Jenkinses had an unusually early breakfast that Friday morning. Between bites the boys threw short frowns at Mary, their eyes questioning. She put on her bravest face. She already had told them that Daddy might come home soon, but not how soon. She wondered how long she would be able to keep getting away with this tepid kind of appeaser.

"You're tired, Mommy," Jimmy said. He turned to Andy and added, "Because she watched sports on TV very early."

"No, I didn't. I tried to find news about Daddy's accident."

"How did it happen, Mommy?"

"Nobody knows yet, Andy. But we'll find out." She filled his cup with milk and turned away to hide the tears welling up in her eyes.

At 7:45 Frank called. "How are you doing, Mary? Did you get some sleep?"

"Doing okay. Joe's resting, in intensive care. Dr. Toro will call in two hours."

"Good. Resting. Joanna told me Mike Doyle will speak on TV, on NBC, at eight."

"Oh. Thank you. NBC. Joanna? At work so early?"

After a brief pause Frank said, "She was in the office at seven with Mike. She's very concerned about you."

"How caring she is."

"Yes. We had a brief chat yesterday in your driveway."

And he gave her his number. If she didn't have it yet. She suppressed her urge to comment and hastened to answer, "The boys love her."

"Of course they do. She's very sweet, but, well, she was nervous on the phone. You haven't heard from me, okay? You know Mike, control freak. She needs her job."

"Got it, Frank. Thanks." As Mary clicked off she wondered why Mike Doyle still hadn't offered her, Joe's common-law wife, the courtesy of a call. Not that she looked forward to it; she feared she might spit out too much of her anger at him, but she asked herself how he felt. He had offered her Joanna's help, but what did that signal? Empathy? Heartfelt support? Appeasement? Image maintenance? She saw herself sliding toward negativity and decided she would have to wait for WEWS, NBC to find out, maybe, who Doyle was. At eight o'clock.

She brushed her teeth, took her nightgown off and splashed a load of cold water on her face. She slipped into her worn Nike shorts and tee-shirt, sat down on the couch and waited, nibbling aimlessly on an apple. Eight o'clock couldn't come soon enough.

News anchor Jack Jones started his morning program on WEWS by describing a traffic accident in Carrollton with significant potential impact on the town and possibly Ohio's hydraulic fracturing industry. "That's a mouthful. Jeff just calls the technology 'fracking,' as do some laymen," he said. His fingers provided the quotation marks and his head pointed at the young assistant next to him, Jeff Simmons. "The vehicle involved was a tanker truck owned by the Supren Company. It transported waste water, flowback and produced water, from wells. Some call it 'dirty water.'"

Jeff's slightly raised eyebrows seemed to signal he had trouble refraining from an eye roll.

Jones offered his and NBC's support to driver Joe Bertolo and family, and to the people of Carrollton, and informed his audience that Mr. Bertolo, a Supren employee, was in intensive care in Akron City Hospital. The cause of the accident was unclear.

He went on, "The industry has become, as we all know, a kind of goose with golden eggs for Ohio, creating jobs and raising standards of living for our state. As a 'good citizen' of Ohio it has made major strides toward shielding the environment and the population from the negative side effects every industry or technology brings with it. It's unfortunate that a traffic accident is already being used in some circles to cast aspersions on the capabilities and diligence of a company that brings great progress to Ohio."

"Cover-your-ass paragraph spoon-fed by Supren and

their buddies," Mary mumbled scornfully to herself. Annoyed, she dipped her toast too deep in her lukewarm black coffee and threw a look at her boys. They were outside, practicing very early distance kicks with gusto.

Jeff took over, his tone matter-of-fact, his speed twice Mr. Jones's. "In a minute we'll have Mr. Michael Doyle on your screens via Skype. He's based in Noredge and manages Supren's sites in several counties. Supren owns the tanker truck involved in the accident with the dirty water. Seems it was on its way to an injection well—"

"We'll get the benefit of Mr. Doyle's knowledge," Jones cut in, "his information and views on the situation in Carrollton, as well as specifics about the accident itself and the chemical composition of the spilled water. But first, Jeff will provide to us a few figures that illustrate the role hydraulic fracturing plays in the economies of Ohio, the USA and the world."

Jeff was barely twenty seconds into his presentation when Mary stood up, turned up the volume and walked out, leaving the door ajar. She didn't need this lecture. *This blatantly partisan industry pitch.* She knew by whom it was written: the graphics had told her right away she had seen and heard it before, more than once on YouTube, and once at a Sierra Club gathering she had "forgotten" to mention to Joe. She felt bad for Jeff, who apparently had been told to present it.

She wanted to catch some fresh air, but the heat hit her as soon as she had taken a few steps. The boys didn't even notice her. She told herself she would do all she could to keep them as carefree as they sounded now, kicking their ball. She went back inside and closed the door.

The screen now showed Mike Doyle. The low-resolution picture didn't serve him well and the sound transmission was uneven. Mr. Jones offered apologies.

Doyle waved him off. "What counts is Joe Bertolo's health, his full and speedy recovery. That's number one. Number two, and just as important and urgent, is a complete clean-up of the spill, for which I offer my sincere apologies to the people of Carrollton. We must save their soil, their air, their health and well-being. Within two hours after hearing about the accident—I was participating in a meeting in Cleveland at that time—I had appointed a superbly qualified engineer to contain the spill, Vince Davis. He's a godsend. A local man, he'll be in constant communication with the authorities of Carrollton, Carroll County and the state. He talks the language of the county. He will be totally transparent with all of you regarding possible dangers and the precautions you should take."

"Great, Mr. Doyle, but—"

"I'm not finished yet, Jeff. At this moment we have cordoned off a major section of downtown, but as soon as we have clarity, know exactly what was spilled, we hope to significantly relax those inconvenient measures."

"Okay, but I have four questions for you."

"One at a time," Jones cut in. "Mr. Doyle must have had little sleep."

Jeff closed his eyes for a split second. "Okay. Number one: what's been spilled? Dirty water. Dirty water is what?"

Doyle nodded. "Good. It's a byproduct of our operation. Waste. Could be from the drilling or just from the operation of the wells, or both. It's 'dirty,' in layman language. It's unfortunately hard to treat adequately, so we inject it into a special well and it'll sit there for...forever. We plug the well. You see, we take care at great expense to dispose—"

"You said 'dirty.' So—"

"Some say 'dirty.'"

"Right. But what is it?"

"Well, we're working to get that answer. The exact one for this case. But I can now tell you that—"

"Just tell us whether the stuff is radioactive, whether it has carcinogens, how scared the folks in Carrollton should be."

Doyle smiled briefly. "I see you did your homework," he complimented the younger man, a trace of condescension in his voice. "The answer is: it's all possible. And we'll find out soon. But I'm sure that in this region whatever we find of that nature, carcinogen or radioactive, will be present in extremely low concentrations. Not an immediate danger at all. To nobody. Not even remotely."

"And to the soil? The run-off?" Jeff Simmons acted like a dog that had gotten his teeth into a piece of cloth and kept yanking at it.

Jack Jones looked uncomfortable.

Doyle now had grown visibly irritated. "The soil." He paused. "Mister Simmons," he said sternly, "Vince Davis is a conscientious, hard worker. He'll clean up this spill in a minimum of time. We've seen very little penetration into—"

"Three days? Four?"

"Cleaning up means much more than just pumping the stuff into a tanker. Checks have to be done, short term, long term. Removing any contaminated layers...I can't commit to a timetable."

Jones kept wiggling his behind. "Mr. Doyle," he asked soothingly, "we all know this is a very serious matter. Can your company assure us that Carrollton is safe, now and in the future?"

"I can't guarantee that a hundred percent, not right now. But I'm telling your viewers that we'll spare no effort."

"Fair enough." Jones turned to his right. "Jeff?"

"How about another kind of effort? Precaution? Prevention?" the young man asked. "I keep wondering what happened. And how it can be avoided in the future. Did Mr. Bertolo drink? Do drugs? Work too many hours?"

"That's three questions. The third one is a 'no' but the first two...I have no way to answer them. Just as I can't assure you he had no personal problems, family issues, money—"

"How about his health?" Jeff's tone betrayed impatience.

"His health, well, we all have a little cough now and

then. Mr. Bertolo as well, probably. But I don't think his health has anything to do with this accident."

"You don't?" Jeff stared at Doyle.

"No."

Personal problems. Mary knew enough. Disgusted, she turned off the TV as smiling Jack Jones looked ready to throw Mike Doyle another softball. She poured herself another cup of coffee.

Her phone rang. *The hospital.* She almost dropped her cup as she grabbed her phone.

Chapter 15

"This is Dorothy from Akron City Hospital. Am I speaking with Mary Jenkins?"

"Yes. Mary Jenkins. Yes." She could barely utter the words, her vocal cords unwilling to function.

"Can I have your date of birth?" Dorothy asked, her voice robotic.

"Uh...." Mary needed a second. "June fifteenth, seventy-six."

"Thank you. Doctor Lima would like to speak with you. One moment."

The doctor seemed to take forever. Mary checked on Andy and Jimmy through the window while waiting and listening to the on-hold music, her heart pounding, her lips dry.

"Good morning, Miss Jenkins. Dr. Lima. I have good news from Dr. Toro regarding Joe Bertolo, your...."

"Husband."

"Yes. He's come out of the coma already."

"Oh my God!" she shouted, gripping the phone hard. She wanted to kiss it.

"Dr. Toro's report says some organs were injured and required surgery. And of course Mr. Bertolo has had a heavy concussion. The surgery went well. The rib cage showed significant bruises. They should heal. Your husband has, however, suffered major loss of blood. Life threatening initially. Also, his right foot has been heavily impacted, and will need surgery as soon as his condition allows."

"Can he speak?" She gripped the phone hard.

"Not really. Not now. He's under heavy sedation. Waking up now and then. Briefly."

"But he would recognize me, right?"

"He might. It depends on when."

"Can I come and see him this afternoon?" She checked the clock.

"You could."

"With the kids?" She heard their shouts out in the yard and Jake's excited barking.

"Ages?"

"Six and nine, almost ten."

"Hmm. I'll have to say no. It would do them more harm than good."

"Oh...." Mary's fears flared up again. And her heart went out to Jimmy and Andy. Would they still have a real father?

"Come between two and three. Go to the front desk and tell them we talked this morning. Okay? I must go now."

"Excuse me. One more question. Will he recover? I mean, completely?"

Doctor Lima sighed. "I hope so—I don't know for sure about his foot. This is not my or Dr. Toro's area of expertise. The hospital will advise on the next steps for that. Take care now."

After the call, Mary still had many questions. How long for the recovery? His foot...would Joe walk again? What could she do to help him? Did he remember anything about the accident? What about the insurance? She had to speak with Doyle. He still hadn't called.

The kids. She heard Andy and Jimmy out in the yard. They sounded totally absorbed in their game, but they too had to be anxiously awaiting news about their daddy. Maybe they were even smarter than she thought and had put on their bravest faces. Acting, as she was.

She swung the door open. "Hey guys!" She raised her fist and exclaimed enthusiastically, "Daddy's better! He's awake!"

Andy dropped the ball and ran up to her, Jimmy in tow. "Did he call?" he asked.

"No. Not yet. He asked somebody else to contact me."

"Why?"

"Because...the person didn't say.... She was very kind."

"I want to visit Daddy," Jimmy pleaded.

Mary had to say no. It tore her heart. "I know." She had to swallow. "I know you do. But he still must rest a lot. The more he rests, the sooner he can come home. I'll go this afternoon to see him, maybe for only five minutes. I'll tell Daddy that you guys begged me to take you with me, but that the doctor said—"

"That doctor doesn't know how much we're missing Daddy." Andy shook his head and looked down.

"I argued with her. But then I thought she knew best."

"Will Miss Joanna stay with us again while you're gone?"

"Maybe. I must hurry now."

She dialed Frank's number. "Joe's out of the coma. I'm going to see him this afternoon. Must find a babysitter. 'No kids yet,' Akron said. He wakes up sporadically and may, *may* remember me."

"So the surgery was successful?"

"It went well, all I know. But he'll need more. His foot. 'Heavily impacted,'" Dr. Lima's words. "What does that mean? Will he ever drive his truck again?" She pictured Joe hobbling over the grass, chasing a soccer ball with the kids.

"Does he remember anything?"

"Well...I don't know. He doesn't speak yet."

"Hmm." Frank sounded subdued.

Mary wondered what it meant. Did he think Joe would not remember? Not ever? She kept the thought to herself. "I should go now. Just wanted to tell you about the hospital's call."

"Okay. About that babysitter. If you don't mind, I'll give Sonya a call. You know she loves kids."

"Oh. Thank you, Frank. Very kind."

"I'll call you."

"How sweet. You're a real friend."

Less than five minutes later he called back and assured her that Sonya would be there shortly after twelve. "She's glad to help and sends her best for Joe and you. She'll bring cookie dough."

"Great. Sweet girl she is. Thank you, Frank."

"Call me anytime in case you'd think I can help. And this afternoon...I think Joe will be very happy to see you."

"I hope he can tell me that. Thanks again."

Mary put the phone down and sighed. The kitchen was a mess. She hadn't cleaned up yet after breakfast.

She walked over to the kids. "More good news, boys. Mrs. Sonya, the teacher, will come and stay with you til Mommy's back from the hospital. I'm sure she'll bake cookies. And she can kick soccer balls very well. Much better than me."

Andy said, "You can play with us now, Mommy. Please."

"But—"

"Yes, Mommy. Please," Jimmy chimed in.

She looked back at the kitchen mess once more, but she couldn't say no.

Ten minutes later she was back inside, putting leftovers into the fridge, filling the sink with cups and plates and spoons, and working herself into a state of anger. She kept wondering why Mike Doyle didn't call.

She noticed the voicemail light was blinking. "Doyle. About time," she muttered to herself and pushed play.

"Good morning, Mrs. Bertolo. This is Mike Doyle from Supren. I'd like to express my support for you and your family. I can't tell you how sorry I feel about what happened to your husband. My best wishes for a speedy recovery, and apologies for the delay, but you can imagine how busy I've been. I must hurry into an emergency meeting about the clean-up in Carrollton. I hope to speak with you in person soon. Thank you."

"Yeah. Thanks for what? For letting you badmouth Joe on TV this morning?" she shouted out loud.

***

By the time Mary turned onto Arch Street to enter the parking garage of the Akron City Hospital she had become a nervous wreck. Had the phone call from Dr. Lima been just a pacifier, a virtual Valium to tide her over until she could see for herself what Joe had become? The fear had grown stronger with every mile she had driven north on Interstate 77. She had visions of life without Joe and couldn't fend off the waves of relentless sadness.

A chill swept through her body and she shivered as she approached the reception desk.

When she was led into Joe's room by Nurse Williams, a young woman with a compassionate look on her face, Mary found him asleep, head bandaged, feet raised, an off-white sheet over his body, arms and legs, two bottles of intravenous liquid and two electronic monitoring devices to his left.

The nurse pointed at an armchair near the foot of the bed. "He's still very weak after so much loss of blood, but Dr. Toro hopes he'll heal," she explained, her voice hushed, her eyebrows raised and doubt in her eyes. "The heavy concussion and his foot are also of great concern. Time will tell. His foot is an issue we can't deal with right away."

Mary's fears were confirmed: Joe's condition was more serious than she'd been told over the phone in the morning. She mumbled, "I know," and closed her eyes, her lips pursed.

"Why don't you sit down and wait, ma'am. He may wake up and even try to speak a few words. I'll be back in about ten minutes."

Mary thanked her.

As soon as she was alone with Joe, she tiptoed to the head of the bed. She didn't touch him, but held her lips close to his right ear and whispered, "I'm here, Joe. With you. We'll get you home soon. Andy and Jimmy wish you well and can't wait to have you back. We love you. You don't answer or nod, but I know you hear me." Tears welled up in her eyes and she took a step back to observe her man.

She sat down in the armchair. The barren room looked indifferent and threatening: a stopover on the way to heaven?

Scenes of backyard soccer fun and Joe's pretend fights with the boys over the biggest piece of bacon came back, torturing her. And would he ever drive his truck again?

Did she want him to? Yes and no battled it out in her head. Maybe Supren would find a way to discard him anyway with some flimsy regulatory argument. How would she fight that, with Joe? Did she want to? Yes and no again. Then the real question reappeared: would he survive? For a life worth living? As a real man? She answered her own questions: he was the man she wanted to marry, no matter how poor or how incomplete his recovery.

She stood up, looked at the indecipherable graphs hanging at the foot of the bed and moved closer to Joe.

Nurse Williams entered the room after a soft knock on the door. "You'd better go now, ma'am."

"Can't I stay a few more minutes? He might wake up, no?"

The nurse frowned but said, "Another five minutes. You understand we must supervise these visits tightly, under the present circumstances. For his good."

"I do. Thank you."

"By the way, you should stop by the reception desk. They want to know whether he has a living will."

"Huh? They...." Her voice broke. "Is he going to—?"

Nurse Williams shook her head and smiled. "It's just a routine matter. It means nothing. They forgot to ask you yesterday."

Mary took a deep breath. "Thank you." She sat down, relieved.

Living will. The words kept coming back as she drove home. Her worries about all the complications and financial headaches grew. Who would help her? Friends? The school? Supren? Supren's HR department? Doyle? How about disability payments? Practical concerns kept piling up in her poor brain that felt ready to burst. She needed answers. She decided to go and see Mike Doyle, right now, quickly, while she still had Sonya at her disposal.

Chapter 16

Mid-afternoon Mike Doyle got a call from Dave Broderick, Executive Vice-President of Supren in Houston.

"Mike!"

Doyle felt pangs in his stomach. "Hi, Dave. What's up?" He tried to keep his tone even.

"I think you know, buddy. What the hell's going on up there in your neck of the woods? Supren's all over the news here. You guys put little Carrollton on the map." Dave didn't sound as jovial as his words suggested.

"Yeah, we sure did, unfortunately. But relax. You know how it works: anything that can give fracking a black eye, the press and TV jump on it. That's no surprise to you or me. Sharks smelling blood in the water. Reporters making mountains out of molehills. Ratings!"

"I know. But you could've—"

"I gave Don a heads-up yesterday. Shot him a quick email. Sorry, I see I forgot to copy you. Busy, man. Getting home at midnight. But be assured, we've got things under control. Give us three weeks. *No más.*"

There was a long pause on the other end. "Don forwarded me your email. He's concerned. The buck stops with the CEO, right? He told me to give you a buzz. Of course, he's been to bigger rodeo's but—"

"We all have. This isn't a big one." Doyle put calm conviction in his statement. *That should do it.*

"Well...okay. If you say so. But he worries, believe me. I'm sparing you his own words." Dave chuckled.

Doyle knew a few of Don's favorite expletives. "I see."

"He doesn't like to get that kind news from TV. He'd rather get it from the horse's mouth. And I don't blame him. He's up to his neck in the negotiations for the Peruvian deal. The life of a CEO. That's why I'm the one calling you."

"I understand. You can tell him with full confidence that we have the experience here to stay on top of this. I have a great young guy on the job who wants to prove himself. Vince Davis. 'If twenty-four hours a day isn't enough, I'll have to start working overtime,' he quips." Doyle smiled at his own mendacious quote. "I believe we'll have this thing cleaned up in two to three weeks."

"Okay, but Don wants to send some of our guys up there anyway. Specialists like Hugh Timmer. It can't hurt and shows Supren's commitment. We should avoid any risk to our reputation in Ohio." Dave's tone had gone full business.

Doyle sighed slowly, without sound. "You're right about that commitment, and our image, but, take it from me, an invasion of Texans wouldn't go over well here. Locals trust locals, particularly if we do a good job, show them we're doing it and keep communications going with the community."

"Yeah. Always those locals."

"You know what I spend most of my time on? Holding hands. 'I understand, I understand Mr. Mayor, we're committed to excellence.' I think you see why I'm not bugging you guys with phone calls."

"Still...."

Doyle scratched his head. This last pause was tough to handle. "Dave," he said, trying not to sound like he was complaining, or begging, "it's a small spill; my top guy, Vince, is doing a whale of a job, and dropping a battalion of Texans here to take over will make it look like we have an Armageddon on our hands. Please ask Don to hold off and let us earn our stripes here. I want to show we can do the job."

"You'd better be sure—"

"Of course. At the first sign of things turning for the worse I'll be on the phone to you in a New York minute. I've been with Supren for just two years and this is a chance for me to prove myself. I'll work my butt off. And I'll keep you and Don posted with daily emails."

"I get it. You want to show us something. Good. I wish I still had your drive. I'm six months from retirement, from fulltime bass fishing. Don't forget to send those emails. Also to Don. And call immediately if anything doesn't go as expected."

Bass fishing. Doyle felt triumphant. "You got it."

"I'm sticking my neck out, you know. But I like your ambition. You're lucky he's swamped with Peru. You and me, we've known each other many years and I'll have to trust you'll deliver the goods. I'll try to get Don's ear on this."

Many years. He's aboard. Doyle was jubilant but kept exuberance out of his voice. "Deal. Don't pay attention to silly press releases or those selected, attention-grabbing TV clips. I'll get you the real stuff. Plus, you guys can call me anytime."

"I'll put my best foot forward with Don, buddy." Dave paused and said, his voice lower, "I remember our good old days together in Oklahoma. Long before Don hired you. I still chuckle—"

"Good old days? What good old days? How good? Just kidding! Thanks."

"Shh!" A sardonic laugh followed.

Doyle smiled and poured himself a cup of coffee.

***

As she drove up Main Street toward the Supren office, exhausted and consumed by grief, Mary mustered all her remaining energy and determination. But she would have to keep the discussion with Doyle short; there had to be a limit to her friend Sonya's patience and good will.

Joanna seemed surprised when Mary walked into the office, but welcomed her with gracious expressions of empathy. She inquired about Joe's condition and reassured her. "I promise you my support for your family, Mary," she said. "I'm not only a Supren staff member but also a friend of your children."

Mary spoke about Joe, accepted Joanna's generous offer, and apologized profusely for barging in on Mr. Doyle unannounced. *Just the way Joe did it once.*

Joanna waved her off.

Mary saw unease on her face. "Is Mr. Doyle available?" she asked.

"Let me check. He's been very busy." Joanna walked to his door, knocked and waited a second. Then she tiptoed in.

Half a minute later she returned. "Mr. Doyle appreciates the opportunity to meet you. Please, Miss Jenkins." She waved the visitor into Doyle's office.

As Mary entered, Mike Doyle stood behind his desk, facing her. He was flanked by two impressive stacks of papers in front of him. He pulled up his pants and stroked his hair, walked up to her and shook her hand. "Please have a seat," he said, sounding serious and compassionate as he pointed to the small conference table with four chairs on the opposite side of the room.

He joined her, his facial expression solemn. "My

apologies for having had to communicate by voicemail, Miss Jenkins. I'm glad you came to see me. Please accept my sincere wishes for a speedy recovery for Joe and strength for yourself. I'm very sorry about this sad mishap."

"Thank you, Mr. Doyle," Mary said, smoothing her light gray blouse and worrying about her hair.

"How's your man doing?" he asked, smiling slightly.

She sighed. "Not well. Worse than I thought. I just drove back from Akron, and the closer I got to Noredge, the darker the future looked. He may not make it. And if he does, what life will he have?"

"Oh? I'm so sorry to hear that. I…." He paused to put up five fingers twice for Joanna, who had opened the door and shown him a red folder.

She disappeared.

"I apologize," he said, turning back to Mary. "The bank is getting impatient."

Mary knew she had to make her case in less than the ten minutes Mike Doyle just had allotted her. She coughed and said, "I hate to be rude, but why did you have to dump on Joe on TV this morning?" She paused and covered her mouth, surprised by her own nerve.

"Huh? I had no intention—"

Infuriated, she forged ahead. "What proof do you have for the disparaging comments you made about him, insinuating something was wrong with him? Something that made him lose control of his vehicle? Personal problems? Do you think he's crazy? A fool? What were those distracting family issues? Which ones? Money problems?"

"Most people have financial issues."

"We have them too—plenty of them. Like everybody else. How are you going to help us?"

For a moment, Doyle seemed taken aback. He opened his mouth but swallowed and said, "Miss Jenkins, let me explain." He had his index up, eyes drilled into hers. "Supren is a social company. We have adequate insurance. We'll take good care of you, your kids, and your husband." He made it sound like he already had formulated the conclusion on this point and shifted his chair.

She looked at him askance. "Okay…and that 'care' includes informing at least the doctors in the Akron City Hospital about the possible, *possible* presence of radioactive substances and cancerous particles in the gases Joe has been inhaling? He may have been half unconscious when the accident happened. Because of that poison."

"Miss Jenkins, I take serious my responsibilities to the community, to Supren, and to Joe Bertolo." Doyle's tone was one of restraint.

"Okay. Why, then, did you speak so cavalierly this morning on WEWS about the clean-up in Carrollton? From what I've read and heard elsewhere, it won't be the piece of cake you described."

Doyle sat up straight, clearly feeling dominant, and took a couple of seconds before answering. "Cavalierly?" he repeated near-mockingly. "How would you know that?

Do you have the right sources, Miss Jenkins? I have a very capable, responsible person in charge there."

"And would he tell you the truth if he knew you wouldn't like the facts?"

"What?" He wrinkled his brows, looking indignant. "Of course he would. I instructed him to, in no uncertain terms. To tell me anything that's on his mind."

"Okay. I can understand that you don't want to splash trade secrets and knowhow on the TV screen, but I feel you should at least tell *me*, what chemicals you use for your fracking and what's in that dirty water polluting Carrollton's air, creeks and soil. I have a right to know what Joe has been handling, inhaling, and spilling on his hands and clothes."

Doyle smiled. "Unfortunately, that information is protected by law. I bet you know that."

"I do," she snapped back, furious. "And you and I know we owe my husband answers. Your answers, not the ones I can read on the web."

He leaned over, his face tense, his hands gripping the armrests of his chair. "My responsibility is to my company first. That's *my* answer."

"I understand. But Joe's part of your organization, so you should feel responsible for any way it's hurt him, endangered or impacted his health. And you know those chemicals did it. May have done it." She came close to choking.

His frown grew deeper. He changed tone. Softer. "Of

course, I must care for Joe and all my employees, but I was making the general statement that I must also defend the image and survival of Supren and ultimately the well-being of the communities we work in."

"Then why don't you call in the clean-up and analysis specialists from headquarters in Houston? Nothing better than that to spruce up your and Supren's image—and take care of our wellbeing here."

Doyle's eyes had become narrow slits. "Houston?" He smiled again. "They can't perform the miracles you want. Not any better than us. We have very capable people on the spot in Carrollton."

"I was just trying to say—"

"Hold it." He sounded controlled but his face spoke volumes. "I know what you're driving at, and it bothers me that you have doubts about our competence and sense of responsibility. You'd better think before you ask such questions. They're, frankly, a bit insulting. I'm starting to understand why the Chamber doesn't like your snide comments. Don't forget you're a city employee. The Chamber and the City Council are close. It's obvious that your husband drove carelessly. Preoccupied, tense, maybe worried."

"I see." Mary kept calm. "Half unconscious because of what he inhaled?" Her question dripped scorn.

"If he inhaled anything it was because he didn't follow procedures!"

She had been waiting for that accusation; Joe had heard

144

it a while ago in this same office. She became provocative, taunting. "Are you certain about that? And that it's really all Joe's fault? That there wasn't any malfunction, or—"

He checked his watch and lowered his voice. "Trust me, I will leave no stone unturned to find the truth, Miss Jenkins, but I must end our discussion here. I hope you understand." He stood up and turned away.

Shaken, Mary waited a moment before she got up.

He came back to shake hands with her and said, "Sorry about that. I have thousands of things on my mind and not enough hours in a day. We'll do the best we can for Joe and your entire family. I know you have a very difficult time."

The door opened. Joanna nodded at Doyle.

"Yes," he said to Joanna and returned to his desk.

Mary hurried home disgusted. Her conversation with Mike Doyle had steeled her conviction that Joe was a victim of his working conditions. Brooding anger overtook her.

When she pulled into her driveway, she didn't remember how she had made it there. She blew her horn. She didn't have the energy to get out right away. She needed a few seconds.

The kids came running out. "Where's Daddy? Is he coming home soon? What did he say?" They had to move back so she could open her door and step out. Sonya stood on the threshold, arms crossed, in control.

Mary embraced Jimmy and Andy. She struggled to sound upbeat as she told them, "I said hello to Daddy for you guys. He loves you and I think he won't be long. How were Mrs. Sonya's cookies?" She put her arms over their little shoulders and walked her boys to the front door. There she let go and threw herself in her friend's arms, crying.

"How is he?" Sonya asked quietly, rubbing her back.

"Joe…Later. Tell you later," Mary sobbed.

Sonya said, gripping Mary's arm, "I think Jake wants to play in the yard, Andy. Why don't you take a little walk with him and Jimmy?"

Mary nodded, feeling helpless. "I'll have to explain, Sonya," she said, her voice weak, as they entered the house.

"You don't have to tire yourself telling me every detail about Joe, unless you want to."

"Thank you."

"I have tea. And cookies. A couple anyway," Sonya said with a smile.

Mary sat down on the couch in the living room.

Sonya turned off the TV and brought her a footstool. "Now relax. I'll do the talking, about your fabulous kids. You should ask me over more often."

"I may have to." Mary had no strength in her voice.

Chapter 17

July 27th was a big day for Mary and the boys: she would be allowed to bring them to Akron City Hospital for a visit with Joe. The night before she had had all kinds of trouble getting overexcited Jimmy and Andy to bed.

A flood of questions emanating from their unencumbered brains made her ride to Akron both stressful and enjoyable. "Invigorating" was a better word.

"Will Daddy recognize us? Can he walk? Smile? Are his bandages all bloody? How many teeth has he lost? Is it true that his room will smell real bad? Maybe he wants to come back home with us? Who's the boss in the hospital?" There was no limit to their creativity and endearing naiveté. She had not mentioned his foot injury yet.

By the time she drove up East Market Street, Andy was hungry and Jimmy needed a bathroom urgently.

"Five more minutes and we'll be in the lobby. Just try to think of the Cavaliers, Jimmy."

"No. I like the Indians."

"The Galaxy!"

"No, Andy! They're in California!"

"On TV too!"

"Mommy, hurry!"

Andy offered expert advice. "Just squeeze your legs together hard, Jimmy. That's what I do in school."

The boys' faces said it all as they entered the room where their father was resting, asleep and snoring lightly. Mary put her index over her lips and whispered, "Let's wait quietly. I'm sure he wants to see us. Wait."

Pudgy Nurse Johnson, standing behind Mary, nodded. She stepped closer to Joe, took a look at his bandaged head and frowned. She smiled at the boys and Mary and said, "I'll be back in five minutes."

They all sat down, Jimmy on Mary's lap.

Andy stared at the equipment surrounding Joe, apparently trying to make sense of it without asking questions.

Jimmy slid off his mother's lap. "I want to look from close by, Mommy."

"Ssh!" Andy said.

Mary nodded to Jimmy.

He tiptoed to within inches of the bed but returned almost immediately, whispering, "Daddy has long gray hair on his face, Mommy, and in his nose. It's not nice."

She nodded, took his little hand, pointed at her watch and held up two fingers. "Two minutes and the nurse will be back," she whispered. "Maybe she'll wake Daddy up," she added quietly. Then she realized that Jimmy didn't really know yet how long two minutes took. He remained standing next to her, silent, lips pursed.

Nurse Johnson came back with a fresh pillow cover for Joe. She pushed a button to crank up the bed head and smiled at the kids. "Maybe your daddy will be able to say hello," she told them, her voice kind and soft.

Andy made a little fist.

"He'll be happy to see us," Jimmy figured.

"Come," the nurse said. "I saw him look at me. He smiles, I think."

Mary thought that was an exaggeration for Jimmy's benefit.

"Oh! Oh, Mommy. Can you help me?" he begged.

Mary stepped close to the bedside and lifted him.

Andy followed her.

"Don't touch his hand, kids," the nurse said.

It was connected to a long tube.

Joe opened his eyes and seemed to nod slowly.

"Look, he talks to me," Andy said, pinching Mary's arm.

She held on to Jimmy while staring intensely at her Joe. He spoke, but Mary couldn't decipher what he said.

"I know what he's saying. He loves you," Nurse Johnson said. "I've been reading his lips for three days. He's still extremely weak because of the tremendous blood loss. He's lucky he made it to the hospital. And then through that four-hour surgery. I've seen people...." She looked at the kids and her voice trailed off.

"He has spoken before, right?" Mary inquired.

"Yes. He has moments of strength. It ebbs and flows. Hard to predict. He's a tough guy. But his blood analysis hasn't stabilized, organs aren't completely functional yet."

"We picked a bad day, the first one we got permission—"

"Daddy's strong, Mommy. The lady's right. He'll get much better soon," Andy opined.

"But I want to talk to him," Jimmy lamented.

Mary sighed. "Let's sit down another ten minutes. Is that okay, ma'am?"

The nurse nodded, her hand on the doorknob.

On the way back to Noredge, Mary had barely made it onto Interstate 77 when Jimmy fell asleep. Then Andy. She felt her boys' disappointment and wondered whether the visit to the hospital had been a good idea.

She switched on the radio and went to WKSU, her loyal friends, counselors, inspiration and refuge. Their signal didn't get through at full strength but she didn't have the energy to search for another channel. She caught snippets of a weather forecast and an update on the stock market as she drove in a zombie-like state.

"And now back to Carrollton," a reporter said, sounding surprisingly enthused. Mary had heard about the spectacular audience the channel generated from the disaster. "We talked to some folks in town...."

Now she was wide awake.

"Carrollton has become a ghost town," she heard local shopkeeper Jim Lynn complain. "I'm not in a blocked-off area, but my business is dead. Roads are cut off and who wants to shop here, so close to radioactive shit and all that other danger? I can't blame my customers for running away, but—"

"Whom do you blame, sir?"

"Who? Everybody. The mayor, the county commissioner, the EPA, the driver, that damn Supren, everybody. But who cares anyway that my business will die? How long is this poison going to hang or sit around? A week? A month? Forever? That fracking business brought me plenty of new customers, but they came with this disease and we may not be able to cure it. Damn poison!"

The reporter went into an explanation that Supren had marshaled the best possible resources for the clean-up: the most modern equipment, and top quality personnel, headed by Vince Davis, an excellent local engineer. Supren wasn't sparing any effort or expense to remedy the situation. He compared this spill to the ones in Pennsylvania and Texas, which were much bigger, and worse.

"So, if this one's so small it won't take long," Lynn concluded. His tone suggested he was speaking tongue-in-cheek. "I also heard of a case where they didn't really succeed in getting the whole thing fixed. Somebody told me of goats dying long after the incident. Crows feasting on their dead bodies died too. I believe it was in Colorado."

Mary nodded. The kids slept like logs.

"If I'm not mistaken, the Colorado problem wasn't a tanker spill, but contamination of a water source deep underground, an aquifer they call it," the reporter clarified.

An aquifer was an underground layer of permeable rock, sand or soil. Its pore spaces were filled with water and interconnected, so water could flow. The layer could be thousands of square miles in size and be found at various depths, maybe as shallow as a few hundred feet.

The merchant sounded undeterred. "Okay. Who cares? Dead is dead. All the same. I wish we'd never seen those Texan oil guys with their 'y'alls'. Or is it Oklahoma?"

"I understand, sir." The reporter paused briefly. "Look, what I can tell you is that Mr. Doyle, the Supren manager, assured us as recently as yesterday that he has full confidence in Mr. Davis. That man is young but already has two clean-up jobs under his belt. Doyle said he felt so strongly about the Carrollton problem and about Mr. Davis's qualifications that he took him off a critical drilling job in Noredge."

"Davis's two clean-up jobs, a joke; Doyle's lying his ass off," Mary grumbled to herself.

Jim fired one more shot. "Full confidence, eh? All fine and dandy. You and me know who's really going to foot the bill for all of this: us, the people of Carrollton and the county. Know what I mean? And Mr. Doyle will walk away with his fat bonus anyway. For my part, he can take it to Houston tonight."

Andy woke up.

Mary cut the radio and hoped he didn't hear her sigh.

Chapter 18

An uneasy calm reigned in Noredge the week after the accident in Carrollton. Supren operations continued at full speed at Rutgers Lake and on Maple Road. Mary noticed that Mike Doyle would show up at Harriet's from time to time and leave an hour or so later. She visited her Joe every day in Akron, without the kids. Sonya Anderson and Jill Smith were the angels helping her out as babysitters.

Mary continued receiving phone calls from friends and being stopped at Lou's supermarket by people she only knew by sight or not at all. Her description of Joe's condition got more laconic and her answers increasingly curt as the day progressed. Many friends cautiously expressed concern and seemed to wonder how she was going to manage without Joe, but she didn't; her hopes for a full recovery grew stronger by the day. She wasn't lying when she told Andy and Jimmy their daddy was going to live and play soccer with them again.

Frank was traveling. "He said he'd better get off his

butt," Sonya told Mary when they bumped into each other at the post office. "He's in New Orleans and Houston for almost a week. Job hunting."

"Yeah. Severance lasts only so long, I guess."

Sonya whispered, "He hasn't seen a cent of it so far."

"Wow. Nothing?"

Sonya shook her head. Then a mysterious smile appeared on her face. "But I'm happy for him anyway. You know—"

"Let me guess." Mary chuckled, her hand on Sonya's forearm.

Sonya frowned. "You think you know?"

"Joanna—"

"She's with him for the weekend." Sonya raised her brows, her eyes quizzing Mary. "Did he tell you about 'them'?"

"Not really. But I have my inside source." Mary pointed to her forehead. "Good for them! I hope they enjoy Houston."

As she drove home Mary's thoughts went to Carrollton. She had heard that several spontaneous demonstrations had been held there and hastily called meetings arranged. Tempers had flared. The Sierra Group and local civic leaders, including some rogue members of the Chamber, were planning a big, organized event with highly qualified speakers and unnamed politicians. Carrollton's citizens were terrified. Some demonstrations had turned violent: the clean-up progress was more dangerous, complicated and slower than the optimistic Mike Doyle had predicted. And the burden on the town heavier. Doubts arose about Doyle's credibility.

"He seems to live in front of the cameras instead of doing his damn job," was the word on the street. "Why would we believe 'Mr. Smooth' any longer? At this snail's pace...."

Health and safety concerns grew ominously; discussions turned more heated and recriminations sounded coarser by the day. Worries about the town's future ran deeper. Desperation set in.

Noredge citizens as well were asking questions more loudly every day. "That's the kind of mess we'll have here someday, too. If it can happen in Carrollton, why not here?"

Mary joined the chorus and was in frequent contact with her Sierra buddies. In February, she had told Joe she'd do "whatever it took" to keep fracking out of Noredge. "I lost the first round," she now muttered to herself, "but this battle isn't finished."

With her Sierra friends Jill Smith and Dan Clark she managed to slip an article into the opinion section of the Sentinel. It pointed at the disaster in Carrollton and asked, "Which town is next? Our turn may come sooner than we think!"

It earned her a heated argument with Mike Doyle over the phone. He threatened her, and even her suffering, innocent Joe. "You know who writes his paycheck. And I can get to the people who write yours," he thundered.

"Thank you for reminding me again, Mr. Doyle. I'm recording, so I won't forget," she mocked.

The recording threat was bluff only, but it had to have infuriated Doyle even more. He waited a few seconds to answer, "Your bill will come due soon, lady. As soon as we're done cleaning up the mess your husband created."

What? My husband "created" the mess in Carrollton? That was a bridge too far.

After that scandalous accusation, she wasn't going to be satisfied with killing fracking in Noredge. She was going to get justice for Joe as well.

***

On July 27th Mike Doyle was on his way home after a long day in Columbus. Interstate 71 looked endless and dreadfully boring.

Nearing Ashland he received a call from David Broderick. "What's up, Dave?" he asked, making sure to sound casual.

"Don't you think I should be asking you?"

"Huh? Yeah. The cleanup, I guess. It's going well. We lifted the cordon for most of the area. The 'noise' is fading. Bloody tree-huggers. We're wearing them out." He chuckled and hoped Dave might as well. Environmentalists were always excellent piñatas.

"It's damn hard to get a picture from your messages, Mike. Pardon my French but they're just shitty platitudes. I can't face Don without more input. It's been almost four days since my call, and I have no idea what to tell him. You put me in a pretty damn rotten situation."

Wow. This was a friend talking? Doyle changed his tack. "My apologies, Dave. Between meetings with officials, my work on the Beta site and overseeing Vince Davis and his crew I can't devote enough time to mails. I figure it's more important to do things right than…anyway, I can tell you Carrollton is shaping up very well. I'm proud of Vince."

"Okay, but you could at least tell him to send me progress reports, detailed, with facts and figures, analyses, costs, measurements, issues. Something we can put our hands on." Dave's tone lay somewhere between demanding and lamenting.

"Sure, of course Dave. I'll make sure he does. Actually, I'll do it myself. The dude isn't the best writer or reporter. Great guy, good engineer, but not a paper man. You'll get that stuff. Promise. Figures." The stacks of printouts on his desk popped up in his mind.

Dave seemed to calm down. "Good. But do it, Mike. By the way, 'The noise fading,' you told me a moment ago. I must say, from what we see in Houston, I must agree. It seems to be dying out a bit. Keep up the good work and tell us about it so we can scratch this one off our list, Don's and mine. Sorry for bothering you so late but I get a tad worried."

"Count on me, Dave. Thank you for your confidence in me." Doyle scratched his temple as he hung up. He floored the gas pedal.

As he swaggered into the living room of his residence on McKinley he threw his briefcase onto the oak table.

His wife Edith shouted from the couch, "Watch it! My tablecloth!"

"Yes! It's mine too," he growled without looking at her.

Just what he needed, a wife in a foul mood. All the way from Ashland he had kept grumbling to himself, unable to find a comfortable position for his tired spine, angrily switching radio channels. He sensed brooding discontent, not just in Carrollton, but also in Noredge and surrounding towns. In TV interviews—short, sporadic exchanges with drivers at gas stations or waiters in restaurants—he saw real or metaphorical fingers pointed at him. And Dave Broderick...Houston...*damned Houston.*

Today's meeting with state officials could have gone better. They had offered their support for the clean-up effort but demanded quick action. He understood "Carrollton" might elicit cries for tougher regulations. They would hamper Ohio's economic growth.

"You'd better look at this," Edith said, getting up and waving the Sentinel. Svelte, tall as her man, she walked up to him with the elegance of a princess. She flung her long raven hair back and said, her Cuban accent reduced to a trace, "More greetings from the tree-huggers. They didn't even hide their names. Here are the heroes." She pointed at the bottom of page three.

He harrumphed. "Jenkins, Smith, Clark. Nothing new. It's the game they play."

"It's no joke, Mike. People stop me in the store to ask why they never see you in Carrollton, sleeves rolled up and commanding the troops," Edith said, reproach in her voice.

Yeah. His wife had her own subtle and not so subtle ways of reminding him of the simmering hostility.

He kicked off his shoes and took out his iPhone. Without looking up he said, "I've got Vince there. He's working his butt off at the site. I know how to manage, empower a hungry young man with a big future. He loves to show his talent. I delegate, dammit."

"But here in Noredge people wonder what they got themselves into when they welcomed fracking. Fracking. 'Is Supren going to be a blessing or a curse?' they ask politely. They pause after the word 'or' and look at me askance."

"Gossip. Bloody fear-mongering by do-nothings." He walked over to the couch and almost fell as he stumbled over his shoes.

"Of the three signees, I only know of Miss Jenkins. She's a teacher," Edith volunteered.

"On vacation, got nothing better to do!" he shot back without looking up from his iPhone.

She lowered her voice. "Are you buying a Porsche, Mike?"

He looked up. "Huh?"

"One of my friends thinks she saw you in a Porsche with

a woman in Canton." She pursed her lips and showed him a pair of wide eyes.

"And?" he shot back. "Yes, I took a test drive. You know I always loved Porsches."

"How long has it been since we, you, bought your yacht? Why did it have to be a Baglietto? In Florida? What for? Just so it can sit in Hillsboro and guard our unoccupied condo? Just so you can get drunk on the ocean four maybe five times a year with your buddies? You do the finances here, but I get worried. What's wrong with a good SUV? And that yacht...*Díos mío!*" Her voice broke.

"I know you get sick on boats, but I came from Houston," he said meekly, surprised by the tears welling up in her eyes.

"So did I. And I'd be scared to death sitting in a Porsche with you after a couple of drinks." She paused. Her voice went from sad to concerned. "Where do we get all that money, Mike? Or do we buy all these luxuries on credit?"

"Just stay out of it!" he snapped and raised his hand.

Catching himself, he stood up, embraced her and caught a whiff of her perfume. He said soothingly, "Sorry, darling. You shouldn't worry about it. We're in great shape. Nothing on credit. Supren treats me well. So well that most of it is under the table. Tax free. You know. I've explained it many times. It's money they have to—"

"Hide."

Mike didn't answer. He had a great deal going, but strict confidentiality was a major feature of it. He didn't feel happy keeping Edith in the dark. He had married her only five years ago—an impressive, beautiful woman he adored. Both had been divorced, he with two teenage children, she childless. He didn't want her to spill the truth inadvertently. He hadn't asked for this kind of deal. He had accepted it but could never tell Edith the details of it or the name of the person who offered it to him.

He sometimes worried about his angry outbursts when she expressed her concern about his work. It was the pressure of the job, he always explained, and each time he said he was sorry. He knew that Edith liked to show off her beautiful clothes, her body, her expensive jewelry— even on their Baglietto last month when he had business friends over on the yacht. She made him show his Rolex watch to friends. And now, all of a sudden, the Porsche was too much? Was this the straw that broke the camel's back? No, it had to be the pressure of Carrollton getting to her.

"*Tengo miedo, amor,* I'm scared," she sobbed. "And who was that woman in the Porsche with you?"

"Cascade has smart women in their dealership!" He felt he didn't deserve the third degree.

Edith went quiet.

He regretted his rudeness. "Don't you worry, *amor,*" he said softly. "I'll take care of us, and you just enjoy it. Deal?"

She briefly closed her eyes. "I guess so," she whispered. She took his hand and guided him to the kitchen. "Our dinner sits in the oven."

"Dinner. Let me get us some wine."

"I have it here."

"Oh good. Dinner. And then? Any dessert?"

She smiled again, her hand on his hip pocket. "*Como no?* Your favorite. *Te quiero.*"

He loved the way she said it.

Chapter 19

rank arrived in Houston Friday night from New Orleans, where he had met with HR and technical staff of an important oil services company. He checked in at the Westin Oaks Hotel on Westheimer Road, in the Galleria area. Viola had scheduled a job interview for the early afternoon of Monday at their offices nearby.

Joanna flew into George Bush Intercontinental Airport the same day as Frank, but at the dreadfully late hour of 11:30 on United 318 from Cleveland via Chicago. By the time she fell into Frank's arms at the baggage claim, she looked like a wreck.

"I barely remember how you got me into this beautiful room," she told him as she opened her eyes on Saturday morning.

"I carried you all the way, you and your bag!" Frank joked.

"I bet you were glad when you could finally drop me down onto the bed," she played along.

"I wondered what all the weight in that big bag was," he said with a straight face.

"Don't you know? My bowling ball, of course." She laughed, curled up to him and whispered, "Divine, Frank. Thank you for inviting me to Texas. My first trip to the state."

He said, caressing her cheek, "I have a Texan friend who raves about Galveston, fifty miles from here, on the Gulf. Galveston Island. Shall we go?"

"Anywhere with you." She kissed him and hopped out of bed. "Do I get the first shot?" she asked, halfway to the bathroom.

"Be my guest." *Literally.* He smiled. Her enthusiasm and spontaneity gave him a warm fuzzy feeling. At his age, he was no virgin, but she made him feel like one. She had for the last month.

"I'll be quick, Frank. Shorts okay, right?"

"I'm sure you'll look smashing in them."

Soon they were on their way.

"Half of Houston must be on the road," Frank complained as he grew irritated at the wheel. The air-conditioning in his rented Ford Focus wasn't up to speed either.

"It's a Saturday. A beautiful day. Let's enjoy the trip," Joanna said, squeezing his leg. "We're together and nobody knows."

"You mean Mike doesn't." He snickered.

It took them almost two hours to get to Pier 21, instead of the Google estimate of about one hour.

"Wow! How beautiful!"

"I'd never heard of this Channel either before yesterday, Joanna." Frank reacted to her excitement as she watched the big ships go by in the Galveston Ship Channel connecting Houston to the Gulf of Mexico. He had his hand on hers as they looked north, seated at their table on the deck of the Olympia Grill. They took their time over their late *bocca d'oro* lunch.

They went for a brief walk on the island and then enjoyed the late afternoon with a leisurely drink back at the Grill, until Joanna noticed that the evening crowd was showing up. They stepped into the car and slowly made their way to Interstate 45 and the bridge, headed for Houston.

"I feel sorry for Mary Jenkins," Frank said as he wormed his way through traffic. "Her Joe...."

The heat still felt oppressive although less so than on the way out; but the congestion was even worse. The gear box complained about the stop-and-go pace. Frank muttered he couldn't wait to drop off the Focus at Alamo.

Joanna sighed. "I worry about Mary too. I had to be the bearer of bad news. Felt so sad for her. But I did my best."

"I know, and Mary told me the kids loved the games you played with them. She's relied on me as if she's known me for ages, but I didn't meet her until about two months ago. At the Rutgers site. She came with my sister, who teaches with her."

"Mary doesn't know about us, does she?" She had her hand on his leg.

"Not sure. I assume she suspects."

"Oh?"

"I never mentioned it to her, but she wasn't born yesterday."

"Please don't tell anybody else Frank. You promised. Mr. Doyle would kill me if he finds out we're such good friends. Strange, but he's kind of...afraid of you."

"Yes." Frank felt a tinge of inner pleasure. He smiled. "Goliath afraid of David. Good! Don't worry, my lips are sealed. See?"

She stared at him and burst into a loud laugh. "Make sure your mouth doesn't freeze that way! Hold it. One second." She dug into her purse and snapped a picture.

"Any good?"

She held her phone in front of him. "Just the way you promised, right?"

"Correct. But I told Sonya."

"Yeah. She saw us together once. Please ask her not to tell. Right away."

"I will as soon as we're back in Houston. We'll send her the picture."

When they reached the Oaks shortly after nine they collapsed onto the bed in exhaustion. Frank reached for the phone to order pizza and a bottle of Chianti. He moved closer. "Now let's cuddle. Real close."

A while later Joanna got up and took her unwilling shirt off. "It's wet," she said, shivering, making a face as she held it with indexes and thumbs and hung it on the back of a chair.

Frank couldn't take his eyes off her as she smiled at him, her long hair all over her sweaty face and dropping down to her small, proudly pointing breasts. "I bet your shorts are full of sand," he said, laughing. He sat up, pulled her close and pretended he was going to unzip them. He dropped his shirt onto the floor.

Somebody knocked on the door. "The pizza man! Already?" Joanna broke away and fled into the bathroom.

Frank opened the door.

"Two glasses, right?" The man didn't seem puzzled but clearly enjoyed asking the question.

Frank smiled. "Yeah. Correct. You've worked here a long time?"

"Long enough. Ages. Two glasses." He winked and threw a glance at the bathroom door.

"You must be one of those two-fisted drinkers," he joked.

"You got that right," Frank joked along as he paid, adding a generous tip.

The waiter left with a grin on his face.

Frank tapped his middle knuckle on the bathroom door. "The intruder's gone. All safe!"

"I heard. Good job. Just a couple of minutes."

Ten long minutes later Joanna appeared, her face one smile, her thin, light-blue hotel robe an elegant swirl, her lips hinting.

"Wow!" Frank kissed her, bending down, she standing on her toes.

"Frank, it doesn't sound very romantic," she said, "but I'm starving. Do you mind? The pizza smells divine." She showed him a pair of big eyes and twirled toward the little table.

Frank poured wine.

"To us," he said firmly, his voice as deep as he could get it, acting as the smooth host.

They clinked glasses.

"We must take care of you, my starving sweetie. I don't want you to faint in my arms," he quipped as he eased her toward the pizza.

"Oh, no? Are you sure?" Her eyes sparkled.

He squeezed her waist. "I trust you can faint very elegantly, but let's sit down."

Half of the pizza disappeared in no time, the Chianti assisting.

"Feels like home, only slightly better furniture," Joanna joked, her "last" wedge disappearing between her lips, her fingers searching for her umpteenth napkin. "To you, my Frank. Frrranky." She lifted her glass.

The way she sounded melted his heart. "I must thank you, darling." He moved his chair closer to her.

She leaned her head on his sweaty shoulder and whispered, "And I thank you. But I'm tired. Aren't you?"

He felt her nervous fingers on his leg. "What kind of tired?" He pinched her hand.

"That kind." She showed him dark wide eyes.

"Same here." He kissed her.

She pulled back. "Same? What a coincidence." She stood up, dropped her robe on the floor and threw herself onto the bed. Her arms summoned him, her nipples exuding impatience.

He flung his shorts toward the table. Halfway.

A deserted half-pizza and a near-empty Chianti bottle were complicit witnesses of a hot Westin night.

On Monday morning Frank, bleary eyed and exhausted, dropped off an emotional Joanna at the Intercontinental airport at seven thirty. The night had been short. She seemed hell-bent on adding a thirty-minute extension in the car. She curled up so close to him and kissed him all over with such fervent passion that more than once he swerved dangerously and had to swallow angry gestures and shouts from fellow drivers through rolled down windows. But he didn't mind.

They stepped out at the curb.

"See you tomorrow," she said.

"I'll be very late. I'll call." He took her hand and dropped his car keys but quickly retrieved them.

A baggage handler smiled, nodding.

"Okay."

"Wish me luck this afternoon."

"I've already prayed for it. And you, don't forget I spent the weekend with my sister Anita in Cleveland." She giggled.

"I'll remember that vividly." He kissed her one more time and answered her wave as she headed for the building, walking graciously.

He felt a fuzzy feeling run up his leg.

He returned to the hotel close to nine and set his alarm for eleven. He needed a nap. A Viola company car would be waiting for him downstairs at one-thirty.

During lunch he ran through the materials he had printed out about the company. By now he had the face of Jim Duncan, his main interviewer, etched in his mind; his verbal bio rehearsed; do's and don'ts memorized; answers to anticipated trick questions formulated on mental cue cards. When he left his room to catch his ride, he tapped his index on his forehead to make sure they were all there.

The trip from the Westin Oaks to the Viola offices wasn't even a mile, but that wasn't walking distance in muggy Houston—unless you wanted to arrive drenched in perspiration, road dust on your forehead and your pants bothering the hell out of your sweaty legs and groin.

As Frank stepped out of the car and entered the glitzy Prosperity Tower, he was both nervous and excited: he was going to talk to a top company in the drilling world. He had been found worthy of an interview with the HR department, three technical experts and maybe the CEO.

"If he's in. We never know where he'll be," the HR assistant had said over the phone. Frank assumed it really meant, "If you clear the preliminary hurdles." He was confident; his month-long preparations for this afternoon had been thorough, and his experience and track record were solid.

He entered the lobby and proceeded to the welcome desk.

A classy female forty-something with a ready smile greeted him. "Mr. ...?"

"Frank Anderson. For a job interview."

"Oh good! You're going to join us. Welcome." She started checking her screen. A sophisticated, athletic-looking woman. Her soft-blue uniform combined perfectly with her olive skin.

"Thanks. But I haven't been hired yet." He had his palms up.

"It's my welcome. You would be a great addition." She measured him discretely and smiled. Snow-white teeth.

"Thank you, Ms...?"

"Miss Turner. Yolanda. Nice to get to know you, Mr. Anderson. You may proceed to the fourteenth floor. Mr. Jackson will meet you at the elevator. Good luck."

By four-thirty Frank had made it into the office of Jim Duncan and faced the mounted moose head staring over the bald man seated behind a huge mahogany desk. The animal seemed to simultaneously protect and dominate the rotund CEO, who was in his sixties according to his bio. Two wooden chairs sat in front of Duncan's desk.

Frank was tentative when he stepped onto the huge Oriental rug, its loud colors screaming at him. It covered the center of the spacious room. A couch accompanied by a coffee table and three leather chairs sat on his left. It faced, across the room, a big, round table overcrowded by golf pictures and trophies.

"Howdy!" The CEO sounded jovial as he managed to rise up from his wide, deep armchair to shake hands. He was a tall, impressive man, but badly overweight. "My boys tell me you're a hell of a guy. That I should get to know you. Take a seat," he said, pointing at one of the three chairs.

Frank sank into the luxurious leather.

Duncan joined him.

The discussion developed well. Frank and Jim Duncan had many professional interests in common, and Jim appeared to be quite an extrovert. They didn't seem to have many acquaintances in common. Duncan's laughs and swear words punctured the air with great frequency. Frank's confidence grew.

"One thing that still bothers the hell out of me about Ohio is that we lost this damn Doornaert deal." Jim waved his hand and shook his head in apparent disgust.

That loss bothered Frank too: he had hoped that Viola would beat out Supren. He thought that Viola would have treated him better. But that was water over the dam. He was now looking for new horizons, hopefully with the Viola company, which was tops in the field.

"Yeah," Jim said, leaning back and scratching his

ample belly, "I wonder what kind of games Supren played. Actually, I think I know what kind." He rolled his eyes and sighed. "They ruined our opportunities in Ohio to a great extent. They creamed off...well, why do I keep bitching about those crooks? They're not worth it. They fired you, I understand?"

"I resigned," Frank responded in a split second.

"Yeah." Jim smiled, nodding.

"They asked me."

"Nicely, I'm sure!" he roared, laughing.

"Rather." Frank smiled back. "The HR department told me—"

"Of course. It's always HR."

"Well...the guy behind it was Mike Doyle."

"Mike Doyle. Hmm. Doesn't ring a bell."

Frank was a bit surprised: the man hadn't spent a fraction of a second looking for a Mike Doyle in his brain before he answered. The name was apparently of no interest to him.

When Doyle had arrived in Noredge, Frank thought he vaguely remembered having heard through the grapevine that a Mike Doyle had been a manager at Viola at some point. He didn't recall who told him. Curious, he had googled the name. Many Mike Doyles. And Michael Doyles. And MJ Doyles. And others. But the name Viola didn't show up. Not on Google, not on LinkedIn. He had concluded his memory or the grapevine hadn't served him perfectly.

"That Doyle has a full plate with so many well sites in Ohio—and on top of that a nasty spill of dirty water in Carrollton," Frank said.

"Ouch!" Jim's hand gestured as if he had just dropped a hot potato. "Wouldn't want to be him. The vultures in the press must be circling over the poor guy. I remember… well, it doesn't matter, we—"

Someone knocked on the door. It opened immediately. A voluptuous lady dressed in white walked in, her stride and glance exuding confidence. She carried a tray with tall glasses and a can. Duncan smiled at her and then turned back to his interviewee. "Ice tea?"

"Oh. Sure." Frank had faked the enthusiasm in his voice. He hated the ever-present sugar in that drink here.

"Make that two, dear."

As he drank his tea, Frank thought of the tons of poison, his word for sugar, that might have been the architects and builders of Jim's impressive belly and buttocks.

Half-way through their first cup Frank heard another knock on the door.

Jim looked at his watch. "Yeah. I know who it is," he said and shouted, "Yes!"

A nervous looking older man walked in, putting his hand up. "My apologies, I didn't think—"

Jim said, "We're done, Lou. Come in." He turned to Frank. "We'll get along fine, young man. Expect a call in three or four months."

"Months?"

"We're going to fit you into our expansion team for Colombia. You understand such things take time."

"South Carolina?" Frank knew of no fracking plans in that state.

"That's Columbia. Ours is Colombia, where they have all that drug business and terrorists. That damn FARC complicating our plans. But don't you worry. Three or four months. Thanks for visiting."

Colombia. "Thanks for meeting with me. I look forward to joining Viola."

"We'll follow up," Jim concluded and turned to Lou.

Frank took the elevator to the lobby level and was half-dreaming as he walked toward the exit door. *Colombia. What will Joanna say about that?*

"Have a safe trip home, Mr. Anderson," said a friendly, enthusiastic voice.

"Oh. Yolanda. How could I forget—"

"You weren't going to run off without saying hasta la vista to me, were you?" She looked up at him, eyes inviting him to apologize.

"So sorry. My thoughts were still upstairs."

She softly rubbed the front of her neck. "Did you get to meet Mr. Duncan?"

"I did."

"Congratulations. I know what that means, most of the time. It'll be my pleasure to meet you again. Soon. As a Viola man."

"I hope so. Oh, by the way, is Mr. Doyle in?"

"One second... Jim? John?" she asked, reading her screen.

"Mike. Michael."

"No. Maybe that gentleman works at another location. I don't recall a Mike Doyle, but I haven't been at Viola that long."

"May I ask how long?"

"Oh? A few days over a month."

She was distracted by a busy-looking older gentleman with quick strides who shouted at her, "Jones in yet? We can't wait. He's late, dammit!"

"I didn't see him, Mr. Hubble. I'm so sorry."

"Terrible!"

Frank waved at Yolanda and she put her hand slightly up. He was on his way to the Westin.

Chapter 20

F rank called Mary Jenkins late afternoon on Tuesday.
"Welcome back, stranger," she said. "How was Houston?"

"Oh? How did you know?"

"I heard from Sonya. Also about you and Joanna but I already knew about you love birds. Kind of knew. Good for you guys." She turned down the radio.

"I see. Thank you—but please don't spread the news. Joanna's scared to death about losing her job. I'm on Mike's blacklist."

"Got on his list, eh? I'm so surprised," she mocked but refrained from sarcastically congratulating him.

"I'm sure you are." He laughed. "But don't—"

"Relax, Frank. I won't tell about Joanna. You sound tired."

"Yeah. Stiff legs. They're just too damn long for an economy ride on a 737."

"Poor thing. Joe—"

"I won't even comment on the size of the nanosnack they offered. On a three-hour flight they could—"

"Joe's better!" Mary cut in, brimming with enthusiasm. "He can sit up in bed and talk to me. And he'll have foot surgery on Thursday."

"Better? Okay! That's a big deal. Really good news."

"Sure is. Thank God. How about you? Did you find a job?" She acknowledged Jake's presence with a good rub.

"Kind of. I had positive meetings with at least two companies. The second one definitely wants me, but I'll have to wait a few months, and I may have to move to Colombia."

"Colombia! *Viva Colombia!* Great! I can teach you some Spanish before you go." Her words were upbeat but she feared sadness crept through in her tone. Frank had been such good support.

"You sure can!" He laughed. "No sweat! In between your job, your kids, Joe in the hospital and what else, Mary?"

She sighed. "You're right, but things will get better. Joe might walk in a couple of weeks. He may even get back into his tanker truck. Not sure. Every night I think about that truck. It turned my life upside down. And Joe's, of course."

"Chin up, Mary. Tough Joe will surprise you."

"I try to believe it…."

"Keep hoping. And if I can help you, let me or Joanna know. She thinks a lot about you."

***

At about six that evening Frank called Vince Davis and asked him for a face to face discussion about the accident in Carrollton.

"Discuss what about it?" Vince asked. He sounded puzzled and a bit reluctant.

"I'll tell you when we meet."

"Mike Doyle might...." After a few seconds of silence, Vince suggested Frank meet him at his sister's downtown apartment on Atlantic Boulevard in Canton at seven-thirty.

"Canton?"

"That's where I am now," Vince said curtly. "Her name's Carla Johnson. James and Carla Johnson. 2076 Atlantic."

"Thanks. I know how you feel about the Carrollton mess and the way Mike's treating you. Don't worry, my lips will be sealed," Frank assured him.

"Get yourself a big Indians hat or something." It felt like an order. From a guy ten years his junior.

"Done. Count on me."

"Okay. Don't be late." Vince sounded scared.

"Got it."

Frank had to wait a good while after his knock on the door at 2076 Atlantic. "J&C," the sign said. Finally, he saw the peep hole go dark.

Vince opened the door.

"Thank you for taking the time," Frank said. When the door closed, he took off his hat.

"This way."

They entered a tiny, sparsely decorated sitting room.

"Take a seat," a nervous acting Vince grumbled. "My sister's not much of a decorator, but...."

"I appreciate her hospitality," Frank said as he stared at a small, lonely Van Gogh reproduction. "I'll make it brief. But first, how are things going at your place, in Carrollton?"

Vince gave him a slow eye roll.

"That bad?"

Shrugs from Vince. "It'll be many weeks before I get back to my job on Maple."

"Your sister—"

"She'll be back in an hour. Dinner with James."

"Oh. Thanks. She's being very kind. You said Mike's still running...." He was briefly distracted by a stack of clothing thrown over the armrest of a small couch at his right. "Still running the Maple site himself?"

"Kind of. But he's the big boss, so what can I say? He's got experience, but it's getting a little old. Anyway, I'm stuck in Carrollton. My wife makes me shower for hours every night to make sure I don't bring a nuclear bomb into the house," he joked, seeming to loosen up. He looked at Frank and added, "Not really much of that radioactive shit in Carrollton as far as we can tell. Women—you know."

"I'm single."

Frank had once noticed Vince with his wife from a distance as they hurried to their car in the parking lot of Lou's. It was late, the same day he had met Vince for the first time. He remembered Mrs. Davis's striking appearance, ultra-petite and ultra-blonde, walking with quick, short steps as she kept pace with Vince, who carried a large bag of groceries.

"But you know about women, anyway." He sounded exasperated. "Maybe better than I do. She bitches about my long absences. Texas girl lonely in Ohio. Mike sends me all over the state and to Pennsylvania, where they know a thing or two about this kind of mess, to Columbus, to Washington. It's a circus. Well, he makes it one. But it's a job. How about you?"

"I'm looking. Tapping my network."

Vince shrugged and frowned. "You shouldn't have much of a problem. You know the industry. Got many years under your belt."

"True. But I'm getting a little pickier. Age, I guess."

"Now, what's up? Why this fancy roundtable meeting?" Vince quipped, clearly forcing himself to lighten up.

Frank looked around. "Something's bothering me about Carrollton. I'm not convinced foul play wasn't involved."

Vince frowned. "Why?"

"Not sure. Maybe it's just me."

Vince frowned again. "Foul play...well, all I can tell you is that minutes after Doyle heard about the accident he called me from Cleveland, sounding terribly nervous. Understandable. He blamed it on Joe Bertolo. His driving. A reflexive reaction, I guess. The man sounded convinced. That was it. No doubts. I tried to urge caution in his statements, how could he be so sure, but couldn't get a word in. Then he told me to hurry to Carrollton. I resisted. No dice. The man went crazy. I loved my work at Beta but didn't want to keep arguing and lose my job. The pay isn't bad."

Frank almost blurted, "I know."

Joanna had told him, pillow talk, that she had heard Mike call Houston to argue for a raise of twenty thousand for Vince. "I think I heard correctly, Frankie," she had said and curled up to him. "So much money."

His eyes trained on Vince, Frank said, "So, you or Mike still haven't heard of any witnesses of the accident? Or any skid marks? Anything else that—?"

"No." Vince sighed, showing a trace of irritation. "Nobody's mentioned anything. No clues. The area is cordoned off and the police have bigger fish to fry with angry townspeople and businessmen facing ruin." He looked at his watch and stood up, seemingly embarrassed for being so rude. "Time flies," he said.

As Frank sat down in his car, he fastened his seat belt and inserted the ignition key. Before he turned it he whispered, "I'm not done yet. Not done yet."

Chapter 21

It was nine in the evening. Mary sat down at the kitchen table, kids in bed, legs tired. She tried to order her thoughts to take stock. Elbows on the table, face in hands, she felt her breath, cold in, warm out. Life had turned into a near-unbearable burden for her and her family.

TV channels and newspapers had discovered "Carrollton." They milked the story incessantly for all it was worth. Commentary was sometimes supportive of clean air and water, but more often inspired by the oil industry's generous support via commercials and political lobbying. Joe was blamed mercilessly day in, day out, Mike Doyle fanning the flames, for the loss of image inflicted on fracking, an industry that created employment and wealth in the region. Some program segments did briefly mention that Joe Bertolo's family proclaimed his innocence and pointed at the man lying in pain in Akron city Hospital. But in most newspaper articles and on TV the concluding sentence was, with minor variations: "Pain and suffering are things the good citizens of Carrollton have come to know all too well through this unfortunate mishap."

Carrollton and, occasionally, Noredge citizens would be paraded on TV screens extolling the wealth that hydraulic fracturing was bringing to the region, and explaining how they personally already had benefited from it. For good measure—Mary's opinion—one or two of the Carrollton spill victims would be brought into the studios as well and asked how they knew the "flowback" water was dangerous and why. That "flowback" euphemism for the waste water that came back up to the surface, and particularly the skewed questioning would drive Mary up the wall: she understood that no complete answers were available, not to scientists and certainly not to the clueless victims. But she wondered how everybody didn't know by now that the truth was hidden from the population by the secrecy laws the industry had bought from politicians.

Jimmy and Andy kept saying they wouldn't go back to school when vacation ended in a few weeks. They had been harassed by kids in the street or at ballgames—and by parents. Their playmates would ape TV anchors and use phrases and words they couldn't have thought out themselves. But Andy knew what they meant. "I can see on their faces that they hate Daddy," he would complain, bitterness and sadness in his tone.

Mary would correct him. "No, Andy. Some dumb older people have told them to say they hate Daddy."

Last night the boy had told her angrily, "They said

that you're jealous of the people who get money from the frackers because you're not getting any. It's not true. You're not jealous."

"How silly, Andy. Don't listen to them. You're right. It's not true." She had cried inside for having harmed her innocent kids.

"I know. I told them."

"Thank you, sweet boy." She had hugged him hard. "And when your big strong Daddy feels better he'll tell them they're very wrong, about everything. And that he didn't cause the accident."

"You know that, right, Mommy?"

"I do."

"How do you know?"

"I'll tell you later."

"When?"

"I hope soon." She had sighed.

Today, anger burning inside her and nobody around to scream at but poor Jake, she decided to take matters in her own hands. Her Joe would not wait for justice any longer.

She would call a town meeting—her town meeting. She was convinced many in Noredge shared her views on fracking and would show up. But where? She feared she wouldn't be able to find a suitable meeting room or hall in Noredge; owners would be reluctant to face the wrath of Mike Doyle. He had the Chamber and the city council in his pocket.

Should she call Frank and ask him for his opinion? He

might enthusiastically approve of her plan but get cold feet once he reminded himself of his severance payment from Supren. Last she heard, only a tiny fraction of it had been paid out. She understood.

She called goodhearted, bearded teacher Dan Clark, her on-and-off connection to the Sierra Club, who lived in a rural area on Manning Road in Hartville, a few miles from Noredge. His barn had been used for occasional parties and small scale art exhibits by friends.

"Be my guest," Dan responded enthusiastically when Mary spoke to him over the phone. When she tried to explain her plans and the reason for them, he stopped her. "I know exactly what you're talking about. I read the papers. I'm with you Noredge guys. Come on over and have a look at my Taj Mahal."

"Thanks! Thanks so much, Dan." Mary had found someone who would give her a lift—roll up his sleeves. "You're a real friend. We should organize our outreach, our thoughts, what we're going to say."

"Absolutely. I've been through some of those gatherings and enjoyed them, plus learned a couple of things."

He had used "we" and "our." Mary got a warm feeling inside. "Tomorrow?"

"Suits me. Afternoon?"

"Great, I'll have the kids with me. Okay?"

"Good! They can play with my goats." He chuckled. "My boys are too old for that. By the way, how's Joe?"

"Thanks. Getting better, very slowly. Foot surgery

Thursday. It's scary. I mean, that too." Dan's question had reminded her that her call was much more about Joe than about fracking.

"Yeah. Good luck to him. See you mid-afternoon?"

"Deal. Thank you, Dan."

***

On the following Saturday around three in the afternoon Mary had taken a seat in the back row and observed the crowd of about fifty that had gathered in Dan Clark's barn. She wore shorts, a loose Nike T-shirt and running shoes.

When she arrived, she had again marveled at the excellent condition of the old, thirty-foot-high wooden structure. "It always shows its age, Dan, but also its dignity and the care you've given it over the years. How impressive it looks today! And how neat. You must've worked night and day since Wednesday."

Dan had shrugged and waved off the compliment with a wink. His wife Lydia, standing next to him, nodded and smiled.

"Thanks, but you're mostly talking about Lydia," he said, putting his hand on his wife's shoulder.

Mary knew what he meant; he had kept her informed of the preparations. The barn's outside had been repainted a modest brown in October. Yesterday Dan and Lydia had finished a little faster than usual their yearly ritual of removing old hay, throwing out obsolete machinery parts, cleaning up unsightly oil spills, spraying, and thoroughly checking out the very basic ten-year-old sound system. This afternoon their impressive John Deere, the pride of the lowly paid teacher, greeted arriving attendees from its temporary, slightly elevated grassy spot between the house and the barn.

Despite two open windows near the ceiling and the valiant efforts of three moaning fans, the heat inside felt like a leaden blanket; but Mary could barely suppress her excitement. She noticed Frank in the next to last row on the other side of the barn, baseball cap pulled down over forehead, oversize sunglasses perched on the bridge of his nose. She smiled: the sun couldn't reach his corner of the barn. But he was here, severance or no severance. *Good man.* She would have to express special thanks to him later, privately. "You've got guts," she would tell him. She didn't know him quite well enough yet to say "*cojones.*"

The crowd was a mixture of young and old, more women than men. Dan and Mary and friends had made dozens of phone calls. They had sent invitations by e-mail to about one hundred fifty assumed environment sympathizers and friends in the region. Dan's Sierra mailing list for Noredge had come in handy.

Fanning herself with a folded copy of the guest list she hummed along with the "*Alle Menschen werden Brüder*" tunes of Beethoven's Ninth that created a festive atmosphere. *Musician Frank must feel at home.* The rustic smell of hay still wafted over the crowd. With her free hand she kept working her phone to avoid conversation with the two youngsters to her right. She had thrown brief, furtive glances at them. They looked a little odd with their tattooed forearms. Were they part of Doyle's shock troops?

"I'm Mary," she had said, offering her hand to the one next to her.

"Nick," he had responded. "And Rudy."

She had returned to her phone.

A tall, beaming Dan, bald on top but sporting a bushy, graying beard and a short ponytail, mounted the two steps up to the wooden platform behind a simple wooden lectern that looked like his own creation. He rang an antique cowbell, forcefully pushed his shoulders down and back and faced the group while waiting for the murmurs to die down. His face was a picture of authority and confidence.

"Welcome all!" he shouted enthusiastically and turned his mike on. "Welcome to my kingdom! We've partied here a good many times, often til much later than our neighbors appreciated!" He pointed at a grinning, corpulent man in the front row. "Today, it's a different story. I noticed you all love Beethoven, but right now I wish we could've had marching bands here to sound an urgent call to arms! A clarion call! Carrollton makes it crystal clear: we're rushing, eyes closed, toward a treacherous cliff. The fracking troops attacking our land, air, and water move ever closer, turn ever greedier and ruin town after town. Gold for some, true, and poison for most, also true. We'd better start calling it what it is: a shameless public robbery! Let's get started!"

Boisterous applause and shouts of "Fracking No! Fracking No!" met his exhortations.

He unfolded a thirty by thirty poster, held it up with both hands high above his six-foot frame and said, "Here are some facts!" He paused. His voice turned businesslike, at times professor-like, when he lowered the glossy sheet and started quoting from it. To most in the audience the arguments and the villains were known. So were the academic sources such as Cornell University, revered by many attendees as their oracle and a temple of truth. Dan Clark admitted that the new technology and industry brought fortune and wealth, but only to the lucky few, many of them because they had chosen their landowning parents carefully. "But it's painfully clear that many other citizens, almost all of us, have to share in the suffering fracking brings!"

Cries of anger and shouts of enthusiasm from the crowd spiked his introductory remarks.

Mary nodded knowingly and studied the two youths next to her. They cried loudly, seemingly determined not to be outdone. They had their fists up in the air when the crowd shouted "Fracking No!" As she looked at Nick and Rudy she couldn't suppress a frown. She abruptly switched to a jovial smile but wondered whether they were acting.

Frank sat stone-faced, as far as Mary could tell from a

distance, right fist under his chin. *The thinker. Rodin.* She chuckled inwardly.

Dan forged ahead. He warned about earthquakes, potentially lethal rotten egg gases, aquifers contaminated by methane and worse substances, horrific traffic jams, exorbitant rental rates, invasions by unwanted strangers and drugs, and unspeakable damage to the atmosphere by methane, which was many times worse than carbon dioxide.

He paused, stared at his audience and pointed at the bottom of his poster. He whispered slowly into the microphone, "See this? Dirty water," and dropped the sheet. "Dirty water! Countless numbers of dangerous chemicals are swimming in it, their names unknown, hidden by secrecy laws or executive orders forced down our throats. In all likelihood, radioactive waste is settling into Carrollton's creeks and sewers and soil. *Right now.* That's what gets to me. The thought is killing me." He lowered his voice even more. "That stuff may kill some of the good citizens of Carrollton. And their children. Their grandchildren. And who comes after Carrollton? My townspeople here in Hartville? The good folks of Noredge? How much of that poison is spilled, everywhere, at every well, anywhere? On every well site, dirty water waits for a tanker that'll truck it to the injection well, where it can cause earthquakes. Just ask the Oklahomans." He halted. There was an awe-inspiring silence. He concluded, sounding emotional and solemn, "How bad will it really get? Does *anybody* know?"

A male in his mid-forties stood up. Dressed in a Polo shirt and slacks, hair slicked down, athletic posture, ready smile, he courteously asked for the floor.

Dan nodded and gestured to him that he should come to the platform.

The man strode forward clearly enjoying the attention as he worked his way through the crowd.

Dan gave him a good stare as he handed him the mike.

"Thank you for letting me speak," the man said, a wide smile confirming his words as he faced the audience. "I'm David Brooks, a proudly neutral expert in the matter we're discussing here. Our Truth in Hydraulic Fracturing Foundation, the THYF, holds views that are greatly at variance with—"

"You'd better say what you mean," Dan told him out loud, and added with a wink, "We're simple folks here."

"Oh. Certainly. I'm sorry. I'm trying to say that I respectfully disagree with many of the statements you just heard. At THYF we fund thorough studies and never lose sight of the overall interest—"

"Of the oil companies!" someone shouted.

Laughter erupted. It resounded over the crowd. Dan looked amused.

Brooks smiled briefly and went on. "The interest of the population in the first place, and that includes the thousands of workers who earn an honest living in the oil industry," he retorted, seemingly unperturbed.

Nick, next to Mary, jumped up and shouted, "Who funds you? Have you read the Cornell study? You tell me what's in that dirty water in Carrollton!"

Mary took another good look at the twosome seated next to her.

Brooks nodded with a benevolent smile in the direction of his young questioner. "You look like a smart kid. I believe you know I can't simply give you a cookie cutter answer. Neither can any scientist at the THYF or anywhere else. Every spill's different, carries water from all kinds of wells. Carrollton...only ongoing tests can tell us what got spilled in that accident." He waited and stared at Nick, apparently hoping this response would do.

"How convenient. Ongoing tests!" Rudy mocked, elbowing Nick as he stood up. "Why are you here? Were you invited?" A murmur sailed through the crowd.

Mary started checking her list. She didn't find any Brooks, not immediately.

The THYF man didn't answer the last question. He fired back, "Our science is completely independent from—"

"You know what chemicals are in the mush they're pumping down! Tell us!" Rudy looked determined to keep digging.

Now Brooks stared angrily at the two young men. "The

composition varies from well to well and it's secret. You know that. Secret by law to protect the country's interests—"

"You mean the oil industry's!"

Jeers and laughter merged into a biting cacophony.

Rudy nodded to acknowledge encouraging smiles and thumbs-ups. "Does THYF know, THYF, what shit Supren's forcing down their pipes? Supren's," he shot back.

"The companies take us in confidence, but first we sign secrecy agreements. I'm punishable by law—"

"And get paid royally by those who entrust you with the information. And you provide them with what they want from you. Figures massaged to your liking. Their liking. Smart, sir. Profitable! But in Carrollton, people may die because of your great deal. I get it." Rudy sat down.

Brooks showed a sheepish smile.

"You laugh?" Nick shouted.

Mary stood up, made her way to Dan and whispered something in his ear while showing him the invitee list. Then she tiptoed back to her seat.

Dan put his hand up and walked up to Brooks. "Sorry, Mr. Brooks. I must stop you here, sir," he said, his tone neutral but firm. "Other guests may have something to say too." He extended his hand in the direction of the mike. His mike.

Brooks moved away from Dan. "Just a moment, Mr. Clark. I'd like to explain one more…."

Suddenly Nick appeared next to Dan and tried to rip the mike out of the hand of Brooks, who held on tightly.

"You scum!" the clean-cut THYF man screamed as he lost his battle to the boy. He threw his empty hands up and looked at the crowd.

"Spy! Traitor!" some bawled, pointing angrily at him.

Dan took over the mike. "Now just get off my property, Mr. Brooks," he intoned. "I don't know who asked you to be here, but I can venture a wild guess. Please leave."

The intruder left without saying a word or looking left or right.

Nick and Rudy high-fived each other and stood triumphant next to Dan, acknowledging applause.

Mary got up, went back to the front and asked Dan for the mike. Looking subdued but speaking forcefully she said, "Most of you know me but anyway, I'm Mary Jenkins from Noredge and—"

"Joe's wife!" somebody shouted. "We love Joe!"

Mary nodded but didn't smile. "Thank you. He's getting better, very slowly. Two days ago he had foot surgery."

"Soon he'll be playing soccer again. I've seen him with the kids," the man kept shouting back.

"I hope so." She pointed at Dan and said, "My thanks to this courageous, generous man for organizing this event! For daring to speak up so clearly. Let's give him a big hand."

Dan waved and said, addressing the crowd forcefully, without mike, "I'm the one who must thank all of you for coming."

Applause followed.

Dan bowed and added loudly, "All except that bastard we just kicked out!"

A standing ovation ensued.

Mary spoke as soon as she felt she could be heard. "This gathering isn't just about Joe. We'll have many more spills and Joes in this state—in the country—if we don't stand up and act. The fracking industry already has engulfed major parts of Ohio. There's nothing we can do about that: the harm is often irreversible. But we can fight to save many of our beautiful towns and neighborhoods where fracking's greed hasn't yet fouled our woods, our land, our air, our water, and yes, some of our souls."

A woman raised her hand. "You're from Noredge," she said, "and so am I. Isn't it too late to save our town? Supren's got two sites and two more on the way."

Mary nodded. "You're right. I'm sure they're planning even more for our town. To answer your question, time is running out for Noredge. We must stop them in their tracks. Now. I propose we draft a petition: not one more site in Noredge! A ban on fracking in our beloved town. I've been offered a lease for my acres three different times. Each time the price went up. But I haven't budged and I won't."

"Why not shut down the first two as well? They barely started." It was Rudy who yelled loudly. "Sierra can help to draft the text for Noredge, and it can be used for other towns."

"Sierra? Could they? Would they?" Mary actually knew

this wasn't the first petition the Ohio Sierra chapter would write.

"I think so. I'm studying chemical engineering in Cleveland, but I'm from Canton. I talk to the Sierra scientists on and off." He showed her a pair of wide eyes and nodded.

Mary looked at Dan, then at Frank, who smiled incognito.

"Mr. Clark and me, we could throw together a first draft," Rudy went on.

Dan nodded.

"Nick, too. And then we'll have to find people to go door to door to collect signatures. Let's try Noredge first." The youngster seemed determined to strike while the iron was hot.

Dan kept nodding.

Mary gave Rudy a thumbs-up. "Good. We have no time to lose. I know that tons of oil industry dollars are flowing into the campaign coffers of judges and congressmen. Big oil wants a state ban on local bans. Some states already have it. It's a race against the clock."

"Who's going to put his signature under the text?" someone in the crowd asked.

"Who? Who? Everybody!" Nick laughed and acknowledged applause and shouts.

Dan raised his voice to ask, "Who's from Noredge?"

Twenty or thirty hands went up.

"Wow! And who's prepared to sign?"

"All of us!" a woman shouted.

He showed a rascal smile. "And ring doorbells in Noredge?"

A joyful back and forth erupted within the enthusiastic crowd.

Mary looked for Frank but his seat was empty. *It's gotten too hot in here for him.* She coughed into the mike and said, "Thank you all. Joe should've heard you." She broke down.

Dan pointed in the direction of his house. "Friends," he shouted, "See those three tables? Lydia's got beer and pop on ice. Beef jerky too. Anybody thirsty?"

A huge chorus roared. "Everybody!"

Staring at the tables and swept up in the euphoria, Mary asked a beaming Dan, "Who paid for all of that?"

"The state of Ohio, of course. Tree-hugger Governor Kasich. Who else?" Dan's eyes sought appreciation for his joking.

"I should've known," she played along.

He whispered to her, "A guy named Frank Anderson footed the bill. Called me last night and asked whether this wouldn't be too much of a burden. My apologies for not consulting you on this." He winked.

"Apologies? Too late! Let me try that jerky before I accept them." She embraced him.

Chapter 22

"I hear it still has great atmosphere and food, Mom. We'll find out soon," Frank said as he swung his Altima onto Cleveland Massillon Road in Bath. He was headed to Lanning's. That stuffy place wasn't his kind of restaurant, and quite a ways from Noredge, but his widowed mother, retired in Boca Raton, insisted she should have dinner at her Lanning's one more time.

"It's *numero uno*, the best of the best," she had said, kissing her fingertips and sounding convinced she knew what she was talking about. "I just love the place. 'See Naples and die,' they say. For me, just give me Lanning's and…. I'd better leave it at that."

He smiled. *Mom and her superlatives.* "Good thing you hit the brakes just in time, Mom. You've got many good years ahead. Your health's good, your spirit strong. We'll do many more Lanning's." He knew she wasn't telling him everything about her doctor visits and the load of vitamins and pills she had to swallow, but he wanted to make this a great evening. Mom didn't make it too often to Noredge, although she had a son and a daughter there. She was staying at Sonya's.

"Yes. And it's cheaper than Naples," she said, laughing. "Particularly for a guy without a job—just kidding." She pinched his leg. "I didn't mean Naples, Florida, you know."

"I've got a good severance payment coming, Mom. It may hit my account before I get my next Visa bill."

Frank had spoken jokingly but his thoughts went back to the event he had attended in Dan Clark's barn less than two hours earlier. In doing so he had publicly disregarded some of the stipulations in his severance agreement, but he had felt he owed his support to Mary Jenkins and the well-meaning folks of Noredge. He had tried to cover up as much as possible with a hat and sunglasses and had taken a seat in the darkest and farthest corner. He had slipped away early, hopefully unnoticed.

It's unlikely that Mike ever finds out I was at that meeting, he reasoned as he turned into the parking lot of the restaurant. He hadn't opened his mouth in the barn. *A damn good event it was.* He chuckled inside.

Mother and son entered the dimly lit restaurant. Frank knew the place but again it struck him as sedate, old-style. It was, however, Mom's undisputed favorite. Chairs were comfortable and richly padded, brown and deep. Table lights glowed orange, corners dark. It was six-thirty. Only three of the fifteen or twenty tables were taken. A good listener could discern a trace of a classical piano concerto being played. Frank's fingers itched.

The maître d' asked for the name on the reservation, took a thorough look at the twosome and ushered them politely, his voice barely audible, to a corner near the entrance. He held Mrs. Anderson's chair when she was ready to sit down. She thanked him.

"Awfully quiet," Frank half-whispered as he adjusted his glasses, but a woman two tables down looked up and frowned.

Mrs. Anderson apparently had noticed: she pointed at her hearing aid. "No need to shout, Frankie."

He showed her an affectionate nod.

By the time his watch said seven-thirty Frank was half-way through his inch-thick, juicy filet mignon, and his mother was having the time of her life with her Plank of Liver. The waiter had silently looked askance at Frank a few minutes before when he came to check the contents of their bottle of Cabernet. Frank had used his palm to signal they were going to take it easy on the alcohol.

"This liver is just too good, Frankie. Epically delicious."

He frowned. "Mom, how did you develop that taste? Liver?"

She shrugged. "As a child. And this dish has been a Lanning's specialty for I don't know how many years. You won't find liver anywhere else this good. My friends in Boca turn up their noses at it. 'How can you eat that, Audrey? It tastes awful and your cholesterol....' I just wink. In Boca I can't even find it on the menu. Gluten free, low sugar, organic, cage free. That's what we have to settle for there." She gave Frank a deprecatory glance.

"You're a free spirit, you—"

"Look at me, the sinner, the dessert nut." She opened her palms so they faced him.

She had a point. She was doing all right. No one would venture to guess even close to her age. At sixty-five she had the figure, the healthy-looking blonde hairdo, the gait, the skin as well as the attitude of a fifty-year-old. She didn't wear glasses. Cataract surgery had taken care of that. "My hearing is as sharp as my mind," she would joke, pointing at her hearing aid, but sometimes Frank had his doubts about that.

"You'll have to come north more often, Mom, I think—" He paused abruptly and, head down, turned forty-five degrees in his chair, away from the entrance.

She held up her fork, motionless, its teeth deep in a sauce-coated chunk of liver. "What's the matter? Stomach cramps?"

"Quiet. Eat," he said, his voice hushed.

"Huh?" Mrs. Anderson sounded puzzled.

"Just wait." He knew he was acting rudely but kept looking down.

"What for, Frankie?"

He turned back, puffed, and whispered, "Whew. I shouldn't have seen what I saw. Got enough trouble already."

"Could you explain?" she asked, looking concerned.

"Just a minute."

"Oh. Yes. I know. Sometimes I'm a little slower nowadays." She winked.

He waved her off. "The jerk who fired me walked in with the wife of the guy who replaced me."

His mother glanced in the direction of the new arrivals. "Hmm. You make it sound complicated, but I get it. Maybe that woman's husband is parking the car."

"It's all valet, Mom."

Frank finally looked up. He saw the couple standing about thirty feet away with the maître d', who pointed at a table in a far corner. Doyle nodded at the man. Petite, blonde Mrs. Davis, complete with impossibly high heels and tight-fitting yellow blouse over what looked like designer jeans, stood next to Doyle. He had his hand low on her waist.

"Oh. But that jerk—"

"Mike Doyle," he whispered.

"Whatever. He doesn't know you saw him, does he?"

"He may, but he didn't make eye contact."

"And the woman?"

"I don't think she knows me."

"See. Don't worry. You show discretion and you'll be okay. He has a problem, not you." She turned her attention to the liver.

Right. He barely listened. He thought of the twenty thousand dollar raise Doyle had given Vince days ago, according to Joanna. Despite his boss's generosity poor Vince had complained bitterly about him in Canton. "How would you like this, Frank?" he had started his lament. "First he tells me how indispensable I am in Carrollton and in the next breath he sends me on a useless trip to Columbus to 'smooth things over' or to Chicago to check on the latest waste removal equipment and technology. Or to Washington. I'm never at home. And my poor wife sits home alone twiddling her thumbs or watching soap operas."

Frank threw a quick glance at Mrs. Davis in the dark corner. He had always wondered why a smart driller like Vince had been taken off the Beta job at Harriet's at such a critical stage of the project. Why did it have to be Vince for Carrollton? Why hadn't Doyle called up the most experienced clean-up crew in Houston? In the country? So much was at stake for Supren. And why did he keep sending Vince out on thinly justified trips while the work piled up in Carrollton?

Mrs. Anderson put her hand softly on Frankie's. "Stop brooding," she said soothingly. "It'll make you old before you…before you find yourself a girlfriend."

Not again. Frank frowned. "Mom—"

"Or is it that job search that keeps bugging you? You won't have any problem with that either, once you put your mind to it. I know my son." She looked proud.

"Thanks. I hope you're right. And I'm on my way to taking care of all of that. Not kidding. I've got a job more or less lined up with a top Houston company, and I'm working my butt off to win the heart of a jewel of a girl I've set my sights on."

"Oh? Who is she? From here? Why didn't you bring her along?" Disappointment overpowered the initial excitement in his mother's voice.

He leaned forward, looked briefly in the direction of Mike Doyle, and said, his voice hushed, "Joanna, a Puerto Rican American, from the Noredge area, beautiful and sweet."

"I don't doubt that but why didn't you invite her tonight? Why are you whispering?"

"I couldn't bring her. That man," he pointed his head in the direction of Doyle, "shouldn't see us together anywhere."

"Or?"

"Joanna would lose her job."

Mrs. Anderson threw her hands up. "Come on. Why? Is that any of his business? And are you such bad company for her? Or she for you?" Her tone suggested she knew the answer to all three questions.

He put his index finger to his lips. "He'd assume she'd tell me too much about his...discussions."

"Hush-hush discussions?"

"I guess so. Some, anyway."

She shrugged. "Don't you have a picture of Joanna? I must approve her, you know." She giggled.

"Here you are." He showed her a selfie with Joanna on his iPhone.

"Wow! You went to the ocean with her? Or is that Lake Erie?"

"I took her far enough away from here. Safe. Galveston."

She rocked her head slowly, her voice fluttery. "Together to Galveston—sounds romantic. Your father and I, we had to behave, if you know what I mean."

"I do. But did you follow orders?"

"Mostly." She smiled.

"I also remember that, when I would be leaving on a trip, you always told me to behave."

She nodded.

"And that I always would answer, 'No way!'"

"That too, and I had to hold back to not tell you, 'Attaboy.'" She studied the picture. "She looks beautiful. I'm tired of waiting for you to get off the street. I hope to meet her soon."

"You will, Mom. Your liver's getting cold."

When they finished their plentiful entrees and their bottle, Frank was happy to hear that his mother wanted to skip dessert and move straight to the Courvoisier ritual, to "get it all moving in here." She had rolled her eyes.

They swirled their drinks and clinked glasses.

"To Joanna," Mrs. Anderson said. "I thought I just heard wedding bells."

He had only taken a few sips of the digestive when she finished hers.

Mike Doyle and his companion were engaged in a close and intense conversation as Frank quietly asked for the bill, signed it and sneaked out, his hand on the shoulder of his slightly unsteady mother.

Chapter 23

On Tuesday, the week after the event at Dan's barn, Mary got a call from Frank.

"Could you meet me in half an hour, for a quick lunch at McDonald's?" he asked. "I'd like to explain my sudden departure from Dan's place, and apologize. And a couple of other matters."

Mary knew why he had acted that way at Dan's but she agreed to meet. Jimmy and Andy were enjoying one of their last vacation days at a friend's house. "No need to apologize," she said. "But we should keep it short. Half an hour. I'm doing laundry. Noon?"

As she slipped into a loose flowered dress she wondered about the "other matters."

At the restaurant, Frank looked nervous. He checked out the nearby tables before he said to Mary, his voice hushed and robotic, "Sorry for taking your time. And my apologies for my disappearance last week. I had my mother in town."

She frowned. *That's the big deal?*

He covered his left cheek with his hand. "Sonya heard that you and I have become the talk of the town. An item. We're seen together too often while poor Joe lies in the hospital suffering." He rolled his eyes.

She laughed, but just for a split second. "It's a joke, right?"

His face told her no.

"But it's a shameless lie. They're nuts!" She made a disparaging gesture and started tapping her forehead with her index.

He nodded. "Quiet. Of course they are, but what can we do to stop that silly gossip? It's out there."

She sighed. "That slander, you mean. What could I...I know what *you* could do. You could tell it all...but no, Doyle shouldn't know that the real 'item' is you and Joanna." She stared at him, not knowing what to say. "I have no idea, Frank."

He threw his hands up, swore through his teeth, and waved the topic away. "Something else, and this isn't gossip," he said. "Seems Mike's spending money like crazy. Flaunting it. His wife's mad as hell regarding the new boat he bought, the Porsche he's looking at—"

"How do you know?" She had stopped stirring her coffee.

"Joanna. Mrs. Doyle let it all hang out to her in a fit of anger. I wonder how much Supren's paying the man. Must be a fortune."

"Okay. And then? He's got a big job."

"Sure. But I keep wondering."

"About?"

He shook his head. "Never mind. Maybe I'm crazy. I just don't understand."

The thirty minutes went by fast. Mary stood up and smoothed her dress. "Let me know when you figure it out, Frank. I wonder how my laundry's doing. By the way, I think you're not crazy, but part of a beautiful 'item.'"

Later that afternoon, when the kids were back home, playing outside, Father Bianchi came to Mary's house. He extolled the virtues of Mr. Doyle, a faithful Christian who meant well with Noredge; he also had nice words for Sonya and Frank Anderson. But he spoke that last name very slowly, with emphasis. Then he discretely warned that some citizens or parishioners frowned at late night visits by "that good man Anderson" to the Jenkins home on Maple Road. He did fully understand that Frank's intentions were praiseworthy and his character generous. "But appearances matter," he concluded with a shy smile.

Damn Doyle, she fretted inside. Obviously he had planted the seeds of slander in the priest's pure mind. She couldn't prove that, but she had no doubt. Barely able to control her anger she answered with a scowl and a stern stare. "Thank you, Father," she said. And she thought of Frank. *The poor guy, smeared for his good deeds.*

She noticed with a trace of glee that Father Bianchi looked somewhat embarrassed. "How about some real concerns?" she tasked, unable to suppress a tinge of triumph in her voice. "Have you also heard complaints from parishioners about a smell, sometimes, when they drink water? And that it looks brownish as it comes out of the tap? I have. You must have too. I'm sure they tell you *everything*." She dropped a good dose of scorn into that last sentence.

She had caught some of these water rumors. Rather than simply accepting insinuations and running with them, she had decided to wave them off. Until now. This morning she had told the kids they had to drink bottled water.

"It's so white, this water," Jimmy said as he tried to spell the word Dasani.

"Does Jake get bottled water too, Mommy?" Andy had asked.

She had nodded.

Good Father Bianchi seemed relieved by the abrupt change of subject. He said he had been approached by parishioners about the water. "But is anything perfect in this world, Mary?" he asked rhetorically. "Only the Lord...." he intoned, pointing upward with a big smile. "Only He!"

She couldn't disagree but felt young Father Bianchi was a bit like her aged aunt, a nun in a strictly contemplative order. "Why would I worry about food for tomorrow, children?" she would ask her middle-aged nephews and nieces, her voice quivering but her pale face a picture of confidence. "Even the birds get fed by the Almighty. They don't worry. They're His creation, as we are, but we're much closer to Him."

"You're so right," Mary answered. "Thank you for coming, Father. I think the kids are getting hungry."

She shook her head as she watched the good shepherd walk to his car. *He's become an unwitting part of the slander machine. Bamboozled by Doyle.*

***

Shortly after the priest left Mary received an ominous call from the hospital in Akron. "Your husband has contracted an infection."

Mary thought Dr. Lima made it sound like Joe had gone out of his way to catch it. "How the…? How did that happen?" she asked angrily.

She gestured for Andy to go outside and take Jimmy and Jake with him.

"We don't know. It's not uncommon. It can be treated, of course. Dr. Maseellal, the foot surgeon, hasn't decided yet whether he'll have to perform additional surgery. He hopes the antibiotics your husband is already getting intravenously will be sufficient. It'll be a few days."

"The treatment takes a few days?"

"Well, all I'm saying is that we'll need a week or so to decide on the surgery. If none is needed, we'll transfer your husband to a specialized facility in Cleveland, with his approval, of course. The Milos Institute. They're very good. Their procedures are very strict."

"Cleveland? For how long?" Mary saw her visits to that facility swallow more time than she could possibly find once school started. She slumped down into a chair.

"A few weeks. But he may have to go on antibiotics for a long time thereafter. Maybe very long."

"You mean forever, right?" Mary sighed, defeated. She dropped her right hand with her phone into her lap. She had heard the story before. A friend's father had suffered that fate for maybe ten years. Then he died.

"We hope not, ma'am." Dr. Lima's tone left no doubt that the conversation had taken too long already.

Mary barely heard her. She was tired and had to make an effort to lift her phone to her ear. She asked, "Can I visit Joe?"

"You can, ma'am, but we'll have to take special precautions."

"Yes. Maybe you should've done that a little sooner." She had blurted it out, frustrated and angry. And scared.

Dr. Lima maintained her monotonous tone. "I understand, ma'am. We don't know how the infection happened, but it's not an unusual occurrence, and impossible to prevent entirely. I'm so sorry. I know you've gone through a lot. You and your kids."

"I'm sure it's not your fault, Doctor. Thank you."

As Mary clicked off she started crying, head in hands, elbows on the table.

"Are you done, Mommy?"

She veered up.

"Can I have a drink?" Andy asked, out of breath, his head barely inside. "We're racing Jake."

"Oh! A drink? Certainly you can, sweetie." She waved him in and embraced him. "I'm so glad I have you."

"Huh? I'm glad I have you, Mommy. Does that make you cry?"

"It does, Andy. It does. Let's have a drink together." She loosened her embrace.

"Yeah. But a quick one. Jimmy might do something dumb with Jake. He's still young."

Mary smiled at her son's juvenile condescension. "Okay. A quick one with mommy."

After the boy rushed back out she let her tears flow. Costs, Joe's long absences both past and future, unpleasant discussions with HR over Joe's employment and care, the bullying of her boys—it all popped up in her head, as it did during her many sleepless nights.

On top of that, Mike Doyle had started a vendetta against her. He didn't seem to waste any opportunity to cast her in a negative, destructive light: Was the Sierra Club paying Mary Jenkins to stoke unrest and unfair criticism of fracking and Supren? Why were those two Sierra losers sitting next to her at Dan's event, as a Chamber member had told him? She had no doubt that Mayor Sanders was in on this smear campaign. Not that all of this came as a surprise: Doyle had to know she was the instigator of the petition that was still being drafted.

That document took more time than she had expected,

but the Sierra folks had taken control and wanted to have all the facts verified, the i's dotted and t's crossed. "It's got to be airtight and waterproof," they said. Kept saying. Dan, Frank and she couldn't argue otherwise: indeed, it had to be hard-hitting, damning, and precise, incorporating the very latest scientific findings. And those kept streaming in. The arguments had to be irrefutable. She had to be patient while fending off unfair comments, insinuations and maneuvers. It had become too much.

Overwhelmed, she started crying, "Joe, Joe, please come home soon. We need you here." A few minutes later she got up and looked out at the boys. They were caught up in their game, thankfully unaware of her misery.

Chapter 24

Late August the new school year started for Mary and the boys. Joe was still working his way back to normal life in the Milos facility in Cleveland, on heavy antibiotics but making steady progress. Mary had to perform miracles to combine her regular duties with sporadic trips to see him at least one weekday. She usually went alone but on Sundays she could take the boys.

By early September the rumors about "a foul smell in the water" had inundated Noredge. They had replaced the weather and baseball as the main topic of conversation among neighbors. Many had switched from tap water to bottles for food and drinks and most feared worse was on the way. Mary thought Father Bianchi had been a bit optimistic about the Lord's willingness to keep the town's water safe.

Arguments pro- and con- fracking had grown louder by the day. Was that newcomer in Noredge the culprit or not?

"The Smell!" The newly arrived odor soon became a godsend for the local TV stations, the Noredge Sentinel,

Akron's Beacon Journal, The Repository of Canton, and others. It had prompted cheers in their boardrooms. It was a juicy topic, a controversial magnet attracting unusually big audiences and keeping them spellbound. People were glued to their TV sets and iPhones because they were fearful, angry, disbelieving or outright skeptical. The latter claimed this smell matter had to be a cruel hoax or an act of sabotage by Greens or other groups opposed to industry that brought prosperity. Fear invaded the city.

Mike Doyle shrugged off initial complaints. "Do you know how much manure a cow produces a day?" he quipped one morning on WKSU. His suggestive question regarding methane from bovine excretion carried a kernel of truth. "Ask the tree-huggers. We bring wealth, jobs and dollars to this place. A hell of a lot more than the cows!"

Mary knew all about the argument that pure methane was odorless. But Doyle smartly kept mum about other organic, possibly harmful substances that often accompanied methane from oil and gas fields and smelled awful. Some feared for lead and manganese.

Soon the odor of a glass of brownish tap water was no longer the butt of earthy jokes or a laughing matter that could be flippantly shrugged off and discarded with a catchy one liner: tests showed methane levels a good deal higher than allowed by the EPA. "If that gas evaporates from the water into people's homes, it can burn," Mary told neighbors and colleagues at school. "And it can cause headaches, nausea and even brain damage. You can die from inhaling enough of it."

Sonya had nodded.

The sporadic, isolated little storms of protest gradually coalesced, grew together into a threatening hurricane that could engulf the town and the region. Noredge's elders had to act.

On September 10th, a Monday, Mayor Sanders faced reporters and citizens at a hastily called public meeting late afternoon at City Hall. Flanked by a combative-looking Mike Doyle, he said he was going to make an important announcement about the water issue.

A thirty-foot-long oak table sporting about twenty-five aging, wooden chairs and, at its far end, American and Ohio flag stands, dominated the narrow, windowless meeting room. On one side of the table two more rows of ten metal chairs each had been squeezed in behind the wooden ones.

Those seated on that side had a huge Ohio State poster at their backs. They looked at a black and white picture of Governor Kasich in front of them and at an antique coat rack. The latter bothered the hell out of those seated with their backs to the governor, their heads inches away from the hooks. The air was laden with perspiration at this late hour and, despite the no-smoking sign, a crisp pipe tobacco smell wafted through the place. Some wrinkled their noses.

All seats were taken. About ten latecomers were

standing behind the third row, some of them leaning on and off on the backs of the metal seats. Frank had gotten wind of the announcement and alerted Mary. Both were seated in the back row.

The mayor opened the meeting, his wide frame blocking most of the governor in the picture behind him as he stood up. "We have been made aware by the EPA of a certain degree of methane contamination of our drinking water, and Mr. Doyle has readily acknowledged the problem," he read from a sheet.

Mary already fumed inside. *The EPA. As if he hasn't heard any citizens' complaints.*

Sanders turned to Doyle, seated next to him, and acknowledged his single nod. He went on, "I've asked you all to join me here so I can tell you we're going to nip this thing in the bud. 'This smell matter,' as some like to describe it." His tone and furtive glances revealed his unstated opinion. He threw another look toward the Texan at his side, who kept staring down but nodded again. "The city owes you and will provide to all of you the clean water we're all paying for. Mr. Doyle, Mike we call him now, will not let us down. He's told me that little, innocuous incidents like ours are not uncommon and almost inevitable. Hydraulic fracturing technology, this godsend for our economy, is unbelievably advanced nowadays, but still not one hundred percent perfect."

"'Hydraulic fracturing.' Our mayor has turned into

an erudite man, you know," Mary mocked in a whisper, elbowing Frank.

A few heads turned.

The mayor forged ahead. "'We've had some bad luck,' Mr. Doyle explained to me, 'but relax. At Supren we know how to fix it. Not really that big a deal.' He's been around this industry for a few years and has been to this rodeo before, as they say." He folded his sheet and turned to Doyle.

"Let me tell you off the bat that I understand y'all's concern," the Texan said, smiling as he stood up.

Sideways glances multiplied throughout the room.

First the mayor's pooh-poohing and now this syrupy 'y'all's.' Yuck. It was too much for Mary but she kept silent.

Doyle made his pitch. "I understand and I promise we'll make you good. All of you. We're citizens just like you. I too hate the rotten smell, but as a veteran of the industry I might be a little less sensitive to it. A bit numbed. Fortunately, we can now say we've cleaned up the Carrollton spill, so we can concentrate on this new issue. We'll take care of it. I'm proud of the team of engineers we have in place now, its expertise. Vince Davis, our key man for the Carrollton matter, rejoined us yesterday at the Beta site here in Noredge."

Some in the room seemed to turn restive.

He paused abruptly and said, "I see hands up. Enough big words from me. I think I'd better answer some of your questions."

A back and forth followed. Number of wells planned for Noredge? Whose fault was it that gas seeped into the water? Where did that happen? Was old water piping the culprit? How many times had Mr. Doyle dealt with this kind of problem? Successfully? In what state? How about providing drinking water to the citizens on an organized, systematic basis? For how long?

Doyle handled it all with aplomb and without even once looking at the big folder he had in front of him.

About fifteen minutes into the question and answer session a thin, unshaven youth in cutoff jeans stood up and asked, "Good evening Mr. Doyle. I'm Seth. Do you have any people from Houston, I mean, any water contamination specialists flying up here?"

"Huh? What channel are you from?" Doyle looked irritated.

"No channel. I'm a freelancer."

"Oh. One of—didn't I just say we have a great group of engineers here who—"

"Any water contamination specialists?"

Doyle let out a deep sigh. "We've got the skills we need. Right here in Noredge. Don't worry: Houston will always be ready to assist. Just one call from me and they'll hop on a plane. I've got my contacts there. But I feel responsible. The buck stops here. With me."

He paused, exuding confidence, his eyes traveling the long ellipse in the room. "I'll personally track down the cause of this contamination, if we even want to call it that, with our guys working their butts off at Rutgers Lake and on Maple Road. This is a driller's job, my kind of job. I'll find the cause with my team. Me, not some bearded vegetarian tree-hugger wasting his days in a laboratory. To me, treating the cause of the problem seems slightly more important than producing tables and figures explaining how bad it is. And, let me tell you again, I'll use any means necessary to get this matter resolved, cleaned up. Even if I'd have to fall on my knees for Houston, but that won't be necessary. Is that clear?"

Sure. Mary was disturbed by the Texan's hype and surprised by the strangely long and emphatic reaction to the young man's simple question. "Does Houston know about this?" she asked loudly.

Doyle had a smirk on his face. "Oh. Miss Jenkins. Good to see you're a conscientious citizen. Somehow I knew that. Regarding your question, would you really think they don't?" He immediately turned to a young woman in the audience who had her hand up.

Mary wouldn't cede the floor. "I doesn't matter what I think, Mr. Doyle. Does Houston know? Supren in Houston?"

"What?" His face had turned crimson red.

Mary felt she had hit a nerve.

He intoned, "Miss Jenkins, the entire Supren organization is informed and stands behind our local team. Good enough?"

She threw her hands up and looked at Frank. He gave her an enigmatic stare. Then a brief rascal smile.

Doyle cut away from the back and forth. "Okay, young lady," he said, pointing. "You had your hand up before I was interrupted by Miss Jenkins."

The woman asked, her voice almost girly, "Can my children drink the water, sir? My two-year-old boy complained this morning—"

"Okay. Okay. Just a moment." Doyle had his hand up and nodded. "Relax, ma'am. Nothing will happen to your boy because of the methane. Man has been drinking water with methane in it since the day water wells were invented. No problem."

"But I heard a house exploded somewhere in our state and I—"

"In Bainbridge! In 2007," Mary shouted.

Mike Doyle looked perturbed but recovered instantaneously. "Right. In extreme situations that can happen." He had addressed Mary. Now he turned back to the other woman. His tone remained soothing. "Even asphyxiation is possible." He paused, his eyes sparkling. "Yes, you heard me right. I did say that. But I can assure you that the quantity of methane we have in our water is tiny. We're light-years away from what we'd need for these disasters to happen. You'll never see any situation like that here in Noredge. I swear."

The lady didn't look satisfied. "But, sir, if—"

"Look," Doyle interrupted again, "I know of fifty ifs and

buts we can discuss here. Talking won't make our water any cleaner. But our team will. They've already started, and I think the best I can do is rejoin them right now. We're all working around the clock. I assure you this problem will be a thing of the past in no time. And we're working with the mayor to set up clean water distribution to all homes. Thank you all."

The mayor stood up and said, "You see we're in good hands with Supren and Mr. Doyle. Don't lose any sleep over methane. It's going to be dealt with, and you'll be pleased. And you will, *will* have all the bottled water you may need. Me, I'm going to have a good glass of tap water." He turned. An assistant waited behind him, holding a tray with two glasses on it. Sanders handed one to Doyle and took one for himself. Both lifted their drinks and shouted, "Cheers!"

Tepid applause followed.

The mayor looked concerned.

Mary rolled her eyes as she stared at Frank. He seemed absent.

"Is anything wrong, Frank?"

He shook his head. "Do you know when we can get our hands on that petition? Can't think of a better time to get those signatures."

"I'll check." She dialed Dan's number but had to leave a voicemail.

Around nine that evening her doorbell rang.

Andy ran to open the door. Neighbor Harriet Woods

entered, mute, looking hurried and panting. She barged straight into the kitchen. "My niece Jennifer told me you were at that meeting," she blurted out without greeting Mary or giving her a chance to remove her apron. "Sanders's. The stories Jennifer heard…explosions and radioactivity, odors, poisons…." It almost sounded like it was all Mary's fault.

"Take a seat, Harriet," she said.

"No, thanks; I see the kids are ready for bed." The woman started sobbing. "I'm scared, Mary. You know about this fracking, so…Jennifer said that that Mr. Doyle is going to solve the water problems. Do you believe he can?" She wiped her nose and shoved the Kleenex into her pants pocket.

"Who knows?"

"Jennifer said many people don't believe him."

Mary tried to keep scorn out of her tone. "I'm sure he'll do his best, but he can't guarantee anything. He doesn't really know how much he can improve the water. He may be promising more than he can deliver."

"But he doesn't ask his bosses in Houston for help, or the governor. Somebody," her neighbor lamented.

"He doesn't now. He'd change his mind if it would look necessary, I think. Let's hope."

"But my land, the water, our fruit and vegetables…." Harriet's tears flowed.

Andy and Jimmy looked at the woman with confused expressions.

She wasn't finished. "I won't get any royalties if…."

Mary looked at her askance. *Yeah, not one cent more than I get.* "All we can do is stick together, all of us, demand clean drinking water and keep the pressure on Doyle. Supren's a powerhouse. It's got to be the entire community against them or we lose. I've been fighting this battle from day one."

"I know. I wish I'd never seen these frackers."

You're a little late. Mary bit her tongue: Harriet wasn't moving anywhere soon. "Maybe it won't be too bad in the end," she said as she eased her visitor to the front door.

Harriet lowered her head and kept nodding. "Good night. Good night, kids."

Chapter 25

When Mary and the boys arrived at school the next morning she checked her phone and found a text message from Frank: "Meet at Johnny's during morning break? Urgent! Revert ASAP."

She almost dropped her phone. "Wait, Jimmy!" she shouted as the boys marched to the front entrance. "Wait. Watch out!" She didn't have to think longer than a split second to know what Frank's message was all about. *The smell. It must be something about the smell.* She felt badly that after the mayor's announcement last night she had had to run off in a hurry. Maybe Frank had wanted to discuss— not maybe. Certainly. He had probably wanted to tell her something he couldn't say over the phone either.

She responded immediately. She didn't care about the spelling errors her trembling fingers made. She could blame Apple.

When she found Frank just after ten at Johnny's, the little coffee shop next to the school, she already knew what was going on—from Sonya. He looked deeply concerned.

"It's the article, right?" she said by way of greeting.

"A hell of a smear job. And not just for me."

"Yeah. A beauty, I hear."

The Sentinel article she noticed in his hand mentioned her in almost one breath with Frank, Sonya had said. It had been written by Mike Doyle himself. "Where is it? The garbage about you and me?"

"Everywhere." He handed her the Noredge Sentinel. "Front page. I highlighted the juiciest parts. Enjoy," he said, disgust and fatigue in his voice. Sadness too. He sat back.

"The bastard. Liar. Lunatic!" Her anger burst out as she started reading.

He observed her, tapping the table.

"Drilling through the aquifer under the Alpha site at Rutgers Lake was done correctly, with all precautions, but the nearly simultaneous cementing operation around the drill pipe may have been done with insufficient care, and is likely to have caused a minor degree of methane contamination of the aquifer. Frank Anderson, who was responsible for drilling and cementing, left the Supren Company. We have ascertained that logs documenting three weeks of operations have disappeared...."

Mary stared at Frank. When pressed, industry officials had to admit that even the most advanced cementing techniques applied with the highest skill and care could leave tiny gaps between soil and pipe wall. They could allow methane to migrate, outside the pipes, up toward the surface and possibly through aquifers that in some cases had to be transpierced to reach the shale rock.

"But 'Mr. Anderson' hasn't been contacted. Not contacted!" He hissed and pounded the little table. He didn't seem to care that two ladies next to him were listening in. "Here's the truth," he thundered, hand rose. "The morning Vince took over for me the logs were intact and complete. He can vouch for that. They must have disappeared into some virtual black hole."

Mary had her eyes wide open. "So...Vince is the one—"

"I didn't say that!"

She felt she had irritated him with that question. "Then who?"

He opened his palms and stared at her. "The operator of that black hole, I guess. Not me."

Rosie, the always tired elderly waitress, arrived with her coffee carafe and asked Mary, "Black, right?" She breathed heavily while she poured and then looked at Frank, who shook his head. She turned and left.

"Any suspect?" Mary asked soothingly, not wanting to fan Frank's anger.

"Not yet. But maybe soon."

"When?"

"Don't know yet. Sorry." He showed her a tired wink and went on, sounding serious, "I'll have to do some heavy thinking. But read on." He pointed at the next highlighted paragraph.

"*Some in Noredge try to mislead the good citizens by spreading false rumors and baseless fears about our industry, which is already making a significant contribution...."* She skipped a few lines as he guided her to another yellow section farther down.

"One of the most vocal agitators, Mary Jenkins, works very closely with Mr. Anderson. Both seem hell bent on exacting revenge for his firing. (We don't subscribe to the rumors that she would be romantically involved with Mr. Anderson. Her common-law husband Joe Bertolo is recovering in Cleveland from the accident he caused in Carrollton on July 23rd). Miss Jenkins also does not accept our well-founded refusal to absolve Bertolo of responsibility for the significant damage he caused by careless driving. She spouts half-truths and complete falsehoods about our industry day in, day out. Her and other amateur comments should be disregarded as well as the petition that, we hear, soon will be circulated under her impulse to impede Supren's operations in Noredge."

She flicked her wrist. "Don't feel too bad, dear 'boyfriend.' We already covered that 'romance.' And he wasted more words on me than on you. What a joke."

He was nearly in tears. "But Joanna—"

She smiled. "She'll know this is bullshit."

"She called me this morning, all upset. Damn Mike. She cried. I explained, and she said she believed me, but...." He shook his head looking powerless.

"Relax, Frank. I'll speak with her. That you're an angel helping me. Nothing else."

"Thank you."

"And it'll be my pleasure to tell Doyle to his face and in Joanna's presence that he's full of shit. How about that?

Well, he may not believe this 'witch who tells half-truths and complete falsehoods,'" she joked. "I'll have to leave my broom at home."

"Good, good." He seemed to appreciate her attempt to lighten up the conversation and showed a weak smile. "Always be careful, Mary. Joe's his employee and you are… vulnerable."

She murmured, "I'll kill the bastard before he—"

"Slow down. I may be able to support you guys."

She knew she was just spouting venom. She looked at him helplessly and tilted her head. "How?"

He shrugged his shoulders and said, "It's simple. We must confront the creep. You and me together. Right away. Today."

"Huh?"

"Let's leave as soon as you're done at school. I'll ask Sonya to keep the kids." He stood up and dropped cash for the bill on the table. "Your break must be over."

"Where do we find Doyle?"

"His office."

"You know?"

He patted her shoulder and asked, smiling now, "Why don't you ask me from whom I know?"

Chapter 26

"Two big points," Frank said as a nervous Mary took her seat in his car for the short ride from the school to Doyle's office.

"More surprises?"

"Shortly after I left Johnny's, I received a rude call from Mike summoning me to his office. I agreed, but added, 'With Mary Jenkins.' He exploded, 'I can't stand that bitch's face. This is between you and me!' he screamed. 'You're going to explain to me how you got rid of those logs. And the back-ups. Where you're hiding them. Or I'll cancel your severance and file suit against you. Or worse. That Jenkins woman has no business being in that discussion.'"

"I see."

"Okay. That was point number one."

"Quite a point. Why do you want me to go with you?"

He chuckled.

The moment Frank had picked her up, Mary noticed

that he was in a better mood than at Johnny's. He and Joanna had talked and made up, she figured.

"Just wait for point number two. It gets better."

"Better?"

"A real doozie, but I had to lie a little. I said I couldn't possibly tell you not to join me because minutes before you had asked me, insisted, to go see him with you. He had attacked you and Joe in public and in the press, and you couldn't wait to tell him some basic truths about fairness and honesty."

"And about those slanderous rumors about 'us.'"

He nodded. "I used your words and some of your fury."

She smiled. "And?"

"He barked that he'd kick you out if you got even close to the front door. So, fasten your seat belt."

It sounded, strangely, like Frank had enjoyed the verbal joust with Doyle. But Mary worried: Doyle had a tight grip on Joe and on her. "I'd better not. You can drop me off and I'll walk back," she said, concerned.

Frank snickered and didn't slow down. "No way, Mary. We're going to win this. For Joe. Mike's going to lose big time."

"You mean that? Win?" She looked at him askance.

"I know that. Maybe not the battle, but the war. Just wait and see. He'll have to walk away tail between his legs. Soon. Believe me. Soon."

In the Supren parking lot they spotted Doyle's BMW.

"Let's go, Mary. Head up."

She feared her nod wasn't convincing.

He patted her on the shoulder and rang the bell. "He'll answer it," he said, his voice hushed.

"Joanna—?"

"Running an errand for half an hour. If she sees my car she won't enter."

Doyle opened the door, looking determined, loaded for bear. His face turned red as he noticed Mary. "Didn't I fucking tell you this was between men?" he thundered, his eyes drilling into Frank's.

"Watch your language!" Frank shouted back, one foot on the threshold.

Mary tried to follow Frank in but Doyle lunged at her and roughly pushed her back out. "Not you. Don't you ever enter this place again or I call the police!"

Four or five passers-by slowed their pace. One stopped.

She stumbled and fell down but quickly stood up, trembling as she rubbed little pebbles off her hands. Enraged, she tried to force her way in but Doyle kept pushing her back with both hands.

A crowd of about ten now had formed. They seemed to enjoy the little skirmish. Two youngsters aimed their iPhones.

Frank squeezed his tall, thin body between Mary and Doyle and breathed, "Mike, you'd better stop this. You'll be all over the TV tonight."

Doyle fired back, looking livid, "You'll regret this, you loser. Get her out of here."

"Loser? Yeah?" Frank's voice sounded ominously low and threatening. "I've got a couple of pictures I took at Lanning's. Not long ago. Mrs. Doyle must have been out of town. Vince too. Or did you have him working late in Carrollton?"

"Huh? You creep," Doyle yelled and paled. He threw a punch at Frank, but missed.

"Calm down, Mike. You let Mary in or I'll bring some sharp copies to WEWS. They love that juicy stuff. You accuse Mary and me of having an affair. Have you looked in the mirror recently?"

Doyle stepped back and hissed. "Everybody knows about you and her. Even the priest."

"Because you whispered it in his ear?" Frank winked at Mary.

For a moment she felt for Father Bianchi, that credulous, pure, well-meaning man.

Doyle's facial expression had turned subdued. His lips trembled. "You've got...got no shame," he stammered, staring at the small crowd and then the ground. "Two minutes."

They walked through Joanna's office area. It was now a neatly appointed space, repainted a light tan, complete with a small polypropylene rug, a transparent polycarbonate desk sporting a combination of three baby pictures, a small reclining chair, a Dell Desktop and a little table with a Flavia coffeemaker and three wooden tabourets.

Doyle strode straight to his office and entered first,

Frank matching his pace, Mary tiptoeing in behind him. Stony silence surrounded the threesome. Lips pursed, Doyle gestured to sit down at his little table. His nostrils were flared, his breathing audible as he stared at Frank. "I hope you'll show at least some class, Anderson," he said, his lips quivering. "Some discretion. I was in Bath with that woman to discuss a painful personal matter. My job requires a lot from me."

Frank looked at Mary, showed her a quick eye roll and said, "We understand. I haven't told anybody."

"If I hear—"

"You won't. Not from me. If you do, I won't be the source."

Mary coughed, turned right towards Doyle and said, her tone neutral, "Mrs. Woods came to see me last night in a panic. She'd heard about the meeting at City Hall—"

"Woods? Who's that woman?" It was a bark. He didn't sound grateful at all for the face-saving shift Mary had made for him in the conversation.

She was going to make sure she measured her words, but couldn't help adding in a little prick. "'That woman,' Mr. Doyle, that woman is the owner of the land your Beta site sits on. She's worried her land will be 'poisoned,' and—"

"Harriet, you mean. Why did she come to you? She knows where my office is. She has my number."

"She's my neighbor. She came late at night, crying. Frankly, I'm worried about my land too. And my family."

"How silly! I've explained at City Hall—"

"For sure you tried. And how," Frank interrupted him, his tone pure scorn.

Mary couldn't believe how confident her friend looked.

Frank went on, "You're full of shit when you write that I screwed up at Alpha or sabotaged it to avenge my firing—."

"I didn't say that!"

"Let me finish." Frank stood up and pounded the table. He leaned over it. His head inched so close to Doyle's that their noses seemed to touch. "Don't underestimate the intelligence of the Noredge people. They're more than smart enough to read between the lines. Get it?"

Doyle waved him off. "It's all in your paranoid mind, buddy. I never meant to—"

"You did. You keep lying. Next point...." Frank righted himself. "You know damn well that both the Alpha and Beta sites sit on the same aquifer. How do you know the methane comes from Alpha? Does it carry an ID?"

Doyle stood up and furiously pointed at Frank. "Let me tell you something, Mr. Anderson. I've handled drilling and cementing at the Beta site myself, neglecting some of my other duties, to free Vince up for Carrollton. I've been at this drilling business 'a few' more years than you. I guarantee you that the operation has been run correctly, no shortcuts in the cementing, no trace of a methane leak."

Frank smiled. "Did you check the Beta logs? For your article?"

"I didn't have to. I know what they say—"

"About yourself. And so, oh wonder of wonders, divine

236

enlightenment led you to your 'honest' conclusion with the speed of lightning: 'It's Alpha!' How can a reasonable person believe you when you open your mouth or hit the keys on your laptop?"

Doyle's face was one scowl. Mary shifted in her chair, her worries intensifying by the minute. How was this going to end? She attempted a weak, "Maybe, Mr. Doyle, maybe you and Vince and Frank together could—"

"You shut up, woman!" Doyle shouted. "Where do you get the nerve to talk about matters you've only read about in activist articles? Scum. And you, Anderson, forget the ninety percent of your severance I haven't paid you yet. You violated the terms of our arrangement. And now you both get out. We're done." He pointed at the door.

Mary and Frank nodded at each other. She stood up and they headed for the door, but Doyle had one more salvo. "Joe Bertolo, he'd better take some driving tests before he shows up for work again. We've hired a good replacement. No trouble with him. Or his wife."

Mary didn't dignify him with an answer. She had long expected that Joe would lose his job and now, after this screaming match, she had given up every remnant of illusion about hers: she had little doubt that Doyle would pick up the phone as soon as they were out of earshot; that he would call the mayor or the school board or both to argue for her dismissal. But she didn't want to mention her concern to Frank now, as if it were his fault.

"We've let the air out of his tires," Frank quipped as they walked back to his car.

"Do you really have pictures?" she asked as he took the wheel. She knew it wasn't very nice of her to stoop that low, but something in her made her want to see them.

He looked straight ahead. "You think I'd lie about that?"

His face told her enough. She elbowed him.

"But I did see him with a woman who isn't his wife. In a restaurant."

"I know he's got a girlfriend. A mistress. Joe told me. He and Joanna heard Doyle boast about her. In his office. His door was ajar. Her name's Galinda."

"You mean Linda. Linda. That's what Joanna mentioned to me. That woman with Doyle in the restaurant was Mrs. Davis, the petite, ultra-blonde with the low-cut blouse. Her name escapes me." He tried to describe her remarkable shape and posture with both hands.

"Okay, okay," she said, giggling. "Hold on to the wheel. I've seen her. Susan. Doyle must have dumped the other one, Galinda."

"Galinda or Linda, I don't care."

"'Joanna sounds very, very nice, Frank. You lucky guy.'"

Chapter 27

Alone in his car after dropping Mary at the school, Frank let his thoughts drift slowly away from the ugly discussion with Doyle and toward Joanna. It was a sweet ride. *Joanna.* Until he started worrying again. How long before she would lose her job? She needed it badly.

He made a brief stop at Sonya's. He wanted company, some small talk. The weather. Lebron James. Dirty water. The price of gasoline and the Prius her neighbor was driving and bragging about.

Later on his way home he wondered how Vince, this heavy-set, plain-spoken, low-key guy with the crew cut ever managed to get together with Susan, that flashy nano-petite blonde. *For how long?*

Shortly before six Joanna called him. "Leaving for home now, darling. Did you get out of the office in one piece?"

"Hmm. Yes and no."

"Oh? What does that mean, Frankie?"

He faulted himself for talking in riddles but he thought it was a fair summary, succinct and clear, for himself anyway. "We got beaten up pretty badly but—"

"We?"

"Mary joined me. She may be in trouble. And I think I lost my severance. I'd better hurry up with Viola or you may have to feed me," he joked.

"Oh, I would, Frankie. Don't worry."

"Thanks. Just kidding. I bet I'll get my severance back."

"You will?"

He chuckled inwardly. "I'll come over and explain. Seven? I'll bring sushi."

"Oh? Park's? Great. Can we make it seven-thirty? I need a shower."

In Noredge a Korean grocer sold every kind of food, including Japanese.

"Seven-thirty."

He stopped twisting the hairs on the back of his head and concluded that a shower wasn't a bad idea for him either. "Cleaning the inside while cleaning the outside," he mumbled, a free translation of what his Latin teacher used to say.

"*Mens sana in corpore sano!*" he roared fifteen minutes later as he checked his gorilla pose in the bathroom mirror.

His nostrils reacted intrigued as he climbed the cement stairs up to a small apartment on the second floor of a four-story complex off Main about a mile north of downtown. An aroma he couldn't pinpoint. Upstairs, Joanna would be waiting for him and her favorite sushi. In that order, he trusted.

Mike Doyle, who had his house on McKinley, wouldn't venture into this area or want to be seen in it, but Frank had parked his Altima at the far end of the building anyway. Peace of mind was worth the effort of an additional few yards' walk. He realized, however, that Joanna couldn't be fully protected all the time from willing sycophants eager to ingratiate themselves with Doyle. It was almost inevitable: one of these days Joanna would have to face her boss and try talking him into not firing her.

The door was ajar. He opened it with his foot. "Service!"

"Just a minute!" It sounded like "jost a minute," but the voice was heavenly.

He waited, standing, holding the polystyrene box and looking at the couch. It was second-hand, his back had told him. The low, dark brown little chest of drawers, a half-empty Coke bottle on top, was an early inheritance from grandma; the three chairs...he had bought them with Joanna at a garage sale. They belonged in a church. The badly curled-up rug menaced the inattentive, particularly the sushi-carrying ones. The coffee table invited him: it often was his favorite footrest as he watched the Travel Channel with Joanna on the sixteen-inch screen.

He went to the kitchen and put the box on the counter. "It's free! You don't need your wallet," he joked, waving a hand to welcome more aroma. "What's cooking here?"

"*Tembleque*. Take a look in the oven."

Before he could comply, his eyes were drawn to the bedroom door, where a glowing, radiating image appeared. *Divine,* he marveled. His heart raced. Joanna in flesh and blood, not some phantasm.

"You like it, Frankie?" She adjusted her left shoulder strap, her eyes awaiting his response.

He stared at the loose-fitting, tan cotton robe. It looked teasingly thin. "Exquisite!"

"The *tembleque* or me?"

He wagged his index and laughed. "What's *tembleque?*"

"Coconut milk, sugar, corn starch and lots of heat. Ground cinnamon on top. A Puerto Rican special for you. *Rico!* Delicious, if I may say so. And…want to feel my robe? Egyptian cotton, the vendor said. Feels cool."

He pulled her close, held her in his arms, and nodded. "Perfect for you. Matches your smooth skin. I adore it," he breathed as he moved his hand lower and kissed her full lips.

She kissed him back, moved away and pointed at the sushi. "Let's go."

With coquettish little steps, her long robe permitting, she walked to the kitchen. He observed the movement of her tight buttocks under the robe and followed, strutting.

"What are you doing?" She smiled as she looked back.

"Walking like an Egyptian." He grabbed her waist. "Behind a goddess."

The windowless, eight-by-ten kitchen accommodated two people but not that comfortably. Joanna always had her plastic barstool at the kitchen counter, which served as table as well. She actually had a narrow metal table, but Frank had only seen it carrying an overload of potted plants. One of her two metal chairs stood folded between it and the wall. Her other one, the stable one, had now joined the barstool.

Frank opened the box and invited Joanna with a formal gesture. She held up a bottle of Cabernet and pointed at the two plain glasses on the kitchen top. Frank picked them up and jovially said "Cozy," as he sat down, wiggling briefly.

Joanna, pouring wine, said jokingly "I see you're concerned, but so is my chair. It hasn't dealt with anything else other than cooking pots and pans and shopping bags for I don't know how long."

They clinked glasses as if holding Waterford, kissed again, and selected their first piece of sushi.

"You stay where you are, Frankie." Joanna stood up and moved her stool so it touched his chair. "More stable!"

"I like 'stable,'" he said and pinched her cheek.

Warm feelings and daring plans set the tone for their conversation. Unlike the wine, some of the sushi would make it to next morning, it seemed, as Frank had expected. They laughed and joked. And Mike Doyle was the great absentee. For a while.

"Now, tell me about this afternoon. I'm entitled to it. I vacated my office so you guys could 'have a real conversation.'"

Frank smiled. He had talked her into finding an excuse for her well-timed errand. "You're ready? The jerk wouldn't let Mary in. He made a scene at the front door. You might see some clips of it on YouTube."

"That bad?"

"It could've gotten worse, but I cut him off at the knees."

"Huh?" It was an open mouth sound.

"With my big machete!" He swung his arm wildly. "I reminded him, not too subtly, that I saw him with Mrs. Davis, dining at Lanning's in Bath, near Akron."

"Mrs. Davis? Susan?"

"Yes."

"Wow."

"He froze. Gasped for air. Walked us in like a beaten dog. He later begged for discretion. I reassured him. Mary had of course heard me, but she and my mother are the only other persons who know about this Lanning's thing. My mom was there with me."

"Susan…." She kept shaking her head.

"I would never spread such a rumor, Joanna, and hurt innocent people. Vince is a good guy. Maybe a little naïve. But I had to defend Mary Jenkins."

"So, Doyle—poor Edith—he must have a new mistress, or one more. Not too long ago he had a Linda."

"Linda? Galinda, Mary said."

"No. Linda." Joanna looked amused. "Linda." The quick slicing motion of her palm didn't leave any room for doubt.

"But Mary told me that Joe and you heard him speak about Galinda. With great enthusiasm. 'Galinda!' Mike had shouted several times. I'm quoting Mary."

Joanna nodded and smiled. "We both heard him. Joe and me. But I clearly picked up the name Linda first. Apparently, it reminded a person at the other end of the line of a Galinda. Just as cute, just as—you know how men talk. 'Yes! Another Galinda! A clone, Jim! A clone!' Doyle roared, laughing. He said he knew that Galinda well."

"Hmm. Joe must have misheard."

"He did. But does it matter? Galinda's a beautiful name too." She took a sip.

"Joe…I don't know…," Frank replied.

Joanna asked him why he kept rubbing his forehead.

"Oh, nothing really," he said and waved her off.

"Okay. Coffee! Coffee paging Galinda! Coffee with *tembleque*? Or?" Her tone was delightfully suggestive. Her wide eyes burned into his as she slowly brushed back her raven hair.

He got up, stood behind her, kissed her neck and felt her breasts. The hard nipples.

She leaned back against him. "Did you hear my long 'or' question, Frankie?"

"I did. Tell me, Joanna, how does cold *tembleque* taste?" He whispered, his tongue licking her earlobe.

"Better than hot." She stood up next to him and reached up for a long, deep kiss. Then she pulled him toward her tiny bedroom. "Let me show you a real Egyptian. Hold me. Unzip my robe."

He took her in his arms.

Her robe dropped to the floor.

Nefertiti? Cleopatra? He had visions.

"Take them off," she whispered, pointing at his bulging pants.

He slowly caressed her naked body with his.

He eased her onto the bed, one arm on her lower back.

She opened her arms.

"I want you," she breathed.

As he entered her she screamed.

They heard a loud knock from above.

"She's jealous, Frank. And I don't blame her. Please love me more," she groaned.

He did. They kissed and caressed and made love until late in the night.

In the morning, the *tembleque* was cold but as exquisite as the company.

CHAPTER XXI

Chapter 28

Turmoil engulfed Noredge. Angry citizens demonstrating sporadically in clusters or in groups in front of the Supren office demanded clarity. "Transparency!" some yelled on TV. Mary was certain that for many of them it was a word they uttered for the first time in their lives. Mothers pleaded for clean water for their children. "Free bottled water from Supren until our water is safe!"

Mike Doyle's Sentinel article had turned Frank into a target of their ire as well. "No wonder Doyle had to fire him. That Anderson is a thief or a criminal or he's in over his head. No matter what, I'm glad he's gone and can't do any further harm. Now let's clean up." These were the words of upset shopkeeper Jeff Dillon. Doyle's libelous claim had hit a nerve.

Mary shook her head when she was confronted by an angry mother wagging her index and shouting, "I know Frank Anderson's a 'good friend' of yours. But that doesn't mean I can't tell you the truth. Good thing that Mr. Doyle plays open cards." Mary rolled her eyes and said nothing.

"That Anderson was fired but the loser got away with half a million dollars, I hear. I don't get it. Must have some big shot high up protecting him," a bystander opined, clutching a shopping bag. She went her way.

An eager-looking young man said, his tone suggestive, "Or...? Or...?" He paused and checked faces. "Could it be blackmail? Maybe Anderson has the goods on Doyle, true or false, know what I mean?" A few nodded, although they couldn't possibly know what the youngster knew or meant. Quick glances among bystanders said it had to be something really bad, something ominous justifying a half-million-dollar bribe.

Mary was berated by Max Goodall, a Chamber member, for instilling unrest and jeopardizing Noredge's future. "Just keep up the good work, lady," he barked, "and soon Noredge will become a ghost town, as so many in the region already have. We're losing our jobs to China. All the rubber business...all gone."

In the last twenty to thirty years the tire industry had moved most of its operations and even offices away from Akron, once the rubber capital of the world, to Mexico, China, the southern US or other greener pastures. Several Noredge suppliers and contractors to the industry had left as well, or automated in major ways, leaving the local economy hanging high and dry.

Goodall was a neighbor on Maple Road. His wife was a

doting grandma. "Don't you have kids, Max?" Mary asked, although she knew he did. "Grandchildren? Don't they deserve clean water that's free of cancer causing agents?"

Her last point was a stretch, but not entirely. Methane was often accompanied by many harmful substances.

He walked away, shaking his head, grumbling.

Later in the day, new EPA figures communicated on WKSU pointed to a worsening situation.

On Wednesday the 12th an emergency session of the Chamber was called for four o'clock. The news spread like wildfire. Mary dropped Andy and Jimmy with a friend and rushed to the Chamber building, although the meeting would be a closed-door affair. Crowds were amassing outside, blocking traffic until the police intervened and ordered all onto the sidewalk. The townspeople, already suffering the muggy heat, now stood compressed and even more exposed to the irritating late sunrays from the west. Two youngsters started distributing Sierra Club pamphlets.

Mary tried to walk in but was rebuffed. She tried to find out, asking around, whether Mr. Doyle had arrived. Nobody knew. Frank was nowhere to be seen. She knew he would be an unwelcome guest, as she felt she was, for at least some in the crowd. Vince Davis was also a no-show.

When the clock said four the crowd didn't disperse but kept milling around, some expressing their almost unspeakable fears for the health of their kids. A few talked about organizing more clean water transport in tankers from Canton. Young adults cracked dark jokes.

Around five-thirty the front door of the Chamber building opened and Mrs. Henning, the wife of Chairman Henning appeared on the steps, smiling broadly, moving slowly. She unfolded a sheet of paper and then gently brushed away unruly bleached curls stuck to her perspiration-pearled forehead. She was flanked on the left by Mrs. Doyle and Mr. Doyle, in that order, and to the right by Mayor Sanders and Mr. Henning. *They're trying the soft touch.* Mary fought to contain her indignation: she was convinced that the text Mrs. Henning was going to read from her sheet had been prepared by men, before the Chamber even met.

The murmuring died down.

It was readily clear from Mrs. Henning's facial expression and demeanor that the Chamber had indeed embarked on a charm offensive.

"I see so many mothers and grannies here. I'm a mother too, of course, and I have four darling grandchildren, so far. How nice to see you all."

"'How nice' indeed. Can't think of a happier occasion," Mary mumbled, huffing.

The man next to her chuckled.

Mrs. Henning went on. The lady's sweet voice was too weak for the crowd. Only fragments of her speech were audible.

"Your concerns are ours too…we want…Mr. Doyle is confident all will be all right…great community…."

A tepid applause ensued. And one whistle.

Mrs. Henning smiled politely.

"Count on your patience and understanding...much appreciated...one town...God bless."

Mary trained her gaze on Mike Doyle, who was all smiles. "A great act," she grumbled audibly. "And not a word about water distribution." The man to her left pursed his lips; the one to her right put his fingers in his mouth to whistle but stopped there.

The Chamber folks and the Doyles stepped down toward the street level and tried to mingle in the crowd.

"Part of the act," Mary snorted.

The man to her right high-fived her.

She moved forward to greet Mrs. Doyle. She felt compassion for her.

"Good to see you again, Mrs. Doyle. Edith, right?"

"Correct. Very good indeed. You are...?" It was a friendly voice.

"Mary Jenkins. We met once before. I hope things will be cleared up and cleaned up soon. We have no time to lose. Absolutely none," she said, heartfelt concern in her voice. She really wanted Mrs. Doyle to take note.

The lady nodded, showing a frown. "I agree, Miss Jenkins. Mary. I love your Texan accent, slight as it is."

"Texan? Oh, really?"

A kind nod. "Where are you from?"

"From right here, but I lived in Lumberton for a few years. Bits of the language must have stuck with me."

"Lumberton? Oh! I know somebody else who's from

that city. Wait…Jim…Jim Duncan. Mike's former boss several years ago." She pulled her husband's sleeve and said, "Mary's lived in Lumberton, Mike. Did you know that? Wasn't your former boss from Lumberton? Jim Duncan? The one who always talked about his football team at Lumberton High? He—"

Doyle suddenly shook his head, his face one angry frown. "*Cállate,* shut up!" he hissed, turning away from the two women.

"But—"

"*Cállate!*"

Edith Doyle's expression was one of growing confoundment during the laconic exchange. She didn't seem to understand what had gotten into her husband.

He means business. Mary threw a quick glance at Edith, who returned her look with one of embarrassment.

A second later, Doyle produced a broad smile out of nowhere, put his arm around his spouse's waist and guided her delicately aside. "My apologies. I *must* introduce my sweetheart to a neighbor," he said to Mary as he walked away, his voice close to smarmy. He didn't wait for her answer.

Mary was puzzled. *Mike Doyle, quarterback of the Chamber's charm team. Quarterback…and chameleon.*

Chapter 29

A t six p.m. Vince called it a day earlier than usual. Tonight was his once-a-month pool night. At Andrew's, the tables were awaiting him as well as three of his buddies: Don, John and Mark. As he left the Beta site and pulled onto Maple Road, he hummed the melody of "Don't Worry about Tomorrow." He looked forward to teaching John a thing or two about billiards. His friend had had the nerve to beat him badly last time.

Vince needed a break. Wednesday night couldn't have come soon enough. His job at Supren gave him more headaches than a human could handle or Tylenol could soothe. Mike Doyle didn't make it any easier. Tonight, Vince refused to think about the jerk who, in all fairness, paid him well.

Fortunately, Vince had a few work buddies and his pool friends. And his Susan. He sighed as he drove. She was a lively, stunningly beautiful woman, a great companion, and the joy of his life.

Lately, however, she complained on and off about their sex life. "Monotonous," she would repine, sulking and often looking for a cigarette. She suffered from "migraines" more than he liked. But he and Susan had great evenings and nights and mornings when her appetite was sometimes almost more than he could satisfy. She obsessed on keeping her body in fantastic shape: massages, creams and injections—he didn't even want to know about them or the dollars she spent. He had to admit he felt proud when he could show her off, parading her into a restaurant of her choice, or to church. But he couldn't get her to attend office parties. "Don't ask me to go brown-nosing to get you a promotion," was her excuse. *Her subtlety-laced version of "no,"* he would grumble inwardly, suppressing the urge to roll his eyes.

When he left home this morning she had been sweet and understanding. "You need time with your buddies, darling. I'll make sure I'm in perfect shape to give you a warm welcome home." She hadn't used her usual "hot," but it sounded so promising anyway that for a second he had thought of canceling pool night and visiting Nan's flower shop.

Only John had arrived when Vince strode to the bar at Andrew's.

The place was dimly lit by the lights above the four pool tables; only a handful of patrons were milling about as it was still early. Seated on a barstool, John was in conversation with Lou, the bartender, their words swallowed by Kenny

Rogers's "Lucille," blaring from speakers in all four corners. The smell of beer and perspiration and the gaping faces of three vending machines across the room joined the two men in welcoming Vince. A TV set's graying screen suspended above the bar, sound muted, showed a baseball game and peddled Geico insurance.

John pointed at Vince. "Evening! Bud Light? The usual?"

"Yep. Can use one. Helluva day, but I'm here." Vince sighed as he took a stool. "So, what's new?" The question was for John.

"Not much. Same old stuff. The kids, Nancy, 'honey do, honey do,' you know. How about you? All good at home? No kids yet, eh?"

John had two little girls.

"Not as far as I know." Vince wondered briefly why Susan had been so sweet and happy this morning.

"Patience, man. It'll happen, whether you order them or not!" John lifted his glass. "Cheers!"

Lou opened a drawer and seemed to check the contents.

"Cheers." Vince nodded, managing a wry smile. As far as he knew, none of his sperm had succeeded in fooling the condom regimen and procedures Susan had imposed from day one. Not even on days she was inebriated.

"How about that new car? Big bucks, man!"

Vince jerked his head back. "Huh?"

"Your BMW. Top of the line, right? Flashy color too. Susan's pick, I bet."

The bartender looked up from the receipts he was checking.

Vince shrugged and frowned. "I've got my Explorer from Supren. Frank Anderson's hand-me-down, but good enough."

"But Susan—"

"She has her little Chrysler convertible," Vince answered, slightly irritated. "We have no BMW."

"But...I'll be damned. I could swear I saw her in that low, silver sleigh, sitting next to you. She saw me, looked up at me briefly as you guys overtook me at that crazy speed. Then she turned to you. I guess you said something to her."

"Me? When?"

"Must've been a week ago. Afternoon. Interstate 77."

"You're shitting me. I never got my ass into a BMW." Vince turned on his stool to face the TV.

John turned as well, took a good gulp and put his drink down with a little bang. "Vince, it was her," he insisted. "Unless she's got a twin sister with the same set of...." He halted his hand gestures. "I could see she recognized me. You don't remember overtaking me?"

"I said I never sat in a BMW."

"Not even in Mike Doyle's?"

"What?" Vince pounded the counter. "Shit! Shit!"

The bartender rolled his eyes and walked to the other end.

Vince raged on. "*Why* did you have to tell me that?" he screamed.

"I'm sorry, man. I said to my wife you must be making good dough at Supren. I'm not jealous. You're working your butt off, of course." The longer his friend talked the more embarrassed he looked.

"The bitch! The bitch!"

John's penny apparently dropped. "Cool it, man. It's always possible that—"

"Too late. You're right. I'm out of here. Sorry, man. I...." Vince broke down. He knew his buddy wasn't making it up.

He drove home in a daze.

He fumed. Whenever he traveled on Mike's orders, he would call Susan on her cell from Columbus or Washington or Oklahoma City; he had heard restaurant or bar background noise too often. Her indifferent responses to his sexual advances had become frequent; the veneer on her faked orgasms was transparent. Her semi-snarky remarks regarding his appearance or gait had grown too painful. Her nervousness at the mention of Doyle's name suddenly made sense. A friendly neighbor had given him a hint, but he had thanklessly waved him off, naïve as he was, and obstinate in his denial. And now John. His buddy.

"The bitch!" he screamed, hammering the gas pedal, a madman. He ran a traffic light and then braked so brutally that his screeching tires scared him. He took a dangerous curve at double the speed limit and swerved dangerously out of his lane, narrowly avoiding a collision. He brusquely swung into an emergency stopping lane and came to an abrupt halt.

"The slut!" He pounded the wheel, then rested his head on it and heard his fast breathing. He tried to take his pulse but lost count. He cried.

Ten minutes later he had wiped his tears and pulled out of the parking spot.

When he arrived at home and exited his Explorer he dreaded walking through his own front door. What was the point? It was over between him and Susan. Doyle had swept her off her feet, dazzled her with his power and money and glitz. *Should've known she wasn't my type*, he reproached himself, feeling empty and deserted.

He turned the key and entered.

An eerie silence met him. Even the refrigerator colluded.

He swung open the door to the garage. Susan's car wasn't there.

He slammed the door shut, went to the sitting room and poured himself a gin and tonic. It took him two swigs to finish it. Then he threw his two-hundred pounds violently onto the couch and almost hoped it would break. He poured another drink. He dialed Susan's cell number, but didn't hit the green button, afraid to hear her giggle, and that painful background noise that might hit him in the face. He offered himself another gin and tonic. He yanked their wedding picture off the wall above the commode, smashed it on the carpet and stepped on the glass.

He fell asleep. Doyle taunted him, with Susan. Vince

swung his sledgehammer at them but missed both. Susan laughed loudly. Doyle winked, an unbearable smirk on his face. Mrs. Doyle cried as she observed the scene.

When Vince woke up he felt Susan's lips on his. Bent over him, one knee on the couch, she caressed his temple and nodded her head at the open gin bottle on the coffee table. He thought he saw concern about his condition on her face. No, it had to be recrimination. His splitting headache reminded him that the gin in his system kept him from making the distinction.

She stood up. "Are you okay, Vince?" she asked calmly while checking the contents of her handbag.

As if she doesn't know or notice. His loud, angry words came involuntarily. "See our wedding picture?" He sounded nasal.

"Oh, my God. Did you...?"

He nodded, his head pounding. "We won't need it anymore. You're leaving me." Deeply saddened he averted his eyes to hide his tears.

She cried. "Somebody told you lies about me. I—"

He was exhausted but managed to utter, "Don't explain. You'll make it worse. It hurts too much." He broke down.

"But I love you, Vince. I always will." She bent down and kissed him again.

He pushed her away. "You love Mike Doyle," he said, dejected. He had made it a statement, not a question.

She kicked her high heels off and curled up to him on the couch. "I want to be with you forever, Vince. I'm so sorry I hurt you. Please, please forgive me. Mike Doyle... I've been so dumb to believe...I'll call him right away. I know you're my only real love. Real." She squeezed her hips against his and wormed her right hand under his back. "Forgive me, Vince. My Vince."

He felt nauseous, his head thumping, his mind racing uncontrolled: he couldn't imagine life without Susan. He had left her alone so often; he had complimented her too seldom for the care she took of her body, to please him; he had reciprocated too little her tenderness and passion. She was so beautiful, much more so than he deserved.

The nausea got worse. He wriggled himself free, sat up and felt even more terrible. "I'm tired," he said, slurring his words. "Just go to the bedroom." He lay down again.

"Leave you here? Alone? Fully dressed?"

"Yes." He closed his eyes.

She shook his arm. "But—"

"Just go. My head hurts."

"Let me bring you a couple of Tylenols."

"Go!"

***

Around seven-thirty Mary's phone rang.

"Jenkins, stop cozying up to my wife." It was Doyle's voice—threatening, scary.

"Oh...she's such a nice lady. I—"

"You heard me. Stay out of my personal matters."

Mary figured he had to be worried that she would talk

to Mrs. Doyle about Susan Davis and Lanning's. She said, "It wouldn't enter my mind to interfere in—"

"Stay away from her. And forget what happened tonight."

"Oh? Tonight? Do you—"

"Stay out of it or I'll kill you." He hung up.

What happened tonight? She was paralyzed, trembling and wondering. *Lumberton? Duncan? Doyle's rude words to Edith....*

"Who was that, Mommy?" Andy asked, looking up briefly from the homework he was doing on the kitchen table.

"Nothing, nothing," she replied, trying her best to sound casual."

"Is Daddy okay?"

"I'm sure he is. Keep writing. It's getting late." Her voice broke. She fled into the bathroom.

After she managed to get the boys to bed she called Frank and relayed the essentials of what happened in front of the Chamber, including her abruptly ended discussion with both Doyles and the deeply unsettling phone call she just had received.

Seconds went by before Frank answered, "Did you talk to Joe yet?"

"No. I'm afraid to. Nothing he can do from where he is anyway." She started sobbing.

"Right. Maybe better not to mention it to him," he said soothingly.

"But Doyle, he—"

"He's probably shooting off his mouth. Losing it a bit."

"You're wrong!" she near-shouted, upset about Frank's cavalier answer. "I know he hates me. That call! He turned livid when I spoke with his wife this afternoon. Why? I never mentioned Lanning's to her. The only thing...It could...Have you ever heard of a Mr. Duncan?"

"Duncan?" Frank had suddenly raised his voice.

"Jim. Mrs. Doyle mentioned that name—her husband's old boss—Jim Duncan from Lumberton, and Doyle went ballistic. For a second or two; then, it was over. And two hours later he says he'll kill me if—!"

"Yes. I heard you. Maybe you should call the police. Tell them to keep an eye on your house. On you and the kids."

"Huh?" *Something I said must have alerted Frank or shaken him up.* "They won't laugh me away? A woman?"

"They'd better not. Do call the police."

"Okay. Shall I tell them about Doyle's affair? Maybe that's what he's so—"

"I bet they already know. Everybody does. Maybe even Edith."

"Hmm. So it must be something else."

"Could be. You'd better call. Tell them I said so. I know Chief Roberts. You never know what people do when they go berserk." He sounded slightly irritated and detached.

"Yes, okay. She hung up and started pacing the kitchen, wondering why Frank had changed his mind. *So abruptly.* She decided to wait half an hour: calm down, have some tea, put her feet up, breathe deep and think it all through. *If Doyle ever finds out I called the cops on him....*

She was barely halfway through her cup when Mike Doyle called back. "I'm sorry...my words," he whispered. "Very sorry. I didn't mean it. I'll never harm you. I had a crazy moment. Got to go. Sorry. I—"

She heard a woman's voice. "Mickey? More tea, darling?" The call broke off.

Edith's accent. Mary put the phone down and reflected. *"Susan" rumors must be getting close to Edith's ears.*

Her tea was cold, her nerves not calmed down. She sought refuge and company on CNN.

The ring tone of her phone ripped her out of her catnap.

"I'm coming home!" Joe's voice resounded through the room. "Freed from prison at last! Tomorrow!"

"Oh? Wow. Great! What time?" The planning compartment in her brain shot into action.

"As soon as you can pick me up. I don't want to stay a minute longer than I have to. They need my bed anyway."

She pictured him packing his little bag, minus pajamas and toothbrush, and smiled. "Okay! Right after school. I'll get Sonya for Jimmy and Andy. I'll call her right away."

"After school, yeah. You can bring the kids."

"Well, don't let them know I told you, but they prepared a special welcome for you. They must be here before you."

Joe chuckled. "Got it. You want to do some good cuddling in the car, right?"

"Would I?"

Chapter 30

Mary broke into tears as she helped Joe step out of the car into the driveway. He supported himself with a cane and leaned on her shoulder with his free hand. He was all smiles. The boys ran out of the house, their arms up, jubilant. Sonya stood on the threshold, waving. Andy insisted to take Mary's place and support his daddy. Jimmy, too short for that assignment, looked on, disappointment written over his face.

"I'd like to hug the boys," Joe lamented, "but I can't." He made an awkward semi-successful attempt with Jimmy. Then he leaned his head down to Andy, but didn't fully reach.

"Did you look yet, Daddy?" Jimmy asked, pointing at the front door.

Joe winked at Mary, turned his head toward the house and exclaimed, "Oh my God! I can't believe it! Did Mom call that decorator? Lucy?"

"No!" the boys chanted in chorus, waving their palms. "We did it all by ourselves!"

Mary and Sonya nodded, their faces serious.

"I love it!" Joe roared, looking impressed and slightly amused.

"We chose the colors, Daddy. The nicest ones we could find!" Little Jimmy jumped up and down.

Sonya showed a quick smile.

The door looked uneasy, framed from top to bottom by an inverted U-shaped band of paper showing a plethora of intense, bright colors.

"Our two budding artists chose them," Mary explained, her eyes big.

"I wrote 'HOME!' on the top, Daddy," Jimmy sounded very proud. "All by myself."

Andy declared he did the "WELCOME!" and "DADDY!" on the sides.

"We used the big ladder," Sonya said.

"And I 'helped' just a tiny little bit." Mary laughed.

Inside, coffee and cake awaited Joe. Sonya served him as soon as he sat down, and then Mary, whom she admonished that she had to take five minutes of rest. "Sit next to Joe. He deserves a big kiss!" she quipped.

"Another one?" Mary shot back, laughing and nestled herself close to her man. She winked at Sonya.

The boys had patiently waited their turn and now wolfed down their cake.

"You see, I'll have to go to the hospital more often," Joe joked.

Mary sighed. Two weeks ago she had started collecting medical bills from her mailbox.

"When can you play soccer, Daddy?" Jimmy looked ready as he rubbed remnants of chocolate cream off his upper lip.

"Later," Joe said. "Later I will. But not yet. Maybe I'll go for hockey first. I brought my stick." He showed his cane.

"Daddy!" Andy's and Jimmy's mutual tones of disapproval left no doubt they had trouble appreciating this type of humor.

Mary beamed. "Finally!" she said, her hands praying.

"No more trips to Cleveland," Joe completed her sentence.

"No. At last I've got you back with me."

"And more or less in one piece. I'll toss that cane in no time. Just watch me." He kissed her as the boys and Sonya looked on.

***

When Mary returned from school the next day, Joe told the kids they should go play outside and handed her an envelope. "I didn't want to bother you at work," he said, looking concerned. "From the School Board. I had to sign for receipt."

"Oh, my God!" Mary leaned her head against his sturdy chest.

"You're not going to read it?" he asked, sounding subdued. "I have. You've got until the end of the month. Then it's...vacation."

She shook her head. "I knew it was coming. I'm so sorry. All I try to do is be honest with myself to save our happiness and our lives."

He nodded.

"I'll find other work, Joe. I have two weeks."

"Read it, Mary," he said soothingly. "You'll see you don't have to blame yourself. It's pure hardball, dirty business, lies and innuendo."

She raced through the text, feeling Joe's breath on her neck as he leaned over her shoulder from behind. His presence reassured her; she wasn't going to be alone in this.

"... *Many of your declarations, actions and demonstrated sympathies inside as well as outside the school have shown a lack of loyalty to the Noredge community and represent a significant impediment to the effective achievement of our educational goals....*"

"So I'm a lousy teacher because I have an opinion. A correct one!" She was defiant.

Joe kissed her neck. "Read on. It gets worse."

"*Your active participation in the Sierra Club network; your involvement in the drafting of a petition harmful to the prosperity of Noredge; your scientifically unfounded public statements against an industry that brings employment to Noredge; your frequent—*"

"Enough!" She started tearing up the single sheet.

"Don't!" Joe shouted.

She stopped and looked back at him, holding the half-torn document.

"We'll need this, Mary. We'll sue the pants off the bastards for—"

She raised her hand to interrupt him. She wanted to say a scornful "Good luck with that," but decided to just sigh. "We're in trouble, Joe."

"Sit down darling. I made coffee. We'll manage." He walked to the sitting room, his cane steadying him. She kept a watchful eye on her man.

"I haven't wanted to scare you, Joe," she said as they were both seated, "but we already have a pile of medical bills."

He nodded. "One came today from Doctor Toro. I'll have to check with Supren why we're not fully covered for my accident. And I'll have to do paperwork to get onto worker's comp, I guess."

"We owe more than four thousand, so far."

"So now we'll be well over five." He pursed his lips.

They discussed their meager savings, the possible sale of their—her—house and cherished land, the necessity of two cars, Mary's jewels—their emotional value much higher than the price they would fetch. There was also the remote possibility of a loan from her cash-poor parents. Needs were very immediate, debts higher than savings. She considered tutoring, temporarily working as a nanny, or another teaching job far enough away from Noredge. "My bad press!" She rolled her eyes. She started to apologize again to Joe, but he waved her off. "You and me, we'll make it. And we'll get our kids into colleges. Good ones. I learned first-hand why."

She called Mayor Sanders.

"This isn't my thing, and what happened…it's not because of me, I can assure you." That's how the politician cut her off when she started voicing her surprise and distress over the letter she received from the School Board.

"But, Mr. Mayor, you have some influence—"

"I have none. I wish I had," he stated firmly, although he had to realize she knew it was a flat-out lie.

"I thought you'd understand my situation with Joe and the kids, and the medical bills piling up. Would you mind explaining to the School Board that—"

"I think you understand, Miss Jenkins, that you haven't made many friends in the right circles. If I may say so the chickens—"

"I get it." She hung up.

"Heard him?" she asked Joe.

"Yeah. Fat Sanders chickening out."

Minutes later her phone rang.

It was Frank. "I heard the big boy made it home! Congratulations. Is he out on the soccer field yet?"

"I'll let him tell you, Frank." She put the phone on conference and handed it to Joe.

"I heard you, buddy. Got to work off some belly fat!" Joe sounded enthused.

"And get rid of his cane!" Mary shouted. Then she shook her head: the little medicine bottle on the table rudely reminded her that Joe would never get off antibiotics. Milos had made that clear.

"Good going!" Frank paused. "I've got another love letter from dear Mike. Registered. He cut my severance by ninety percent to zip. They've paid ten. 'Non-compliance with the articles of the agreement.' You can figure which ones," he laughed. He hadn't sounded bitter. He had good job prospects and probably a sizable egg nest to boot.

"Yes, I can, Frank. Got my love letter too. Fired," Mary said flatly. "Joined the club." She didn't mention their own meager savings.

"What? You? It's Doyle, the bastard. I'll...." He paused and lowered his voice. "I know what injustice this creep has inflicted on you guys. I'm with you. Call me anytime. For anything."

She sighed, emotional and overwhelmed. "How kind of you, Frank. But we won't bother you. We'll manage, we think."

"Don't be bashful about asking for assistance, okay? Heard me? And I'll keep plodding, digging into Mike's business. Looking for his Achilles heel. May find more than one."

"Not more than two," Joe joked, shooting an encouraging glance at Mary.

She didn't appreciate the banter. "Achilles heel?" she asked. "You think so?"

Frank chuckled. "Yes. No joke, Mary. Remember I said it. By the way, how about getting together, you guys, Joanna and me? Quietly. At your place? We'll bring dinner. I'll take care of it. Tomorrow night? Six-Six-thirty? Okay?"

"We'd both love that. You're too much, Frank, but thanks. See you tomorrow."

She clicked off.

Chapter 31

Two days after he found out about his wife's affair with Mike Doyle, Vince got a call at the Beta site from Frank around four-thirty in the afternoon. The drilling proper had ended weeks before and the complicated completion work on the well was in full swing. The banging and clanging were still so loud that he had to shout. "Is it urgent?"

"Yeah. Kind of." Frank sounded more intense than his words suggested.

"Give me half a minute. Call you back." Vince headed for the parking lot, nervous, his strides long and fast. *Maybe Frank already knows about Susan and Doyle. Maybe all of Noredge knows.* When he reached his Explorer, he looked to his left while opening the door and noticed Doyle stepping away from his BMW about ten vehicles down the line and heading for the site.

In no mood to dignify his boss with even a single word, Vince dove into his SUV. He shut the door noiselessly, suppressed his reflexive impulse to start the engine and then called Frank. "Got to make this short. The elephant is hanging out here."

"Oh. I see. Him. You sound a little short of breath. Did Hathi trumpet loudly as usual?"

"Hathi?"

Frank laughed. "Disney language. Or Kipling. One of my many silly habits."

"Hmm." Vince kept silent for a few seconds, looking to his left. Then he said, "I managed to stay out of his sight, for now. Afraid he'll catch me when I get back to the van. I'm in my SUV."

"Okay. You mean '*my* SUV!'"

"Yes. Thanks for breaking it in. What's up?" Vince was in a hurry. He now realized that Doyle might be looking for him and make a scene about his absence.

"Sorry, you sound like you've got to run, the boss waiting. Nothing good I'm afraid. Something fishy's going on with Beta. Trouble. Don't know exactly what, but you're the man at the site and Mike's up to no good."

"You know?"

"The grapevine."

Vince was dumbfounded. "Huh? Grapevine? Who's that?"

Frank said calmly, "Can't tell you, Vince, but you should believe me. I'm trying to help you. Mike's after you now, for Beta."

"After me?" *Susan dumped him. The jilted adulterer seeks revenge.* Vince feared the worst but didn't feel he had to level with Frank about personal matters. His cheekbones trembled but he forced himself to speak loud and indignantly. "How silly! I did just a couple days of the drilling here. The first days. Preparatory work. Mister Big took over, remember. He, Hathi himself banished me to Carrollton. Beta's his baby." He turned his head ninety degrees and stared at the busy site. A couple of crewmembers were gesturing playfully, apparently having a good time joking around.

"So what, Vince? You and me, we weren't born yesterday, were we? You know Mike's been lying like hell about the Alpha logs, right? On paper and on tape." Frank sounded ominous.

"Yes."

"So, would elephant Hathi have any problem lying about Beta? And screwing you? The man has no shame."

"Everything was fine when he took me off Beta." Vince was furious with Doyle and sadness over Susan inundated his heart again, waves of hurt hitting him.

"Something else—"

"Yes! Keep it short." Vince shouted, irritated, convinced he was going to hear about Susan.

A pause followed. "I know you don't want to confront him—"

"That's my decision, isn't it?" Vince snapped. He was close to the boiling point.

"Of course. But listen. I don't believe that we know for sure what happened in Carrollton. How it happened."

"Huh? Why?" *His damn Carrollton again.*

"Just my gut feeling buddy."

Vince sighed, feeling listless. "Thank you, Frank. But I have enough on my plate already. I'd better go now."

"I understand. No sweat. Just know I'm ready to back you up if you want me to."

Vince felt empty after the call. His boss had to be waiting for him in the van, but he sat back a minute, took a drink of water and fiddled with his iPhone. *To hell with Doyle.* He temporarily forced himself to forget he had to hurry. He had to let it all sink in. Think. A few minutes longer.

Should he make peace with Susan after a weekend of bitter arguing, explaining, reproaching? Wednesday night had been his only one on the couch, but in bed they had avoided touching. Breakfasts had been painful affairs, conversations limited to the strictest necessities. When he came home yesterday evening he found her on the couch, a People magazine in her hands, her eyes swollen.

By now he had given their relationship a lot of thought, envisioned all kinds of scenarios for life without her. None came even remotely close to making peace with her. He was ready to wipe the slate.

When he arrived in the control van Henry, the young IT wizard, shot him a strange glance. "Vince," he said after a cough, "I'm sorry. Mr. Doyle stormed in here ten minutes ago. I don't know what's going on but he wanted me to block all access to the logs."

"The logs? We have to halt operations?"

"The drilling logs. Only. No access to them, for nobody, for the next three weeks. Except for him. He shouted his orders and ran out. I already changed the passwords." He shook his head and opened both palms.

Vince stared at him. "Did he ask for me?"

"Nope. He was in too much of a hurry to get out of here." Henry seemed to suppress an eye roll.

Vince tried not to frown. "Oh. I see."

"You see?"

"I think so. Never mind." He walked out and strode back to his car, convinced Doyle was ready to somehow make him into a scapegoat.

Upon his return from Carrollton to the Beta site at Harriet's, Vince had noticed that Doyle had worked at remarkably high speed: during the drilling process Doyle had used very limited time between drilling successive portions of the well—much less time than considered safe by most experts.

After drilling each portion of the well cement had to be applied, between pipe and soil, and it needed enough time to set. The time spans Doyle had allowed for setting were extremely short. That was a risk neither Vince nor most experts ever would have taken.

Had Doyle applied a special new technique or a secret new cement composition? Vince hadn't commented, afraid to insult the boss, but he now feared the man might have created Noredge's water problem.

"Why did he rush things like that? Why such dangerous haste?" Vince wondered in disbelief, talking to himself as he drove home. "Just to get another feather in his hat? Or an even fatter bonus check?"

He shrugged and didn't bother to answer his own questions. "Screw Doyle. Screw Supren!" he mumbled. "I have a life too. I'm going after him. He's toast!"

He parked his car in the garage, next to Susan's little Chrysler, and opened the door into the kitchen.

He found Susan on the couch in the sitting room. She had been crying again. Tears were something he always had trouble dealing with. He looked away.

"What's wrong, Vince?" she asked, sounding subdued. "I mean, you're early," she quickly added as she stood up. "And...relaxed."

Her words surprised him. He supposed he had talked himself into a better mood during his short ride home. He had even caught himself whistling. Letting it all hang out, saying "to hell with the creep" apparently had worked wonders for his mind. But, at the top of his list of remedies, he had discovered a miracle drug: revenge. Frank had set him on the path and Henry, the IT guy, had put him in motion. Vince was going to go for it. "Beta," he had kept repeating. "Going for broke."

He was ready to straighten out matters with his wife. "Let's talk, Susan." He spoke softly.

Slowly rocking her head, she put her hand on his waist and buried her head in his shoulder. "Will you forgive me,

Vince? I want to live the rest of my life with you. No one else, ever."

It was the fifth or sixth time she had told him that. He had refused to give her a clear answer, doubting her loyalty. This time he wanted to forgive, even if she hadn't asked. "You're my wife, Susan, and my love," he whispered.

"Oh! *Thank* you, Vince. I love you so much." She smothered him with kisses.

His tears flowed as freely as hers. "I forgive you, but not that bastard who got your precious head spinning. I'll kill him." He had spoken his threat almost inaudibly.

She jerked her head back, eyes wide. "Don't hurt him. You'll go to jail."

"No, no. Just a way of speaking. But he'll pay! I'll sue the pants off him. For sexual harassment!" He immediately realized she wasn't an employee of Doyle's. "No," he added, "for much worse." He pulled her toward him and embraced her.

They kissed and whispered sweet words.

"I'm ready, Vince." She squeezed him harder.

"To sue?"

She shook his body. "For you."

"Me too. But I'll need a shower."

He let the water wash away his aches and pains; as he bowed his head and let the pulsating waves hit his neck, he felt his anger toward his wife rush down through his body, form a vortex at the drain and spool downward, spiraling away into the past.

***

Late in the evening, Mike Doyle felt a vibration on his left leg as he lay on his couch browsing through the Wall Street Journal. He looked at his watch. *Ten p.m. Some people are shameless.* He dropped his paper and reached into his pocket. *Dave Broderick.* Doyle was in no shape, and had no desire, to get into an uncomfortable conversation.

Two minutes later he checked his voicemail.

"Mike, wherever you are, this is getting out of hand." Dave sounded exasperated. "We're friends, and I deserve better from you. No need to tell you what I mean. I look like a fool. This methane stuff got to Don before I'd heard about it from you. It's been going on for days, it seems, but I haven't heard shit from you. Call me back. I fear Don's going to go after you. And me. I was dumb enough to stick my neck out for you."

Doyle looked at Edith.

"It's about the water, right?" she asked, looking worried.

"Yeah." He shrugged. "Some guy Dave complaining. I'll get back to him tomorrow, at a decent hour." He picked up his paper from the floor.

Chapter 32

"Could you have the garage door open and your car in the driveway, Mary?" Frank sounded slightly embarrassed over the phone. It was about five-thirty on Saturday. "I'd like to park inside. We'll be carrying food."

Mary smiled. Frank wasn't lying, but he wasn't telling it all. She figured he would close that door as soon as he had driven in: the Supren crew still worked around the clock seven days a week across the street at Harriet's. "I know, Frank. Thanks so much. And Joanna won't have to worry about being seen with you."

"Oh? Yes, that's right."

Mary winked at Joe, who had overheard the conversation. She had trouble understanding why Joanna wanted to keep hiding her relationship with Frank, just to cling to her lousy job. She knew it had the poor girl drudging impossible hours, serving a detestable boss who imitated her accent, despised Frank and made fun of her in front of businessmen.

"Why doesn't she just run away?" Joe asked.

"All I can think of is that maybe Frank wants Joanna to stay close to Doyle. Maybe she's both Frank's lover and spy?"

Joe didn't respond but went for another practice walk without his cane, floundering from the kitchen table to the sink, resting, holding on, then on to the refrigerator, resting, then to a chair—only to sit down and ask for his cane.

At ten to six Frank's car entered the driveway.

"Don't run out, guys," Mary said to Jimmy and Andy. "Stay here. Wait until Mr. Anderson knocks on the kitchen door from inside the garage. Then you can open the door for him and his friend. And help them carry the food." As if Frank and Joanna were bringing five-course meals for four adults and two kids. "And don't let Jake in," she added nervously, checking her nail polish.

She wore her favorite silky tan blouse over a short black skirt showing much of her shapely legs on high heels. Joe's glances had complimented her on her free-flowing, volumized hair as well.

When Andy opened the kitchen door, Joanna stood in front of him, smiling, purse dangling on left arm, her right hand supporting a twenty-inch glass platter. "Hi big boy. I remember you."

"What a beautiful salad!" Mary exclaimed. "You guys did too much work."

"Freshly made. Frank and me." Joanna walked in, her face dripping pride.

Andy offered help, but Mary held him back. "You might drop those cute little tomatoes."

A smell of burned meat wafted into the kitchen as Frank followed behind Joanna. He carried a stack of polystyrene boxes, controlling his white tower with hands and chin, his glasses uncomfortably askew.

The kids stood uneasily idle. Jimmy touched his nose and pointed at the contents of the boxes.

Andy nodded. "Steak," he whispered.

"You're spoiling us," Joe said to Frank. "Thank you so much."

"It's not the Ritz Carlton quality you must have gotten used to at the Milos Center—"

"Right, but it seems close, smells close," Joe roared, tapping his cane on the floor.

"Take a seat," Mary said to the guest-caterers when finally they had their hands free. She pointed at the metal chairs around the kitchen table. "Let's chat."

All managed to secure a seat on five metal chairs and a small stool. Mary held up a bottle of Merlot and handed it to Joe. He opened it and poured the wine. The adults clinked glasses as did the boys, plastic cups filled to the brim with pop. Mary renewed her welcome to the guests.

"We'd better start the meal," Joanna said, "or the hamburgers will get cold."

"Hamburgers?" Jimmy asked, his voice hushed. He looked at Andy.

"I was close. Almost same as steak," his brother mumbled.

The conversations started. All the bad news that had come in on Monday and Friday was no match for the exuberance about Joe's return home and his prospects for a near-full recovery. Dinner was a festive affair, the mood upbeat, Mary's joy contagious. The boys listened in on the discussions, which the adults adapted somewhat for the ears of their youthful but keen listeners.

Around eight, the playful tunes of *"Eine kleine Nachtmusik"* alerted the partiers. Frank dug his phone out of his pants pocket and said, his voice low, "Hi Vince."

The adults instantly became quiet and put their forks down.

Mary captured a few words from Vince. "Beta... Carrollton...."

Joe raised his heavy eyebrows.

As Frank listened, frowning, he gestured to Mary, suggesting it might be bedtime for the kids. "We have to discuss."

She nodded and, eyeing the boys, pointed silently in the direction of the bedrooms.

They pouted with reluctance, got up, said "goodnights" and "thank-yous" to their parents and visitors and filed out of the kitchen, feet dragging. Andy muttered something inaudible to Jimmy as they exited.

Mary tried again to listen in on Vince's call. Joe and

Joanna continued their meal, handling forks and knives with extra care.

"What?" Frank exclaimed, his eyes shouting surprise. "The logs? Cementing...How fast? ...What? ...Incredible... Ultrafast? Damn right! Man! ...Yes, I agree...Could we go...? We must talk first...Can you come over here? I'm at Mary's...." He turned to the hostess, questioning her with his eyes.

She gave him the okay sign.

"Okay, buddy. Ten-thirty-four Maple Road." He paused and chuckled. "Of course you know. Across the street from your second home. Bring your bulletproof vest!" he roared. "Hathi may be watching you!"

While they finished their dinner and waited for Vince, Frank explained that in Vince's absence Doyle had summarily blocked access to the drilling logs at the Beta site.

"Wow!" Joe said. "The Beta logs? Doyle? Why? To hide... what?"

Mary shrugged. "Who knows what he's up to? But he sure seems to be going after Vince now."

Joe nodded. "Yeah. And Vince after Casanova, who's been messing around—"

"Okay, Joe," Mary said, her hand on his forearm, "the kids have perfect hearing." She stood up and went to the bedroom. "Brush your teeth with Dasani, boys," she said as she closed the door and returned to her guests.

Minutes later a car blew its horn. Mary hurried to the

front door and waited on the threshold for Vince. The young man looked disheveled as he dragged his heavy frame out of the car in slow-motion, but once he started moving toward the house he suddenly got an air of determination about him.

Frank came to the door as well. "He's tired, but it looks like he's grown some balls," he commented. "About time."

"I must get him a chair," Mary said and ran back inside.

Once in the kitchen, Frank introduced his visitor, who nodded curtly and said, grinning, "Heard a lot about you guys."

"Take a seat," Frank said. "My God, I couldn't believe my ears! That gentleman, Mr. Michael Doyle wants to throw you under the bus for the methane that must have flowed up from the Beta site into our aquifer. You didn't say that when you spoke about those logs, but that's what you meant, right?"

"Yep. I bet that's what he's going to do: blame me."

"For sure? You heard from someone?"

Vince lowered his voice. "I didn't, but I've convinced myself—"

Frank put his hand on his shoulder. "Join the club, man," he said. "Mike tried to finger me for polluting the aquifer with methane from Alpha. He had no proof. I shut him up. At Beta *he* did almost all of the drilling. Himself. And now he's hiding the logs. His ultrafast cementing must have created the methane problem. Of course, he's going to blame you. It's your turn."

Vince had to blow his nose. "You know Doyle literally chased me away from Beta like a dog when I'd barely started drilling there. I never understood why."

"I think we may have figured it out," Frank replied. He paused and looked around the table. "Once the spill in Carrollton happened he got you away from Beta in a big hurry. Too big. Agreed? As if he had been waiting for the accident."

Hmm. Mary was unconvinced. "Doyle needed a good man in Carrollton," she countered.

"Yeah," Frank mocked. "One with zero experience in clean-ups. Sorry Vince. I bet Supren's got plenty of spill experts in Houston. Doesn't that accident look a bit too convenient for Mike? Suspiciously convenient? To me it does." His eyes were wide.

Vince's expression grew dark.

Joe looked on in disbelief.

Frank leaned his head. "Couldn't it have been a set up? Carrollton gave Supren a black eye, but it also offered Mike an excuse to pull Vince off the drilling job so he could take over Beta himself. And create the mess we now have at Beta and in our water," he intoned.

"What?" Mary had her palms up. "Why would he have planned to create all these problems? How could he have wanted to?"

"Who knows? Hard to understand he would've, indeed. Looks like we'll have to find out." Frank eyed Joanna.

She had morphed into a sphinx.

Vince nodded. His eyes traveled full circle around the table. "I've decided to speak up," he said. "I don't fear losing my job any longer. The bastard will sack me anyway." He paused and sighed. "The moment I arrived at the scene in Carrollton I saw motorbike brake marks, skid marks, on Route 39, about fifty or a hundred feet past Joe's wreck."

A brick hit Mary's stomach.

"What?" Frank sounded indignant. "Why didn't you—?"

"Let me finish," Vince begged, red-faced. "A traffic sign was knocked down and an old oak tree had lost some bark. Not sure that happened at the moment of Joe's accident, but it couldn't have been much earlier. The brake marks led straight from where Joe went off the road to that tree."

"And you didn't tell Doyle?" Frank sounded angry. He turned and stared at Mary and Joe.

Vince put his hand up. "I called him right away, of course, but he snubbed me, scolded me, and ordered the area roped off immediately. He hissed. 'If you mouth off to the police, one word, I'll kill you. I'm in control, remember! Me!' I couldn't believe my ears. I was still very new in my job at Supren and bit my tongue."

"So you did tell him!" Frank now sounded even more upset.

Vince nodded, looking sheepish.

Frank shook his head, dejection written over his face. "Too bad you never mentioned that to me. To us."

"I'm sorry. I think you understand."

Frank muttered something indecipherable through his teeth.

"By now that evidence must be gone," Mary said, feeling powerless.

Joe took the floor. "Mary must have asked me a hundred times whether I remembered anybody hindering me and causing my accident. But I just recall waking up in the hospital with a splitting headache, and Mary said that was days later. If she would've known this...too late now...." He shrugged.

Frank tossed Joanna another smile and gestured with his chin that it was her turn to speak.

She threw an apologetic glance at Mary and Joe. "Frank and I have kept a secret," she said almost inaudibly." She turned to Vince, compassion in her eyes. "Two days after the accident," she went on, "a crying, young Asian woman burst into the office. 'I need money,' she screamed. '*Monnaie. Maintenant.* Now!' I think she might have been Vietnamese. 'My boyfriend's in the hospital. Supren must pay the bill! The boss promised! *La compagnie!* We have no *assurance.* Where's the man? My boyfriend's leg is badly injured. His arm too. He needs surgery.' She sounded hopeless. And out of breath. Shaking."

Joe frowned. "How did the woman know where to find Doyle?"

"She said, 'Everybody knows where Supren's boss's office is. I drove here and asked. I'm a cook in Medina.' I asked her for her telephone number but she refused. 'I'll come back, we need money, he has to pay,' she said, still crying and lamenting in French."

"And Doyle?" Mary asked.

"Not there. He arrived an hour later. I told him about the woman and that she refused to give me her phone number. *Dios mío!* I thought he was going to explode—or kill me! I couldn't believe how angry he was. 'You have no right…!' he thundered and stopped. He pointed his index an inch from my nose and hissed. His voice was so low I could barely understand him. 'Don't you ever mention that lady's name. Or that she was here.' She hadn't told me her name. I wondered why he didn't fire me, but Frank later explained to me why he didn't."

Frank smiled.

"Doyle had to be able to keep you silent, Joanna," Mary said. "Did she come back, the Vietnamese?"

"Oh no! *Nunca.* Never." Joanna sliced the air with her hand and let out a long sigh.

Vince didn't look convinced. "All fine and dandy, Joanna, but we have no proof. And, if I heard Joanna right, the Vietnamese didn't say anything about an accident."

"Indeed, she didn't," Frank interjected. "So far we only had Joanna's word, but now we also have yours. That's two. We can make them work as proof, against Doyle's. I'm ready to confront the bandit. You, Mary? Vince?"

"Make it work…?" Vince seemed to be figuring out how, but deferred to Frank. "Now? At this late hour?" He checked his watch.

"Any hour's fine. Now's perfect. Every day counts, Vince. Let's go. You and me." Frank turned to Joe, who winked. "And Mary. Right now."

"Wish me luck," Mary whispered to Joe.

Ten minutes later she was rolling her eyes and ringing the bell at 1426 McKinley. The stately Doyle residence looked threatening in the dark. The lighting needed maintenance. A dog barked.

"It's the neighbors'," Vince explained. "He doesn't bark when I come alone."

"I think they're doing popcorn." Mary nervously threw her hair back, exhaling heavily.

They hadn't heard any footsteps when Mike Doyle opened the door.

Barefoot, red tee-shirt reaching over belly, shorts barely visible, toenails pointing like daggers, he planted himself on the threshold to face Mary.

"Almost ten! What's the matter? Are tree-huggers that rude? You know where my office is!" He tried to slam the door shut but Frank jumped forward and stopped him with his shoe.

Doyle looked livid. "Get out of here or—!"

"Are you threatening me again? Forgotten about the pictures?" Mary asked, teasing.

He backed off, his eyes firing anger. He opened his mouth as he noticed Vince on the side but didn't say anything.

Frank and Vince moved forward, gently pushing Mary over the threshold.

"Apologies for our lack of manners, but we're in a big hurry. We just want to make sure about a couple of things. Whether we understand them correctly," Mary said politely, standing almost as tall as Doyle on her high heels.

Without saying a word, Doyle ran back toward a door leading to what looked like a sitting room, carefully closed it, and returned. He panted, his voice low. "Say it. No shouting. Two minutes. Shameless you are."

Frank took over. "We have the name of the biker who caused Joe Bertolo's accident in Carrollton. Why did you pay him, or his Vietnamese girlfriend? Just because you felt so bad for them?"

"What?" Doyle recoiled. He looked back in the direction of the sitting room. "Where did you get that crap?" he breathed.

"You know damn well where," Frank said.

"Where?" Vince jumped in. "I'll tell you. From the tree and the traffic sign. I told you but you shut me up."

"I didn't! A tree? A Vietnamese?"

Vince looked at him askance.

Frank smiled. "Mr. Doyle, your memory's failing you. Happens to the best."

"I'll sue the pants off you guys for slander if you ever...." The Texan kept his voice low and looked intermittently at the door behind him.

Frank winked. "Oh. Slander! You know a thing or

two about that shit. I've made a few copies of your latest article, your labor of love in the Noredge Sentinel. For my grandchildren, you know. Couldn't have said it better myself. Neither could Mary, I bet. Mary my lover, right? You're excellent indeed at slander."

Doyle had listened with surprising calm. Until now. "Get the hell out!" he hissed. "Out!"

Frank didn't budge. "Soon, Vince Davis will get the Mike treatment, right? You destroyed my name and Vince's is next in line. Another article in the Sentinel, another smear job, and I know why."

"You!" Doyle shouted. He threw a lightning-fast glance at the door behind him.

Frank paused and went on, "You played it well: all proof of Vince's innocence has been blocked, hidden. Or destroyed? Which is it? No drilling logs at Beta. Bad luck, Vince! Or maybe you could make them available again, Mike, those logs? Supren might want to see them too—after your thorough study of Vince's 'screw-ups.'"

Vince had teared up. Mary felt sorry for him.

Doyle kept silent, seemingly pondering his response, chest heaving.

Mary went for the jugular. "Why, Mr. Doyle? Why do such bad things happen? Almost simultaneously? The spill in Carrollton, my poor husband saddled with heavy antibiotics for the rest of his life, and a foot that will never again kick a soccer ball with his kids. And now the methane? Why can't our kids have clean water any longer?

Do you know why? Is it all an act of God? A God in a bad mood? Or what?" She shot him a fiery glance.

"Doesn't headquarters ask you these questions? Don't they want the logs?" Frank asked. "Haven't they insisted?"

The dismissiveness on Doyle's face made it clear that this was none of Frank's business. "They're fully briefed."

"By you. Just you. Bamboozled by you. Bribed? Blackmailed?" Vince mocked him scornfully.

"You? You too, Davis? You'll pay dearly for this," Doyle fumed.

The door to the sitting room opened briefly, then closed again.

An eerie silence enveloped the limited space of the hallway. It made even the vacant, imposing antique hall tree appear uneasy, standing solemnly. Then, a torrent of anger and vitriol overtook the place, as Doyle shrieked, "Out or I get my gun!"

"Let's go." Mary already had her hand on the door knob. "Good night, Mr. Doyle. Please say hello to Edith."

In the car on their way to Mary's place Vince, from the back seat, stuck his head between her shoulders and Frank's. "I don't get it," he said. "Doyle keeps accusing Joe, his own man. Trying anyway. That's accusing Supren. He's cutting off his nose to spite his face. Crazy."

"Not if he wants to spite his face," Frank laughed.

"What?" Mary and Vince asked in chorus. "Hurt Supren? Not crazy?"

"Not if he wants to spite his face." Frank had gone for a chortle as he repeated his sentence.

"Are you serious, Frank? Why would he?" Mary was perplexed and looked back at Vince.

Frank said, "All we know is that he did. But why? Beats me. I just have some wild idea. Too wild, maybe. I joke a lot. I like joking. Playing games." He started laughing loudly.

"Like when you said you knew the names of the Vietnamese woman and her boyfriend?" Vince asked.

Frank looked in the rearview mirror. "You could say that, but most of what I said was true. I just used some opportune extrapolation. I know it's a little risky," he added as he made a left turn onto Maple Road.

Mary frowned, silent.

Frank hurried to the front door, ahead of Mary and Vince, who had started a discussion outside the Explorer as they stepped out of the vehicle.

Joanna embraced Frank passionately and kissed him. "Thank God! You're back safely!"

Mary noticed tears in Vince's eyes.

"I'm losing my job, Mary, but I'm so happy," the young man said, his lips trembling. "Susan and me, we're a happy couple again." He wiped his cheeks and stepped into his SUV.

"Give her my best, Vince. And take good care of her." Mary waved as he drove off.

Chapter

O n Monday morning around seven, Frank prepared his cereal, skim milk and blueberry breakfast and sat down on his bar stool. With his elbow on the granite kitchen counter, chin resting in hand, he combined spooning with thinking.

When he had dropped off Joanna at her place around ten-thirty last night and wished her sweet dreams, she had said softly, "You too, darling. Dream about me all you want." She had tapped her index on his cheek and quipped, "But not about that stunning Galinda, remember?"

He had shaken his head vigorously and laughed, recalling their '*tembleque*" conversation a week ago—and how it had ended delightfully in her bed.

"Galinda," he had said to himself when he arrived at home.

He had googled the name before, as soon as Mary had mentioned it to him. A long time ago. The web had told him Galinda was an actual girl's name.

Today he had woken up around three and tossed and

turned until daybreak. Restless. Last night at Mike's he had bluffed about knowing the name of the Vietnamese, and it had worked. A little later, on the way back to Mary's, he had gone out on a limb, another one. Long and thin, this one, he now realized: he had blurted out his provocative "if he wants to spite his face" about Doyle without much thought behind it.

Had he joked too expeditiously? Actually, the words had exited his mouth spontaneously, because his mind was simply working overtime and convoluted. It was dealing with too many thoughts, assumptions and ideas simultaneously.

But something had put him on that strange track: Galinda, the word that kept popping up on his mental screen since his *tembleque* night with Joanna.

"Galinda" had stubbornly clung to him from the day he first heard the name, but now it reappeared again and again in vivid colors on his screen. Joanna had reignited its flame when she wished him good night yesterday: "No dreaming about Galinda!"

Galinda. He had often wondered who the man was at the other end of the line when Doyle had his roaring "Galinda" discussion. A "Jim," Joanna had said. She and Joe had partially and unwittingly overheard it. "Jim." From what Joanna had told Frank about the relaxed timbre and the wording of the conversation, the man had to have been an old buddy of Doyle's. But the latter had reacted with swift and inexplicable anger against poor Joanna because she had had the nerve to knock on his door during his loud, friendly conversation. Why was Doyle so irrationally upset about that innocent knock?

Frank recalled that Mary had told him about another instance when Doyle reacted brutally without real provocation: when Edith spoke of Jim Duncan from Lumberton on the steps of the Chamber building. Doyle had rudely admonished his wife in Spanish. He apparently thought that Noredge people wouldn't understand him, and likely never imagined the possibility that Mary spoke fluent Spanish. Or he was simply too angry to control himself.

Doyle had seemed overly sensitive, twice, about his connection to a person named Jim. Could that Galinda man have been Jim Duncan? The Viola boss? Was the fracking world that small? Was this Jim Duncan the same man who, during Frank's job interview at Viola, had acted as if he didn't know Mike Doyle, although for some reason Frank always had thought Doyle had worked for the man at one time?

Did Jim Duncan lie to me? Why?

Half-way through his meal, Frank got up, opened up his iPad, went to the Google site and typed "Galinda Jim Duncan" into the box. Hundreds of articles and sites popped up featuring Galindas and Duncans galore, but no connection between them. He tried "Galinda James Duncan." Apparently no romance between Jim or James Duncan and a beautiful Galinda ever made it onto the web. Why would it anyway, a trivial affair? He gave the Mike Doyle-Galinda connection a try, with little conviction. No success. He gave up.

The clock said ten and he told himself he was a fool for wasting a beautiful morning. He looked in the mirror, rubbed his stubble and decided to go for a jog out east on McKinley.

He couldn't get his thoughts off Doyle. As he ran faster and faster, anger spurring him on, the townhouses and then the luxurious residences flew by him unnoticed and at shorter intervals. His absentmindedness cost him a slightly twisted ankle because he failed to notice a sudden dip in the sidewalk. By the end of his run he had thought things through: Joe and Mary's suffering—physical, emotional and financial; Noredge; Carrollton. Frank was convinced they weren't accidents. "They're damn crimes. Not serendipity. Crimes. Mike's," he mumbled while breathing heavily. "Too much points in that man's direction." *But why? Someone tell me why....*

Who could answer the question? Who would? Who was hiding the truth? Hiding something? The man who had probably lied to Frank in Houston? Duncan? The man Doyle didn't want to be heard associating with, Duncan?

Frank decided he would fly to Houston to see Viola and get himself an audience with Duncan. It certainly wasn't a foregone conclusion that he'd make it into the man's corner office again, but he bet on Yolanda, the sophisticated receptionist in the Viola lobby. She had shown keen interest, twice, in chatting with him when he went to meet Duncan late July. *I bet she might just find a way to sneak me in,* he chuckled inside. *She'll have to.* After all, Viola's big honcho had shown real interest in him for Colombia. Frank would express his continued interest in the job. "Despite an offer from another major company," he would tell Duncan with a straight face.

He would also drop in at Supren, a short taxi ride from Viola, and express his concerns about the goings on in Noredge and Carrollton and, last but not least, his loss of severance. It wouldn't be easy, though, to get into the right offices at Supren: he was a fired employee. That wasn't the exact legal term, but it was reality.

He had barely toweled off after his shower when his phone rang.

"We're going to Houston," Vince said, snickering. "Tonight."

"We? Tonight?" Frank was puzzled.

"Doyle and me. Supren woke up, I guess. About time. No, too damn late. I don't know whether I can stand being in the same room as that guy," Vince quipped.

"Did he ask for the meeting?"

"Are you kidding me? He hates their guts, and vice-versa I'm sure."

"Great! Good luck, buddy. I wish I could be a fly on the wall. Enjoy!" Frank's pulse rate had doubled. *I'm not going to be in that room, but I'll make sure I won't be far away.* One way or another he would get a few words in at Supren, whether they wanted to hear them or not. And he would see Jim Duncan, welcome or not. He'd fly to Houston tomorrow. *No, tonight. Whatever the hotel bill is.* He called Viola and asked for Yolanda Turner.

"She'll be in at two-thirty. Do you want her voicemail?" the operator asked.

Shit. "No, thanks. Could you just tell her...no, no message." He didn't feel he could ask for Miss Turner's cell phone. It would be a long wait until three-thirty Eastern.

At three-forty he got through to Yolanda. He helped her remember who he was, an easy task. "The guy from Ohio" description wasn't even needed. He told her he would appreciate a few minutes with Mr. Duncan.

"And it has to be tomorrow, Mr. Anderson?" She sounded disappointed.

"If at all possible, Yolanda."

"I'm so sorry, but Mr. Duncan is traveling. How about next week? It would be great to see you again here."

"Can't do, Yolanda. I should see him tomorrow. In person." He lowered his voice. "My future at Viola may depend on it."

"Oh my God! We do want your friendly smile here, Mr. Anderson."

"Thank you, Yolanda." He sighed loudly and waited, mentally directing his energy at her through the phone.

She broke the silence, her voice a mere whisper. "Listen, I'm not supposed to do this, but I know you'll treat this information discretely." She paused.

"Of course, Yolanda."

"Mr. and Mrs. Duncan are at the Greenbrier. You know that chic place in West Virginia? They're attending a working session of Interoga, the worldwide association of oil and gas companies. They'll fly home on Saturday. Please don't tell anybody I gave you this information."

"My lips are sealed. Count on me. I know that association. Actually, I now remember reading that the Interoga meeting was going to take place this week. Mr. Duncan won't be surprised that I try to find him there. Thanks again for telling me he's attending."

"I'm so glad I could be of some help to you."

"I won't forget your kindness, Yolanda. *Hasta la vista.*"

He hung up and called Mary on her cell. "Our Galinda-boy is at the Greenbrier til Saturday morning. I'm going to catch him."

"Doyle?" She turned the radio down.

"Duncan. We should leave tomorrow morning. Early."

"We? Duncan?"

"Yes and yes. You're Mike's number-one victim. You suffer from polluted water as we all do, but you've also been fired and almost lost your husband. You've been threatened by Mike, can't pay your mortgage because of him. And I forgot the bullying your kids have to endure. I need you there when I smack Duncan in the face with the truth. Make him hear and see what Mike has wrought, with his help, I think."

"Hmm. I see...."

He pictured her rubbing her chin.

He pushed a little harder. "Jim Duncan told me in Houston, in July, that he didn't know Mike. You remember you told me about Doyle's *'cállate'* bark to his poor wife, right? Mike didn't want the name Jim Duncan uttered, correct? Jim. That's one. Then the Galinda discussion Joe and Joanna overheard. Mike was furious about it. Because it was Duncan at the other end of the line? It was a person named Jim. See? Both Mike Doyle and Jim Duncan act as if they don't know each other. But I bet that they do and that the Galinda guy was Duncan. I'm going to confirm it."

"And then?"

"Then we'll…there must be a reason why they've been lying. We're going to find out what it is. 'It' may be something ugly."

"And you think—"

He pictured her deep frown and her glance at Joe, whose cough he had heard. "The same as you, I bet. That 'it' may explain Doyle's strange behavior."

"'Strange?' Does he deserve that euphemism?"

Frank understood the lack of conviction in her voice and her feelings about making up a story for her absence from school. "I smell success, Mary. But I need you there."

"Jimmy and Andy—"

"Call before school hours and leave a message. Say you must urgently visit a very ill relative in West Virginia." He laughed. "We'll need four to five hours each way. Shall we leave at six? Before the kids can ask questions?"

"The school…they may find out I'm lying."

"Why worry about them? You've already been—"

"Fired."

"Yes." He couldn't immediately find a less bitter word.

"Joe—"

"You want me to talk to him first?"

"He heard you. He's nodding and laughing. And making a big fist."

Chapter 34

Mary and Frank had barely gotten out of her driveway Tuesday morning when she was overcome by guilt. "I may have ruined it all, for my entire family," she lamented, sobbing. "Who knows how Supren will treat Joe once he's more or less recovered? If the way they deal with me on medical bills is any indication, I don't see much hope. In a few days I'll see my last paycheck and then we may soon end up on welfare." She took another tissue and blew her nose. "Sorry, Frank. I must tell somebody."

"No problem, Mary. Believe me, this is not the end of our story with Supren. We still may come out victorious and the Chamber and the mayor red-cheeked. That's why we're headed to White Sulphur Springs. Greenbrier here we come!" He raised a fist and smiled encouragingly at Mary.

"But most of Supren's big bosses are in Houston."

He shot her a jovial nod. "We'll get to them too. Later. They might not be as bad as we think. Mike has tried to bamboozle them, kept them in the dark about the disasters he's created for us. But right now, he's in Houston with Vince. The chickens are coming home to roost. You might get a courteous call from Supren. With apologies." He tapped her on the shoulder. "And then from the school board! Then the mayor. We may see them falling like dominoes!" He offered her a little plastic box. "Care for a mint?'

"Thanks. You're trying hard to make me feel better, Frank. I hope you're at least half-right. I have to scrape by on the few thousand dollars we have in the bank. My property has lost at least twenty percent, compliments of Supren, but my mortgage hasn't dropped." She laughed scornfully.

"Banks like fracking money, but don't want to hear about shrinking home and land prices."

"Andy needs new soccer shoes. He's growing like a weed. I had to tell him to wait. I may ask a friend for a hand-me-down." She sighed.

"He's becoming quite a guy. Good kid. Jimmy too. You can be proud." Frank spoke firmly, nodding.

"They are."

His words were encouragement for Mary. The real thing. Her boys were her pride. That was a fact—not some dream in the future that needed a carefully phrased description prefaced by lots of contingencies. This, the boys, was now. This she had. This kept her marching.

They took a break in the Parkersburg area, over half

way on Interstate 77. Fresh autumn air welcomed them on their way from the car to the McDonald's entrance. Once they opened the door, grease and detergent odors took over.

"We'll hit Charleston pretty soon. Then Interstate 64, less than an hour of it," Frank explained as he attacked his Quarter Pounder.

Mary nodded. "And then? How are you going to find Mr. Duncan?"

"One way or another, Mary. Easy. I remember him from Houston. Tall, more than rotund, bald, sixtyish."

She laughed. "Easy? I bet eighty percent of the men at the Greenbrier this time of the year fit that description!"

"Okay, but he looks *exceptionally*...sixtyish."

"That'll do it," she said without batting an eye.

Frank had an incoming call. "Oh, you? Vince?" He switched to conference. "Mary's with me."

"Guess what? Doyle's a no-show. No message. Houston guys are asking me. How would I know? You seen him?" The young man panted heavily.

"Nope."

"Thanks, got to go. Sorry."

"Understand. Take care, buddy."

Mary rolled her eyes. "Doyle chickened out."

Frank snickered. "If Vince knew where we're headed...."

A few minutes before noon the majestic main building of the Greenbrier appeared. Massive, white. The awe-inspiring structure kept Mary and Frank silent as they drove up the long, flowerbed-lined stretch from Main Street to the entrance.

"Pictures don't do it justice," she marveled after a while. She had seen it on postcards.

"Almost a hundred years she's been around in this shape, the grand dame," Frank said.

"So much history!"

Joe had googled the Greenbrier last night. "An old thing," he had told Mary. "They say it's been around since 1778. I wonder how many times it's burnt down. Seven hundred rooms and twenty restaurants. You might get lost."

The guard at the front offered valet parking, but Frank refused and was summarily banished to a far-off lot with his Altima. "That's what I get for being parsimonious," he quipped. Mary and Frank knew they were out of their league at the Greenbrier.

"This quarter-mile walk is a blessing for my joints anyway," Frank said as they made their way from the car to the hotel. "Let's try the check-in desk first. They're not supposed to give room numbers of guests to strangers, but who knows?"

Mary didn't comment. She admired Frank's optimism and drive. And generosity. She felt he was here much more for her than for himself.

At the desk a short, smiling man wearing the name tag "Sergio Winters" welcomed them with a broad smile. "Mr. and Mrs. ...?"

"We're not checking in," Frank said, smiling back. "I'm here to meet one of the participants in the Interoga conference. I'm a member as well, but not attending this particular event. I'd like to briefly meet Mr. Jim Duncan, an old acquaintance of mine. I assume he's here. Would it be possible to call his room for me?"

Sergio looked left, at the colleague next to him, and answered without checking his desktop, "Duncan... Greenbrier policy doesn't allow me to confirm that Mr. Duncan is a guest. We have special security for the time being, too. The conference...."

Frank turned to Mary and mumbled, "Struck out."

"Since you know him, we could just wait around and have a drink or snack. Try our luck," Mary suggested.

Sergio winked for a nanosecond.

"Okay. But let's stay close to the desk, Mary." Frank pointed at a small table nearby.

"Why?"

"For the view." He and Sergio exchanged brief, knowing looks.

She frowned. "The view" was a collection of elderly ladies with a few men mixed in, having tea or coffee at the numerous small tables spread out over the immense black-and-white checkered lobby floor. This space was called the "Upper Lobby" as was posted at the entrance. It was aristocracy as she imagined it. On one side a bar welcomed guests. It carried the name "Lobby Bar."

They sat down. She took her iPhone. Frank kept throwing glances in Sergio's direction.

Ten minutes later the colleague next to Sergio stood up, pointed at her watch and disappeared.

Sergio walked up to Mary and Frank, looking discrete, carrying a folded sheet of paper. "Mrs. Duncan is Cuban, right?" he said, while checking the immediate surroundings.

Frank and Mary nodded.

"My mother, too. The Duncans should be back around two, I guess. Mr. Duncan and some of his friends like to read newspapers here in the afternoon. If you find him, don't mention me. Just say you supposed he was attending the conference. It wouldn't be a lie, would it?"

"It wouldn't." Frank smiled.

"Okay, then. I suppose this is yours," Sergio said as he handed the sheet to Frank.

Frank looked at both sides. Mary noticed it was a blank sheet of stationery.

"Thank you," Frank said, a rascal smile on his face. He folded it.

"*Con mucho gusto,* my mom would say. And good luck."

"May I ask you for an envelope?"

Sergio seemed pleasantly surprised. "Sure. Please come with me, sir."

Frank carried his light blue trophy when he returned from the desk. He sat down and furtively took out his wad of twenty-dollar bills. He unobtrusively slipped three of them into the folded sheet that still lay on the table. He paused briefly as an older male guest wearing a red jacket and supported by a cane—and a younger woman—hobbled by and tossed him a smile. Then he inserted the sheet into the Greenbrier jacket and winked at Mary. "I'll catch Sergio later."

They patiently watched the comings and goings and took turns to peek, from a short distance, into the exclusive, stuffy Lobby Bar where a famous chandelier hung. It had been used in the production of the movie Gone with the Wind.

Their stomachs complained on and off, but neither Mary nor Frank could afford to leave their spot for a snack: they assumed prices would be exorbitant anyway, and, worse, they might miss Duncan. Frank insisted that Mary be with him at any time. "I need you with me," he insisted. "I want Duncan to have to look you in the eye. Noredge has suffered too much. *You* have."

Except for a couple of quick trips to bathroom they stuck to Frank's plan. Powerbars and two small bottles of water had to appease their stomachs. No morning golfers had turned up in the Upper Lobby by two o'clock.

Then traffic started picking up. More and more pants sporting all colors of the rainbow made their entry, steps short, speed mature.

Seated at a table about twenty feet away from Sergio, Mary and Frank kept a close eye on him.

"I wonder whether he's had a chance to check the blue envelope in his pocket," Mary murmured.

"It should buy us a little help, maybe a hand up or a quick index in our direction. I would recognize Duncan, but I might miss him in one of the arriving clusters."

"Right. A little," Mary replied, her eyes trained on two jewelry-laden matrons parading by. In no mood for optimism, she resumed their earlier conversation about the situation in Noredge. "The damage has been done, Frank. We may score a little victory, maybe get Mike booted out of town, but Supren will continue. We've got Alpha and Beta. Soon we'll have to welcome Gamma, Delta and so on. Once they reach Omega they'll start all over again with Alpha1, Beta1. We're doomed."

"A mini-Oklahoma in a few years, the whole deal. Earthquakes…."

"What boring names for those wells! Alpha. Beta. No imagination. Is it too much effort for these frackers to spruce things up a little?"

"Yeah. Well, some companies do. Enerplus has a Mars and a Plato, and a Porky Pig! Hell, why not a Pluto or some nice-sounding girl's names?" Frank quipped. "Like Venus—"

"Or Doyle's 'Linda,' the one before Susan," Mary said scornfully. "Or was it *Ga*linda?" she elbowed him.

Frank guffawed. "Yeah?" He raised his hand. "Wait! Galinda? Could it…?" He had his mouth open. "Were Mike and Duncan talking about—?"

"A well? Wow! Google!" Mary grabbed her iPhone.

"Look for Galinda and Viola. Quick!"

"Yes, sir!" She had already started.

He vigorously tapped the table with his pen.

The tapping stopped. He said, his voice hushed, "That's him. Him." He pointed his index, hand resting on stomach. "The yellow pants. Baby shit color." He jumped up. "Stay here. Keep your eyes on me." He exhaled deep. Steps clearly forced, but measured, he headed toward the man in yellow, who now was only twenty feet away from Mary.

Frank greeted him. "Mr. Duncan? Frank Anderson."

For a couple of seconds the man seemed puzzled, checking Frank's plain polo shirt and faded jeans. He frowned. Then he produced a huge smile. "Of course! Our man for Colombia," he said loudly. "How are things in…?"

"Noredge."

"Yes. I'm bad with names."

Frank waved it off. He glanced for a split second at Mary, his eye roll telling her, "He's bad with names. Yeah. We already know that." He turned back to Duncan. "I see. So, you may have forgotten the name of that guy with the Vietnamese wife too."

A young woman walked by, a crying little child on her hip. Onlookers across the room looked on, apparently wondering how much the Greenbrier had lowered its standards.

"What? Vietnamese wife?" Duncan acted puzzled.

"Never mind the name. How much did you pay the guy to run that dirty water tanker off the road in Carrollton?"

The Texan shot Frank an angry stare. "Carrollton? Pay? What is this? Are you nuts? Buzz off! I'll—"

"You may not know that guy's name. But I bet Mike Doyle does," Frank mocked.

Duncan's mouth fell open but he seemed to recover almost immediately. "Doyle? What Doyle? Out of my way," he grumbled angrily, "or—"

"Here!" Mary shouted as she ran to Frank and showed him her iPhone screen. "My apologies, Mr. Duncan. Here it is, Frank! Galinda! Pennsylvania…disaster for the Viola Company…terrible mismanagement with cruel, lasting consequences…the well plugged…Galinda! There's more." She felt like jumping up and down.

Frank looked incredulous. Then jubilant. "Galinda? he said. "You heard that, Mr. Duncan?"

The big Texan turned crimson red. "Get lost!"

Why didn't we think of this earlier? Cloning Galinda. Cloning Galinda. In Noredge. A bad, dirty Galinda in Noredge. Another one. But why? Mary wondered inwardly as she enjoyed seeing Duncan's lips quiver.

Passersby slowed down, intrigued by the commotion. Several seemed to know Duncan and mumbled in low voices.

"Galinda! You want to read it for yourself, Mr. Duncan?" Frank asked scornfully. "Here's a picture."

Mary noticed wide eyes in the circle that had formed around the threesome.

Duncan started moving in the direction of the front desk.

Mary and Frank followed him.

The oil honcho turned around, looking livid. "Get away from me. Bad things can happen to nosey tree-huggers." He lightly touched his hip pocket for a second, his voice low but his eyes speaking volumes.

"Huh? You're threatening me? For asking you a question?" Frank taunted him.

Mary's phone rang. *Joe?* "Hold on, Joe," she said hurriedly. "Wait! Wait!"

Duncan moved closer to Frank and breathed, standing inches away from him, "See this?"

Mary, dumbstruck, saw him point his gun at Frank, his hand at hip height and covering most of the weapon.

Frank shouted, "A gun!"

A guard ran to the scene, weapon drawn. "Hands up!"

Frank raised his hands.

Mary, legs trembling, hurried a few steps away but remained on the phone, concerned and panicky. She kept talking to Joe, her voice hushed, her phone touching her lips, "Okay. I repeat. You okay, kids at school. Correct? What? ...Doyle wanted to kill me? Kill *me*? Correct?" She felt her legs weaken.

Duncan tried to slip his gun into his front pocket but the guard thundered, "Drop it! Hands up!"

The Texan looked destroyed as he dropped his weapon into a fauteuil. He had to have friends in the small crowd that observed the scene.

"Come with me, hands up, both of you," the guard said. He picked up the weapon and motioned Frank and Duncan into a corner close to the desk.

Mary followed within a few feet, shaken and now half-whispering into the phone, "Okay, Joe. You're all safe. Yes...a knife...the police...Principal Summers...I see. I'll call back in a minute. What? Yes, I'm okay... yes, a gun, but okay! Don't worry. Call you soon...a few minutes. No, no. I'll call. Love you. What? You told him what? ...Carrollton and Beta? You did? My God! ...yes, I'm okay. He did what? ...Doyle was forced to...the police heard too? ...Duncan? Viola? Call you back...yes, right away." She cut the call.

"What's going on?" The guard looked very annoyed as he questioned both men. "This is the Greenbrier, you know."

Mary hurried closer and blurted, pointing at her phone and then at Duncan, "He caused two serious environmental disasters for the people in Ohio. In Noredge and in Carrollton."

Frank's head jerked back.

The guard stared at Mary, eyes wide, then a deep frown.

Duncan shouted, "I did not. Not! How could I? Crazy. I never—"

"Mike Doyle did and you paid him!" Mary shouted. She nodded at Frank.

The guard gestured for calm.

Duncan fired back, "Horseshit! You have no proof! Who's that bloody Dole? Never heard of him." His jaw was shaking. His hands came down.

"Doyle," Mary said.

The guard blinked.

Frank smiled. "Never heard of him? I know you took him off the Viola directory, but you were overheard talking to him."

Duncan looked bewildered. "Impossible!"

"By two people in Noredge. About Galinda."

Duncan's eyes froze. He appeared close to slumping down.

The guard pursed his lips.

"That Doyle just confessed you paid him for the dirty job, Mr. Duncan!" Mary interjected. "Mike Doyle. To the police. In Noredge. At my house. My husband confronted him."

"Huh?" Veins in Duncan's temples were ready to burst. "Pure crap!" he yelled.

Mary pushed her phone under Duncan's nose. "See this, sir? My husband just called me. Doyle stormed into my house with a knife. Less than a minute later, the police showed up. They said Doyle had come from the school. Where I work. He'd looked for me there first. The police—"

"The school must have alerted them," Frank interjected, sounding overly enthused.

Mary looked at him askance and nodded, slightly irritated.

The guard frowned and motioned with his hand that Mary should continue.

"The police found my man hands up, a knife at his throat. Mike Doyle's knife."

"He had to have gone berserk." Frank added, studying the guard's face.

"Kind of," Mary went on. "He cried like a baby when he was arrested. My husband screamed at him that he had destroyed downtown Carrollton and fouled the drinking water of Noredge. 'It's not me. I had to do it, had to do it, Viola made me do it! Duncan!' Doyle sobbed."

"Do it? Do what? The knife attack?" The guard sounded incredulous as he addressed Mary.

"No, sir. Creating that mess in Carrollton and the one in Noredge."

"That bitch!" Duncan jumped in, roaring. "She accuses me but has no basis. Just a few idiotic words from this guy Doyle. He's clearly lost it."

"I think it'll be your word against Doyle's in court, Mr. Duncan," Mary opined. "And against his bank accounts." She checked with the guard, feeling she was out of her league.

The man used his hands signaling he wanted calm.

Duncan still fired back. "Those Supren bastards are

pumping oil and gas from under our leases. Illegally. They pay off the local officials. They're scum."

"So, you're saying this is your revenge, right? All that sabotage and the misery you caused is just a little revenge?" Frank mocked. "On the guys who beat you in the Doornaert deal? Or stole a few barrels of oil from you?"

The guard seemed confused.

Duncan screamed, "What? Revenge? *My* revenge? *My* sabotage? Did you hear me say that? I'm saying that Doyle, whoever he is, must be a real creep. That's all I'm saying. A dirty thief stealing Viola gas. And a liar."

"Mr. Duncan," the guard said, "come with me until the police arrive."

He turned to Mary and Frank and put his hand up. "My apologies. Let me assure you this isn't Greenbrier fare." He tilted his head towards Duncan, who was staring at his shoes.

"We appreciate your intervention, sir," Mary said, still shaking.

The guard nodded.

Rocking his head, scowling, Duncan avoided the curious glances of hotel guests as he was led away.

Mary called home. "We're both okay here, Joe! I must have scared you."

"Okay? Whew! Good! Me too! A gun, you said? Duncan? The kids are still in school. Sonya said they weren't told anything about the knife."

But they'll find out in no time. "Oh, thank God. I was so concerned. I hoped—"

"A gun! But you guys made it out of that place in one piece. Two pieces!" He sounded over the moon and triumphant. "I admit I worried a bit about you guys."

More than a bit, she knew. "A gun, but not one shot fired. And we netted the other crook—Doyle's paymaster. Duncan."

"Yeah. So we caught the big fish."

We? "Yep. Right. We. Frank heard you. He's got a big smile."

She switched to conference.

Joe went on, sounding more than ready to report, "The other one, 'big shot Doyle,' I thought he'd shit in his pants like a two-year-old when the two agents stormed in. He fell down in the old chair, on a pile of mail!"

Mary guffawed.

"When the guy was handcuffed I told him a few truths, to his face. The police were all ears. I said he'd arranged my accident and then pulled Vince off the Beta job at Harriet's—"

"So he could do the drilling there himself," Frank added. "And screw up the well. Himself."

"Hi Frank. Yeah, right, himself, while having a fling with busy Vince's wife."

Frank leaned closer to the phone. "And the police, what did they—?"

"They were stunned. I told them that you could give them all the technical stuff."

Mary jumped in. "And that you don't remember that anybody tried to run you off the road in Carrollton."

"I did, Mary. Also that I didn't think Doyle wanted to kill me in that spill. I don't think that was his plan, but what do I know? And I got damn close to meeting my creator. I just said Doyle must have wanted to have that spill. Had planned it."

"Good! And Principal Summers acted very swiftly and smartly. The agents wasted no time either. We owe them a big thanks. Them and Summers." Her thoughts went to her firing. She knew the principal felt badly about it.

"Absolutely. Sonya called me. She sounded worried as hell. She told me that Doyle had stormed into the reception area looking out of it, brandishing a knife and screaming, 'Where's Jenkins, the slut? I got something for the bitch!' They said you weren't in. He bolted without a word. Thomas Summers called the police right away and they knew where to go, in a big hurry."

"I'm sure Frank will call his sister right away and reassure her we're okay, Joe."

"Safe travels."

"See you soon. Love you!"

Chapter 35

"**A**nd now…?" Mary stretched her arms and yawned as she woke up on Wednesday morning, wondering what she had actually accomplished yesterday with Frank at the Greenbrier—*really* accomplished. She turned toward Joe, her eyes questioning him.

"You're asking me? Doyle's toast," he replied, lying next to her, hands under head. He whistled. "From what you and Frank told me I gather things didn't go too well yesterday for that chap from Viola either. All the same, those big shots. Crooks and actors. I guess that's how those shysters elbow their way to the top."

"I'm so glad Doyle didn't hurt you." She caressed his face.

He shrugged. "The creep didn't have a chance. The police were awfully quick, but I would've gotten a hold of his knife anyway."

Mary lay on her side and beamed at her man.

He turned to Mary and put his hand on her hip.

"The loser looked like he was going to faint," Joe went on. "He begged, almost whispering, not to be handcuffed. Whining like an old lady."

"You mean like me?" Mary teased.

Joe smiled. "No way! You're a spring chicken. You don't whine. Not ever. Not that I remember!" He caressed her forehead and moved her brown hair backwards, freeing her cheek for a kiss.

"But now…." Mary sighed. "Nothing's changed. Alpha and Beta are still in full swing, Beta spewing its poison. I must contact Dan about the petition first thing. We have to stop that damn fracking. I'd better get going."

Joe chuckled.

She knew he was admiring his Mary, who had managed to get her way partially—so far, anyway.

When she reached Dan Clark on the line at ten-thirty he sounded exuberant. "Congratulations for yesterday, girl!"

"Oh? Thanks, Dan."

"I heard from Frank. Caught them, eh? One in the Greenbrier and one here. I wonder where Doyle slept last night. Not with any of his mistresses, I bet." He burst out in a fit of laughter.

Mary didn't react. "What a day it was. *Whew!* But we're not done. We do need the petition for the next step. Urgently."

"Yeah. Strike the iron while it's hot. We were basically ready with it a couple of days ago. But the precise science isn't easy, you know. One little goof and we lose credibility. So, we're checking and checking. You guys have been speeding up matters for sure," he joked.

"Kind of. My apologies to Rudy and…?"

"Nick. And a few others."

"Those crazy young guys, Nick and Rudy. I think we should ask them to add to the text the scheme Doyle used to ruin Supren's reputation, mess up their operations. It's called 'friendly competition,' I guess. Or 'sabotage.' Viola must have been furious about the dirty tactics Supren used in the takeover fight of Doornaert."

"Right." Dan chuckled. "And that Duncan. In the slammer too—another lonely mistress somewhere last night, I bet!"

Mary pictured him rubbing his beard. "It's no joke, Dan. He ruined lives and companies and careers."

"Sure. But Supren in Houston doesn't have clean hands either. They've been incredibly negligent. They gave Mike Doyle free rein to do whatever he pleased and let him ride roughshod over those who dared to object. Supren and Viola, they've ruined the entire fracking industry's image in Ohio. Screwed themselves!"

"Huh? Well, yes. Right on. And with our petition we'll give them a hand to fully complete that act," she echoed him jokingly.

"Yes! Our petition. Our contribution. Our kind of Vaseline! Free of charge!" Dan roared.

She chuckled. "You're getting carried away, my friend.

Anyway, I don't think Nick and Rudy will mind too much that we're messing up their labor of love once more with that new input."

"To the contrary. They'll get a kick out of it. Don't worry. I know them." He paused and intoned, "They'll send you their bill."

She liked that humor better. "I get that, Dan. Four hundred dollars an hour as usual. Anyway, if you want real detail on those cementing shenanigans, you should call Frank."

"We'll get it all fixed. Don't worry. How's Joe?"

"Thanks. Joe's great. You heard all about the knife, right?"

"Everybody knows, Mary." He laughed. "Thank God he didn't get hurt, again. By the same creep. Take care. I'll get back to you."

***

At six o'clock on Monday they had gathered on the deck of Dan's place in Hartville: Mary, Joe, Frank, Joanna, Rudy, Nick and grill master Dan with his wife Lydia.

"This isn't exactly an occasion for a party, but one has to eat," Dan commented jovially as he proceeded slowly and with care along the circumference of the circle his guests had formed with their chairs. He dropped hot hamburgers onto the buns lying on their paper plates, whether they had asked for one or not. "From a charcoal grill. We don't have any of that methane gas in the Clark household."

Lydia stood up, pushed her hair back and said, smiling, "Over there, guys. Help yourselves." She pointed at the window ledge, where napkins, pickles, fruit and condiments were waiting to become part of the event. "And there." Canned drinks sat on a table, a few steps away from the circle. She and Dan waved off the rave reviews for their production. "It must be that you guys are really hungry," she quipped.

Silence reigned for a few minutes.

Mary and Joe had arrived a little late. She kept eyeing Rudy. He had a folder lying on the deck, under his metal chair. "So that's it, Rudy? Our not-so-secret weapon?" she asked.

"All of it. Warts and all, but we think it's presentable now." The young man bent down. "Come on, guys," he said, talking to his documents, a slight groan reflecting his physical effort. "You've been patient enough. Show us what you've got." He got up and handed three-page copies to all attendees.

"Do we call this a Sierra document?" Frank asked, racing through the text.

"No. No mention of Sierra, but we got the imprimatur of my boss," Nick responded. "It's a 'People's' message."

"You sound like the Pope, or a Bolshevik, Nick. At least like a Howard Zinn, 'People's message.'" Mary quipped.

She didn't wait for a comeback but started reading right away.

To the attention of Mayor Sanders:

We, the people of Noredge, say "NO" to fracking!

We demand the immediate cessation of all hydraulic fracturing activities on our territory; the plugging of all wells; the revocation of all outstanding permits; and the permanent prohibition of all future permits!

Our petition is based on the grievous suffering of children and adults alike because of the well-documented drinking water fiasco in Noredge and the great damage done to the town of Carrollton, where a disastrous spill of poisonous dirty water from fracking occurred. Both tragic events were caused by the Supren Company.

The aquifer that has provided drinking water to Noredge since the day of its incorporation has been polluted by Supren's Beta well on Maple Road, as our documentation below demonstrates. The Supren spill in Carrollton took place under questionable circumstances, but recent events have demonstrated that the company bears the full responsibility for it.

We are confident that the assertions expressed in the preceding paragraph would readily be confirmed if contested in a court of law.

We call on you, the Noredge authority, to accept the measures proposed in this document!

All in Noredge want clean soil, water and air, and long-term prosperity!

Submitted respectfully: Name:
Address:
Signature:
Date:

Frank looked up and gave Rudy a thumbs-up. "We can go to war with that, buddy."

"How about the notes on the next pages?" Joanna asked, sounding concerned. She pointed at the first lines on her second sheet under the title "Scientific and Economic Justification."

"Don't worry, sweetie. It seems hard to understand for many people, but we need it," Frank said, smiling at his lover.

"It's like the fine print on a sales contract. But the text on the first page is in pretty big font and shows some not too academic-looking exclamation marks. We have both scientific and economics activist language." Dan chuckled.

Mary ran through the two additional pages diagonally: Cornell Impact Study; Impact of Methane on Public Health; Composition of Dirty Water and Secrecy Surrounding it; Ten-year Economic Projections for Noredge; Fracking Legislation; Oklahoma and Pennsylvania Case Studies. Detailed Analysis of the Causes of the Carrollton Incident and the Cementing Issues in Noredge. A plethora of topics and arguments and calculations that would deter, she figured, all but the well-versed lawyer or scientist.

"You don't really have to read all of that," Nick said,

sounding defensive. "We put it in to show we're not—you're not—a bunch of boneheaded screamers and troublemakers."

"Yeah. The first page would do for this bonehead," Lydia commented, raising her hand and winking at Nick.

Mary kept silent.

"Now we have to roll up our sleeves!" Dan exhorted his friends. "I'm ready and I'm even not from Noredge. Knocking on doors, cajoling, arguing! Winks or threats, jokes or tears, whatever it takes!"

"Noredge has fourteen thousand people. Say, twelve thousand adults. How are we going to reach them all?" Frank asked, his eyes running the circle on the deck.

"We can," Mary said. "Let's assume we have four thousand front doors to knock on. We all work our butts off for ten days. Each of us and some more friends, say about ten in total, make thirty house calls per day. In ten days we talk to six-to-eight thousand people. I bet we get four thousand signatures. That should be enough for Mayor Sanders and his city council to—"

"Check his Pamper," Nick said, snickering. He was nibbling at an apple.

"Thanks, Nick," she replied with a smirk. "But we need copies to stuff in mailboxes and to carry with us."

"I'll get us five thousand copies, my treat," Frank volunteered. "I know a guy in Cleveland. We might ask five or six youngsters to stuff a couple of thousand mailboxes at night."

"We can ask the Sentinel," Joanna suggested timidly.

"They're in the pockets of the fracker bunch," Joe said, shrugging. "Sorry, Joanna."

"How about WKSU? They've been bugging me for an interview since Saturday morning," Mary said. "I stalled them so I could have the petition with me. I'll sneak in a plug."

"Or two or three, go for it!" Dan shouted, his fist up again.

"How about this young chap, Jeff Simmons of the Jack Jones show on NBC?" Frank wondered. "That lad has his head screwed on right."

Joanna got involved again, looking keen and excited. "Let's add a couple of lines at the bottom of the first page," she said, her eyes checking with Frank, "to tell the people they can of course run copies or scans and send in their signatures."

Nick dug up his iPhone.

"Of course, Joanna! To our address," Joe said.

Mary dropped her copy. Was this real? Her Joe volunteered that? She stared at him, proud and shaking her head in disbelief. "Of course," she repeated. "Of course! You guys have my phone number too. It's also my fax."

"Got your e-mail address too," Nick said. "How about this little blurb at the bottom of page one? *Feel free to print your own copy or scan and send it with your signature to Mary Jenkins, by mail, fax or email.*" He showed it to Mary on his iPhone.

"Perfect! Thanks."

The others nodded but Dan looked pensive. "Back to Mary's math of a minute ago," he said. "We have six volunteers here, right? But Joe shouldn't—"

"Should!" Joe shouted. "Count me in. Me and my cane!"

"Right. It will speak volumes, Joe," Lydia jubilated.

"So, we need another six volunteers or more, and a bunch of youngsters to roam Noredge streets at night and stuff mailboxes." Dan looked ready. "My heart goes out to the few boxes that might get skipped, feeling left out."

"Yeah, Dan." Lydia rolled her eyes.

Frank stood up and stretched his legs. He gestured at Joanna they should go. "I'll have the copies at your place by tomorrow night, Mary."

She was already writing a list in her head, of additional volunteers—and their kids, for the mailbox stuffing.

Chapter 36

O n Tuesday, Mary was a guest on NBC for about eight minutes, including her introduction by Jack Jones. She immediately felt young Jeff Simmons had her back when he asked her compassionately whether she was okay when she was about to enter the make-up room.

Both Jones and Simmons skated over Joe's pain and the suffering of the general population. They concentrated on the failed Doyle knifing attempt at her residence and the incident at the Greenbrier. *Ratings,* Mary scoffed inwardly.

Six minutes into her time slot, Jeff kindly threw her a softball. "Where will all of this lead us, Miss Jenkins?"

She suppressed her smile and recited Nick's lines at the bottom of page one of the petition, complete with address, phone number and email address, all hers. She added, "If we want to go with this where we should go for the good of all citizens, you've all got to sign our petition! And get your signatures to me today!" Her eyes drilled into the camera. "Sign!"

At that moment, Jack Jones reminded Jeff that they had to go to commercial.

***

"No, Andy. Not this big house."

"But Mommy, my friend Bobby lives here. He told me his father will sign."

"No. Mr. Jackson won't. Bobby doesn't know." Mary didn't want to waste her time. It was around seven p.m. Jay Jackson was a vocal advocate for the fracking wave.

She had to cover at least twenty more houses tonight. This was the second day of the canvassing operation. By now, at least a quarter of the Noredge mailboxes had been honored with a copy of the anti-fracking petition.

Andy had insisted on joining his mother. She had told him that this knocking on doors and pleading, begging for signatures would get boring after twenty minutes and three conversations about dirty water and air. Her warnings were no match for his excitement. So Mary and Andy were one of the nine volunteer teams covering all of Noredge, each in the section that Frank, the master organizer, had allotted to them.

The eastern section of McKinley, Mary's section, was a tough nut to crack. The residences were upscale and the mostly well-to-do residents hadn't really suffered that much from the fracking. The wells and drill sites spewed their gas, dust and noise far west of them, at least for now. Many houses here had private water wells. Of the nine residents she had addressed so far, five had turned her down.

Mary and Andy skipped the Jackson residence.

"Come on, Andy. With the next house we'll do very well." She needed a quick success for the boy to compensate for his disappointment. Mrs. Chambers, three houses down, was a sure bet.

"You're skipping two more houses, Mommy."

"We'll do them later. The next lady's really nice, but she may be leaving soon for a party. I know her well."

Mrs. Chambers was all Mary had expected and more. "I'll go and visit neighbors who might not be at home tonight. And I commend you, Mary, for your courage and commitment."

Andy listened in but Mary wasn't sure he understood all those beautiful words.

As they walked back to the second skipped house, the first past the Jacksons, her mind wandered. She pictured Joe getting out of the car and making his way up the steps to knock on various doors. She was sure he'd speak convincingly. *But he'll do five to ten houses, and his weak ankle will catch up with him.* He might persevere a little longer physically though; she knew him. He would, however, have a hard time with the disappointment of cold refusals like "we don't do politics" or footsteps inside after he rang a bell and the door stayed closed. Or a slight lifting of a curtain as he approached a house. Trying more productive back entrances was a step too far for him in his condition, as it was as for Mary, who feared dogs.

Her heart melted as she thought of Joe volunteering their personal email, snail mail, and phone for the very visible, public responsibility of receiving and counting signatures. And checking for potentially embarrassing duplicates. Her eyes had to have told him she wanted it that way. She knew that was the reason why he had answered for her at Dan's, exposing himself to vitriol and worse from Supren and many of the city elders. He had decided to be with her on this, all the way.

She felt grateful to Frank. She said thanks within to the many who also, at this very moment, were fighting for the petition: three young people from the Sierra Club, Dan and Lydia, Joanna, Jill Smith from Canton and three of her colleagues at the hospital, one from Medina and two from Hartville.

When the Andy-Mary team arrived home at nine, past the kids' bedtime, Joe wasn't back yet. Jimmy was watching cartoons with the sitter and Jake.

Mary called Joe.

"Hold on…just a second, Mary…. Okay, back. Just got number forty to sign up. Didn't want to go home with less. I'll be there soon."

"Forty? How's your foot?"

"My foot? My cane's getting tired! See you in ten minutes."

Sunday was a day off for the canvassers. "We'd rub a lot

of people the wrong way knocking on doors," Frank had suggested. It had to be a day for church, family and rest.

Mary and Joe didn't keep just a running tally of the signatures. During morning hours Joe copied on the Jenkins laptop each and every name and address connected with arriving signatures and at noon he backed up the list on a flash drive. Faxes and emails kept pouring in. "We may have to raise money for ink and paper and who knows what? Our printer may call it quits. Will we need a TV ad?" he had asked Mary. She had sighed, thinking of her dreadful checkbook situation.

When by noon they had finished their phone updates with their comrades-in-arms and completed the count of signatures that had arrived by mail, fax or email, they were disappointed.

"1451." Mary sighed. "Our second week will have to be better, Joe."

"A good bunch may still be sitting in the snail mail pipeline."

She looked at him askance.

He scratched his head.

They calculated they might end up with a total of four thousand at best by the end of the second week. Not a great number compared to the adult population. Mayor Sanders might laugh them out of his office.

"We'll just have to work harder and longer hours, Joe," Mary said.

He tapped his chest with his index. "Me, I'll start at

nine. *Nine to nine,*" he sang to the tune of Dolly Parton's "Nine to Five."

That afternoon Joe drove the kids to a birthday party.

When he returned and opened the front door, Ravel's Bolero pumped through the living room.

Mary called him from afar. "Welcome back, Joe. Lock the door. We must celebrate." By now he had to have detected her perfume, and when he strode into the bedroom and pulled her against him, she wasn't surprised that he was already erect.

Foreplay had no chance. His explosion of love and desire couldn't wait. The untouched glasses of wine Mary had poured waited patiently on the side chest, seemingly full of empathy and understanding as the lovers caressed and relaxed.

"'Celebrate,' you said, Mary. Celebrate what? Our fantastic 1451?" he asked as his fingertips grazed her right breast.

Between soft groans she whispered, "Your liberation, Joe. You threw off the yoke of Supren, of the fracking gang, and set yourself free. It's worth more to me than anything else."

"Free of my job too, of course." He sighed. "Doyle didn't fire me...but *someone* did."

"Me?" She felt pangs of guilt.

He laughed. "You? No. Me. Joe Bertolo." He caressed her cheek. "I'll manage, don't worry."

"Yes. We'll manage. Lie a little closer."

***

By late Saturday evening of the next week the final signature count had rounded the cape of thirty-six hundred: a disappointing figure.

"Some people will never stick their neck out, Joe. They're sheep being led to slaughter without giving a peep," Mary lamented as she walked into the kitchen, where Joe was doing his counting. She yawned.

Joe stood up. He pursed his lips but put his hand on Mary's waist and massaged it softly. "We'd better hurry with this thing, sweetie. Our water isn't getting any better. I don't care what the mayor says or promises."

Clean water tankers were still diligently making four rounds a week, covering all sections of the city, delivering their precious cargo into all kinds of containers. Citizens also could pick up five gallons a week per person at four stations set up on the main streets. But Mary had heard Supren was considering cutting back on the funding.

"Our 'dear' mayor." Mary's eyes stared at Joe from under a deep frown.

"You think he'll resist? Three thousand plus isn't something to sneeze at. He has to think about his reelection next year."

"Will he run again?"

"Do your eyes tell me you think no?" He seemed puzzled.

She had to admit to herself that she hadn't heard any rumor that Sanders wouldn't run, but she showed Joe open palms and big eyes. She reached for the Jim Beam cabinet, looking back at him, and poured two drinks. "It's late," she said. "Let's relax now. I'm going to take two good showers."

"Huh?"

She offered Joe his drink and lifted her own glass. "This is my first one. The inside."

"Cheers. I'll join you." He winked. "For both showers."

On Sunday morning Mary contacted Frank at ten o'clock. "Good morning. Sorry to rip you out of Joanna's arms so early, but Joe and I think we should make our move ASAP with the mayor."

"Huh? With our current number of signatures?" Frank didn't sound too enthused. Was he afraid they would look like fools? Losers? Or did she interrupt something important this morning?

She forged ahead. "It's up to thirty-six hundred now. We may get another hundred tomorrow. People are suffering and wondering. I think our result of just two weeks of canvassing will come as quite a shock to the poor man. Should we try for Tuesday noon? People will be out to lunch, so we might get a bit of a crowd in front of city hall when we march in."

"Hmm."

She heard him mumble, presumably to Joanna.

He coughed. "The old man must have his feelers out," he said, his voice still a bit hoarse. "He'll already know our results more or less. He may refuse to see you. Us. May try to run out the clock while he consults with a bunch of lawyers."

"He can't possibly think thirty-six hundred is peanuts."

"Who knows? He can think anything he wants. He may say they're not officially certified or something. I have no idea. I'm no politician."

"Me neither, but I bet you he'll cave." She caught Joe's thumbs-up and smiled.

"Cave?"

Frank's short, somewhat curt answers now had convinced her Joanna wasn't pleased with the early Sunday morning call. She felt an internal giggle. "He will. First thing tomorrow morning I'll ask him for an appointment for Tuesday noon and tell him what it's about, as if he doesn't know."

"I wish I could be as—"

"As naïve as me? We must show confidence, Frank."

"Okay...."

At nine o'clock on Monday Mary called City Hall and asked for the mayor. He wasn't in yet, but Mrs. Cole, his assistant, was kind enough to relay a message. "Can I tell him what it's about?"

"Guess," Mary said. She knew Mrs. Cole well.

"Oh. I should know, of course. We all know, right?"

"Could we make it tomorrow at twelve?"

"Twelve.... Call you back, Mary."

Twenty minutes later the mayor's response came, through Julie Cole. "He'll be glad to meet with you and your friends at noon tomorrow. For *thirty* minutes," she said matter-of-factly.

Mary smiled. She knew what Julie thought. "I appreciate the mayor's time and attention. Thanks for the appointment at such short notice," she said courteously.

"Our pleasure. See you tomorrow."

Joe had listened in. "That was easy. He must think our figures are ridiculously low. Easy to laugh off. But I bet he's wrong and risking his job." His pointed index showed his conviction.

"Or he's not running," Mary shot back, a bit nervous. "Let's start packing for tomorrow's show. And I must alert Frank."

They managed to squeeze the bundles of petitions into three old cardboard boxes. Mary tried to lift one. "Piece of cake," she said and puffed.

When they gathered on the steps of City Hall minutes before noon on Tuesday, a crowd of onlookers and sympathizers had formed. The trio had spread the news here and there. A slight drizzle tried to temper their enthusiasm, but they marched up the steps undeterred, to a cacophony of applause, cheers, hoots and whistles. Harriet watched the scene in silence. Mary felt a touch of compassion for her but it faded fast. She had to concentrate on Joe. He had insisted on carrying one of the boxes. Frank followed them, with two boxes, silent and looking lost in thought. *Maybe he thinks it's all futile. Anyway, he wants to be a good sport.*

Julie Cole opened the front door before they could ring the bell. Mary checked her hair in the glass cover of a hallway photograph showing a younger, smiling Dick Cheney cutting a ribbon. She smoothed her blouse and took a deep breath.

The mayor's door was open. He was standing in front of his huge desk when they entered. The short, paunchy man checked his watch.

Telling us he's hungry. Mary chuckled inside.

"Come in. You can drop those boxes in that corner," he said curtly, pointing, "and take a seat."

"Thank you." Mary said.

His sturdy table was round, made of chestnut wood that didn't have one visible scratch. The chairs were heavy, hard to move, but felt comfortable once she was seated. She looked at a picture behind the desk of a fly-fishing Sanders. She said, "Looks like—"

"Wyoming," he said, smiling. "The good old days." He groaned as he lowered his wide frame into a chair. "You guys must've been working overtime."

He sounds jovial. It must be Wyoming, Mary thought, surprised. *Or is it our low count? He must have heard.* She lifted her hand, her eyes asking Sanders, "May I?"

He nodded and let a sigh.

She coughed lightly. "I think you agree we have no time to lose to solve our water problem, Mr. Mayor."

He slowly closed and reopened his eyes, a long, calm blink. "I agree. We're dealing with it with appropriate haste. I'm convinced that we'll be able to maintain an adequate drinking water supply, a major effort, until the engineers come up with a permanent solution. Soon, I think." It sounded like a line he had used a hundred times—delivered with confidence bordering on arrogance.

"Meanwhile we should stop making matters worse," Frank responded. "More methane creeps into our aquifer every second."

"More than just methane," Mary added. Her eyes checked with Frank. His nod was close to unnoticeable.

Nobody reacted. She felt she had the floor, and indeed no time to lose, so she cut straight to the chase. "Mr. Mayor, I assume you've read our petition?"

"A few times." His tone was flat. He started tapping the table, his eyes daring her.

She leaned her head toward the boxes. "Joe and Frank have carried in more than thirty-six hundred signatures from well-meaning concerned citizens."

"Thirty-six hundred? Hmm. Not even half the population."

"No, sir."

"Uncertified, right?"

Baiting me. She knew she had to keep her indignation in check. "Uh. Of course. We don't claim they're 'certified', but we've counted meticulously and honestly, my husband and I. We've discarded duplicates and obvious fakes. Feel free to contact any of the signees to verify. We're decent, honest people."

He waved his hand. "Thirty-six hundred means nothing, anyway. Certified or not. Our population is over fourteen thousand."

She wanted to respond, "Including at least two thousand children. We have signatures from more than half of the households," but she bit her tongue. She said, "We know that many more—"

"I can tell you firsthand, right now, Mr. Mayor," Joe jumped in, raising his voice, "that you have many more Noredge citizens, thousands, who keep silent but feel exactly the same as the three of us here." He looked at Mary and Frank. "But many of them are afraid to speak up."

"Afraid of whom? Me?" The mayor's exaggerated laugh betrayed his anger.

Joe evinced a look of concern and lowered his voice. "I wouldn't put it that way, Mayor Sanders, but every citizen knows by now the power Supren has here over...over everybody. My wife lost her job because she—"

"That was a school board decision," Sanders snapped.

"Was it?" Mary's tone was scorn-laden.

The mayor's face had turned red and his forehead started showing pearls of perspiration. "It was. Keep your insinuations to yourself."

She took another deep breath and asked, "Will you accept the terms of our petition?" She paused and waited for an answer or a nod—anything.

The mayor didn't react.

"If not," she went on, "somebody may have to run against you next year to force—"

"I'd welcome competition," Sanders nickered. "I'll beat them to a pulp, as I've done for more than a decade. And your petition? It's unpatriotic, unworthy of serious discussion."

"Unworthy? Have you read pages two and three?" Frank asked. He suddenly seemed to turn combative, and winked furtively at Mary.

She was convinced that the text floated a few levels above the mayor's pay grade.

"I haven't," he said dismissively, waving his hand, "but my technical guy tells me it's a bunch of misleading, tendentious gobbledygook." He looked at his watch. "To answer your initial question," he turned to Mary, "number one, no, I personally don't accept your proposals. And I suggest you don't try to scare me with empty political threats. Won't work."

"I don't have the slightest intention to threaten anybody, Mr. Mayor."

He ignored her. "Second, you guys should know that this kind of decision has to be taken up by the city council. Third, let me advise you that the petition's chances in the council are nil: too much is at stake for the community. We're losing jobs to China; our tire businesses are going down the drain; we're getting whacked by cheap imports; and the US is being milked dry by Saudi sheiks. Maybe that should be page four of your petition." He sat back, his eyes drilled into Mary's.

Frank said, "We understand the procedure you have to follow. How soon can the council meet?"

"Governor Kasich may want to get his two cents in too, so it may take some time. Mrs. Cole will let you guys know the decision and I'll confirm it in writing. Don't get your hopes up too high." At once he stood up. "Thanks for coming."

The trio looked at each other as they proceeded to the exit of the building. The mayor's attitude had apparently drawn Frank out of his earlier defeatism. He kept shaking his head. "This can't be the end of the story. Too much is at stake. What the hell can we do? What more?"

"Go to court. Sue Supren for negligence. Barricade the access to their wells." Joe sounded ready for action.

"Kidnap...whom could we kidnap?" Frank asked, his tone quipping but his facial expression showing desperation.

Mary had kept quiet. She understood Frank needed a dose of black humor to quash his disgust. "Okay. Okay. Are you guys done? How about something serious: I'm not done. With Sanders."

"Yeah. We can always blackmail him. With one of those—"

"Stop joking, Joe. I can do better than that." She was determined. "I'm going back in there. You stay here. Mister Mayor's lunch can wait."

Frank wrinkled a brow. "Why go back? Are you going to be long? Joanna's waiting."

"Long enough to spoil his appetite. He'll listen, dammit. Til I'm done with him." She was already on her way.

Joe looked incredulous.

"I'll show you. Just wait," she shouted.

She strode by Julie's desk, which was vacant, headed straight for Sanders's office and barged in unannounced.

He almost dropped his sandwich, his expression one of bafflement, which quickly changed to one of irritation. "Two more minutes," she said, nervous, her throat dry, index and middle finger trembling in the air. She swallowed and steadied herself. She felt his eyes diagnosing her as he offered himself another bite of his sandwich.

His look became one of amusement while he took his time to clear his mouth. An eternity. Then he asked, chuckling, "Got more signatures? Take a seat."

"Thanks. I'm running against you next year." She had blurted it out before she was in her chair.

He sat back and produced a big smile. "Great! Be my guest, honey. Friendly competition."

"I'll beat the shit out of you."

He frowned, a condescending smirk on his face. "Oh. Not that friendly."

"Stop joking. I've got a mailing list of over three thousand, you know. All keen, informed voters. And Joe's silent legion may be a lot bigger."

"So that's why—"

"Why I launched the petition? So I could run for your office? No. But now the game's changed. You refuse to listen to your citizens. I have to kick you out. And I will. And then I'll implement the petition. Me."

He leaned forward and lowered his voice. "Calm down, Mary. Calm down, girl. First of all, the council hasn't decided anything. Hasn't even discussed your document."

"I have no illusions. You more than hinted how the vote would go."

In a split second his face had turned livid. "What? Don't you twist my words. You're being unfair." He stood up and gestured she should leave. "I don't take rudeness very well."

She got up too and moved close to him.

She felt his heavy breathing and smelled his perspiration, but didn't let it bother her. She was going to get out the big guns. "I will go, but just one more thing. I demand that the city sue Supren. For mismanagement. For neglect. For disregard for the community. It's your duty."

"The council—"

"Forget your bloody council. Supren will sue Viola in any case. That's obvious, right?"

He looked taken aback for a moment. Then he said, "Obvious? Well, they have the right, of course."

"Viola will countersue. They've been seriously screwed over in the takeover battle of Doornaert."

He leaned his head. "You know?"

"We'll find out, won't we?"

"Huh?" He smiled.

"I bet we'll have a couple of very interesting lawsuits, or more than two. They'll open city and company books, Supren's, Viola's and Doornaert's; interview corporate, city and county personnel, even corporate lawyers; look for bribery, permit shenanigans and tax evasion; scrutinize private bank accounts and international transactions...." She ran out of breath.

He shrugged. "You don't know a damn thing about such—"

"I bet some Supren top executives will be more than happy to cooperate with the authorities," she went on. "They'll talk about bribes left and right, improprieties to save their necks when the Doornaert take-over story gets unraveled and they have their backs against the wall."

He frowned and nodded slowly, a patronizing smile over his face. "Let them, Miss Jenkins. You don't know what you're talking about," he said. "I suggest you get out of here."

Mary tried once more. "I do know what I'm saying about that takeover: Frank Anderson has contacts at Viola."

"Good for him. I asked you to leave."

"I will."

As he sank back into his chair she heard him murmur dismissively, "In over her head."

She summarized her mayoral lunch spoiler as she walked to the exit with Frank and Joe. "I tried to scare him, but he waved me off," she concluded. "I don't think he's feeling very well though."

At four that afternoon Mary received a call from Julie Cole at home. "I have a personal message from Mr. Sanders for you, Mary. He had to go home early today. He wanted me to tell you that he'll be glad to insist with the members of the city council that they approve the petition you have submitted. He'll be in touch with you soon."

Mary resisted her impulse to shout. "That's great, Julie," she said politely. "Thank you. I sensed all along he would—"

"Mr. Sanders cares deeply about the citizens of Noredge. Talk to you later. Congratulations."

Mary ran to Joe, out in the yard. "He accepts!" she screamed, hands up.

"Sanders?"

"Yes!!"

"Yep. He's smarter than I thought. Call Frank, and Dan. And…everybody."

She fell into Joe's arms.

He picked her up and swung her around.

"Slow! Your foot, Joe!"

Andy and Jimmy punched their fists in the air.

Chapter 37

That night Mary and Joe made love as if there would be no tomorrow. And if they were wrong about that, they didn't care anyway.

Later, as they lay exhausted, their blood still pumping, Mary ran her fingernails over Joe's chest. "It's almost heaven, Joe."

"If there is one, sweetie, this must be damn close."

"Yes...." She sighed.

"Yes but...? I heard you. You know, those bastards who fired you...I think they might change their tune. Get you back to the school. Can Miss Mayor be a teacher too?" He pulled her onto him.

She felt his warmth, giggled and tucked her head into his elbow.

He rocked her lightly. "Can she?"

"I have no idea. But you're skipping a few steps on that ladder to heaven." She turned onto her side. "And I'm not so sure Sanders had a *real* change of heart—"

"Oh yes. I'm sure he did, for now," he joked. "That

weathervane flipped over at the speed of lightning. But a little too rapidly for my taste. Apostle Sanders on the road to Damascus…. How long before he makes a pit stop and pulls another one-eighty? And he still could come up with the excuse that he can't get the votes at the council."

"He won't do that. I bet he'll fight his members tooth and nail not to let that happen: miraculously converted tree-hugger Sanders must have their consent because he plans to grab his opponent's trump card out of her hands. 'Bye bye Mayor Jenkins,' he must figure."

"Okay. I see. Okay. No one-eighty now. But how about after the election, if he wins?"

"I'll win. I have to and I will: I have another ace tucked away in my pocket."

Joe smiled. "Yep. Calling him a crook. Should be easy."

Cutting right to the chase, my Joe. "No. No name calling—"

The bedroom door squeaked. A little boy entered, a couple of steps.

"Jimmy?" Mary grabbed the bed sheet and pulled it halfway over her upper body.

"Mommy, I forgot to do my homework. Are you cold?"

"Oh," she said softly, suppressing a chuckle and covering Joe with the sheet as well. "No. Not cold. You can do it tomorrow morning. I'll wake you up twenty minutes early."

"Ten minutes, Mommy? It won't take long."

"Ten. Okay, go to sleep now."

Jimmy left and closed the door.

Mary tossed a smile at Joe, jumped up, ran to the

door, locked it and gamboled back to bed, back into his muscular embrace.

He looked at her, amused. "Locked it well? Andy may have homework too," he teased.

She frowned, her eyes twinkling. "Back to Sanders. No name-calling, I said. No name-calling, but I'm sure Sanders must fear I might. I didn't flat out accuse him of selling out to frackers. But I used not-so-subtle provocation: the Doornaert deal, all those Supren and Viola lawsuits on their way. I bet he was shaking in his loafers when I threw that at him. He bent but he didn't break—didn't explode in anger."

Joe showed a big smile, nickering. "The shyster didn't take the bait, eh? But his ears must have been burning. Bribery. Kickbacks. Permitting shenanigans."

She shook her head, chewing her bottom lip. "He even managed a couple of condescending smiles. He had a hell of a time trying to maintain a façade of courtesy, but it held." Her eyes lighted up. "No explosion, Joe. No violent anger. Know what that means? Don't you think that any honorable person confronted with my kind of insinuations would go ballistic?"

"So you're saying he had to be playing dumb. Dumb but smart. Pretending he didn't get the message. But guilty as hell."

"And even hoping against the odds that credulous Mary might believe his hands were clean. Or trusting that shy Mary would be too timid to ever call him out."

He squeezed her waist. "Or that 'Lady' Jenkins is not so naïve or shy but will refuse to play the dirty card."

"That could be. I will."

"Huh? Refuse? Then you don't have an ace." Joe sounded a bit irritated.

"No, not that kind. I don't want to stoop that low to win. I won't have to." She shivered and curled up close to him. "I'll have to play it cleverly. Not act cheap. I'll have a plan. Noredge's people are smart enough to read between the lines."

He slowly rocked his head. "Hope so."

"Noredge will surprise you, my dear Joe. And so will I. Watch me, your future Mayor. Want to bet?" She rubbed his stubble.

"No. I want to cuddle."

***

Mid-December the Noredge City Council agreed six to three on a city-wide fracking ban. Mayor Sanders, who had argued and voted for it, called an immediate halt to Supren operations at the Rutgers and Maple Road sites, and declared no new fracking permits would be considered.

"Good," Joe commented. "But I wonder about mid-May. After the election."

"Which I will win. No need to sigh," Mary retorted.

The city erupted into jubilation and celebration. Mary basked in the glory. But water distribution had to continue, even as Supren was closing down its sites.

"Mayor Sanders will have to keep after them Texans or...." The threat was heard at grocery stores and bars all over Noredge.

Mary would nod and complete the sentence in her mind. Rumors about her challenging the mayor swirled. She kept mum but was already planning her course, sometimes under the puzzled stares of Joe. Reading up on environment and energy and climate change; making phone calls to organizations she found on the web; contacting clean energy advocates. People stopped by at home to offer donations. A Californian group offered help in vague terms, adding that cleaner forms of energy "existed."

She let it be known to friends and neighbors that she was available for tutoring at her home. Joe's workers' comp amount wasn't nearly enough to tide her family over "until better times will be upon us," as she would say with a sigh. And it could be cut to zero any day now.

By mid-January Supren had plugged the Rutgers and Maple Road wells with loads of extremely expensive cement.

"No more methane fouling our water," Mary stated proudly.

"Not in the next twenty years," Frank corrected her, sitting across from her at the kitchen table. "Then?" He rolled his eyes. "Cement doesn't last forever, you know."

"Right, stranger," Mary said. "Then what? Not your

problem. By then you'll have long run off to California with Joanna, I guess?"

Frank smiled. He had just returned from a ten-day trip all by himself to the state. "Twenty years. At that point the city will have to tell Supren to re-plug, whatever the cost."

"Oh yes," Joe quipped. "Re-plug as ordered by Mayor Jenkins."

"Who'll have retired by then!"

"Yes, Mary. Well, me too. I'll be playing soccer with the grandchildren." Joe put his hand on her shoulder and winked at Frank.

***

"Harriet seems to avoid us," Joe observed one evening. "An hour ago I saw her walking in her yard, staring at the ground, shivering in the cold."

"Let her. She's got her signing fee anyway," Mary grumbled. "It should compensate royally for her messed up yard, and buy her a warm overcoat."

"But you've killed her royalties—not that I mind."

"And hopefully saved her and our drinking water. Okay?" The phone rang. Mary took the call. From Chuck Dombroski, so the screen said.

"Am I talking to the lucky girl who married Joe Bertolo?" the caller asked without introduction. "Well, um...yes...."

"I'm an old buddy of his. From college. Chuck."

"Okay. I'm Mary. Hold on. Honey! Chuck Dombroski for you!"

Joe jumped up from the couch with surprising ease. "Dombroski? I'll be damned."

She handed him the phone.

"Chuck! I thought you'd fallen off the earth, man. All good? What's up?" Joe sounded thrilled and showed Mary a "great guy" thumbs-up.

Chuck laughed. "If your lady looks as great as she sounds I'll have to meet her someday!"

Joe's sheepish grin told Mary this was Chuck language.

"I can hear you loud and clear, Chuck. Please go on! I want more," she joked.

"Good. We should get together. Look, I heard about this Carrollton disaster and discovered last week that Joe was the driver. I should've called right away, but I guess better late than never. How's my college buddy?"

"You mean the one that dropped out after six months? Just fine. Thanks. Recovering well but up to my neck in this fracking shit like everyone here. A real mess."

"I know. Working yet?"

"No. Workers' comp for now...until the commission cuts me off."

"Yeah...."

"And my wife lost her teaching job trying to be a good citizen."

"All because of Supren, Chuck," Mary explained, half-shouting.

"Heard that too. Sorry about your bad luck. So you're done with Supren, Joe?"

"I won't touch bloody Supren with a ten-foot pole, buddy."

Chuck chortled. "Of course not. Sue the bastards. You'll make a fortune."

"A good friend told us the same," Mary jumped in again. "Maybe—"

"Sue them, I say. I have a lawyer. Meanwhile, you may know that about ten years ago I went into business for myself. I own four nurseries, all in Ohio, one close to Canton. East Canton."

Joe's eyes lighted up. "Oh? I had no idea. Pretty close to our neck of the woods."

"Yep. And I could use some help there. My Canton manager will retire in July and I'm looking for a reliable guy. One I can trust with money and who can deal with people, treat customers fairly with respect, coach young workers out of high school and so on. Mature. I thought that sounded like you."

"Do you know that Joe coached high school football for years, Chuck?" Mary asked.

Joe gave her an "of course he does" frown.

"Do I know!" Chuck roared. "Let's be clear, the job won't make you guys rich. I'm sure I can't match those ridiculous Supren wages. But we could talk about that. Find a way, if you like."

Joe kept rocking his head and staring at Mary. "Well, I know how to grow tomatoes, potatoes and corn and—"

"Sunflowers and roses and pumpkins," Mary added.

Chuck snickered. "You'll learn, and I've got a couple of specialists who travel to my locations. What I need is a steady hand. I could come over and have a drink or two, talk about the old days. I live in Bath."

"Yes. Good. Mary and me want to hear more about your lawyer, too."

A week later Joe worked his first day at "Dombroski's" in East Canton.

By the end of March the level of methane in Noredge's water had dropped to acceptable levels, but most citizens continued drinking bottled water and all insisted on continued free distribution. The mayor complied, no questions asked. "Of course," Mary mocked.

"Just squeeze that Sanders lemon and the juice will flow. Til election day," Joe quipped. "By the way, where the hell are Frank and Joanna? Haven't seen them in ages."

Mary nodded knowingly. "Our friend must be exploring new horizons. I think he's had it with fracking. He's hinted he might take some courses. He can afford coasting for a while. Sonya told me Supren paid his severance a couple of weeks ago."

"I bet he had built himself a good nest egg already. Quietly. That severance may be just gravy. My old boss Jeffrey told me the smart bachelor amassed a fortune in the Dakotas working crazy schedules for two or three years in the Bakken fields and having nothing to spend his dough on."

"He may. Whatever. Good for him. He never bragged

about it." She sometimes wondered why Frank didn't buy himself some fancy Mercedes or BMW.

***

Sanders started his reelection campaign with an article in the Sentinel and a city-wide mailing of a reprint, including a photo that had to be at least ten years old. He listed his accomplishments over the last four years and offered apologies for the drinking water issue.

"We have confronted the problem head-on, restored the quality of our water and are taking measures to recover damages from Supren, a company that, despite iron-clad assurances of safe operations and strong employment growth, has let down the good citizens of Noredge. In a further step prudent management of the city's finances will enable us to lower real estate taxes...more money in citizens' pockets...compensating as best we can for the suffering...a better place to live...." The text climaxed with a promise screaming loudly, "Not one of our children will have to drink polluted water in Noredge! Not one! Not as long as Mayor Sanders runs the city!"

"He should've used more exclamation marks," Mary noted dryly as she handed the paper to Joe.

She kept to her busy schedule of quiet preparation. Under the radar. Soon she filed the papers required to make her candidacy official. She, and Joe time permitting, started separate daily canvassing efforts once more, knocking on every door listed on their petition lists.

Two weeks later a Sanders flyer made the rounds ridiculing Mary, his only challenger so far, as a dreaming tree-hugger with no consideration for the economic wellbeing of Noredge. "Sickly emotional about her land which she inherited." Sanders proudly stated he had risen from nowhere through hard work and built up his life and business from scratch. Then he had started serving the community as mayor, living in a modest house on small acreage. Acquired acreage. "What's her merit?" the flyer asked. "Having chosen the right parents? So she could afford to forgo leasing fees and royalties while blaming neighbors with more limited resources?"

Joe would react angrily to such language, but Mary remained calm. She refused to repeat publicly the biting words she had spoken to Sanders in her private meeting with him the day she dropped off the petition. "We'll never be able to match the upcoming attacks the Chamber will be happy to finance for Sanders in print or on radio and TV," she said to Joe, without complaint.

The assaults on Mary intensified. She was "a fired teacher. A failed teacher. A neophyte at running anything, let alone a city, who would drive Noredge off a cliff. A Sierra Club stooge. With two small kids to keep her plenty busy."

She didn't lose her cool. Her own personal calls on voters, in their houses, and Joe's frequent reports raised her level of confidence. "The wind's blowing in the right direction, Mary," he would say as he plopped down after another round of visits. The man combined his five or six days a week at Dombroski's with knocking on doors during weekends and evening hours.

Frank, back in town, assisted under the radar. Mary knew he was also contacting energy companies and environmental organizations. He seemed to have discovered his real calling, this petroleum engineer. "Branching out in new directions," he said when Mary asked him for the umpteenth time what he was up to. Lately he had delivered those words with a tinge of mystery in his tone.

Mary showed him an inquisitive frown. "I know you're keeping a secret from me, Frank. You don't trust me," she teased him.

"Yeah." He smiled. "It's about time I tell you. I'm going into solar. Panels."

"Huh? In California."

His eyes sparkled. "In Noredge."

"What?"

"Putting money in a partnership. To help Noredge. I believe in it. Get the city back to work. Jobs, Mary!"

Neighbor Jack Wiltse's angry face appeared on her mental screen. He had blamed her yesterday for the loss of his job at Supren.

"Wow! Frank!" she exclaimed. "Oh my God I knew it. I *knew* it. I told Joe you were going to end up with something like that. 'In California,' I said. But here! In Noredge! Partnership with whom?"

"I can't divulge his name yet."

"Tell your partner I want to join."

"Huh?" Frank cocked his head, his eyes questioning. "Just like that? With somebody you don't know anything about?"

Mary knew she had sounded a little wild and naïve. "I do know you. I trust you're dealing with an honorable person. I'll join. I'd be a very small partner."

"You mean it?" He lowered his head and stared intensely down at her.

She nodded firmly. "Sure I do. Don't you think I can help? I love solar. I'll take a loan. I have collateral. Land."

He looked at her askance. "Will Joe—?"

She shrugged. "It's my land. And he'll love to help. We've talked about such things."

Frank nodded but looked unconvinced. "You did?"

"I told you I knew what you were up to. Kind of knew anyway. Joe will be with us. He expects a legal settlement from Supren—without a lawsuit. Could be a good sum. Really good."

He looked perplexed. "Wow! A settlement…."

"Dombroski's lawyer helped us."

"Good for you guys! Okay. Well, I'll talk to my partner."

"Put a good word in for us, will you?"

"Should I?" He showed her a serious face but then burst out laughing.

Mary started plotting.

***

Late April, less than two weeks before the election, the rumor mill said that Sanders was in trouble. "She's going to kick his ass!"

A nervous-sounding Sentinel executive, Mr. Gray, called Mary right after breakfast a week before Election Day. "For the benefit of the city we would like to organize a debate between you and Mr. Sanders. He has gracefully accepted."

Bullshit. He must have begged them. I don't need this. She and Joe already had spoken to at least thirty percent of the voters. And Frank now had joined the effort. "Maybe I should gracefully decline, Mr. Gray," she answered, smiling at Joe and mouthing to him, "Debate."

"You think so? May I ask you why?"

She detected a tad of reproach in the caller's tone. "You sure can. You might have noticed that our dear mayor has been spreading garbage about me. Loads of it. I haven't responded. But if I'm on the stage with him, I'll have to react, and I don't want to get into the gutter. I like things civil."

"We want civility, too. Our moderator would control the tone of the exchanges, Miss Jenkins. We intend to focus on the plans both candidates have for the city. Well informed citizens—"

"Promise me you will tell Mr. Sanders that I'll walk out the moment he starts talking trash."

"As I said—"

"Yes or no, sir. I have no time to waste. Send me an email to confirm. Thanks." She cut the call.

Joe gave her a thumbs-up.

"Piece of cake." She winked.

"Did he say yes?"

"I don't know. His problem."

Friday night, four days before the election, the Odeon movie theater on Main Street was packed twenty minutes before debate time.

Two minutes before eight Stan Perkins appeared onstage. He was the sedate, grandfatherly moderator from the Sentinel Mary and the mayor had agreed upon. The two candidates accompanied him. Mary pointed and waved at Joanna, Frank and Joe, who were seated side by side in the front row. Joe raised his fist.

The debaters took their seats.

Lively discussions within the crowd faded as Stan raised his hand. He introduced incumbent and challenger and invited them to state their qualifications and goals, time limit two minutes.

Sanders read from a sheet a basic summary of his first announcement in the Sentinel. He received polite applause. Mary thought he sounded angry and entitled. She detected some nerves as well.

She spoke about the need for long term prosperity in harmony with a healthy environment. "No contradictions there if we're smart enough to bank on the constant progress technology makes every day." She got the same plain audience reaction as Sanders, but hers was followed by waves of murmured comments, questioning frowns and whispers. *Okay. Got them wondering.*

A courteous back-and-forth developed between the contestants, on budgets, regulations, garbage pick-up, school hours, law enforcement and more. Sanders's experience gave him the upper hand, but he kept mum about drinking water.

About half an hour into the debate, Mary made an abrupt turn. She pointed at Frank. "Mr. Anderson, sitting right there in the first row, former Doornaert employee and technical whizz, has proposed to me that Noredge pursue an interesting tentative proposal from a solar manufacturer to set up shop in our city."

Sanders's head jerked up. He stared at moderator Perkins, who opened his palms and looked somewhat helpless.

Mary showed a slight smile. "Over the last few months, tough times for all of us, Mr. Anderson has been studying the nuts and bolts of solar power. Yes, solar...." She paused. "He developed very interesting contacts. He's helping one of them locate a new operation in Ohio and Mr. Anderson wants it in Noredge. So do I."

Gasps spread through the crowd. Mary heard some handclapping.

"I hope you're not trying to bamboozle the good folks of Noredge, Miss Jenkins, with one of those pipedreams thought up by some pot-smoking guys in torn jeans."

Sanders turned to the audience, his face soliciting concurrence, but he quickly went back to Perkins. "Let's stay on the topics that matter."

Mary jumped in before Perkins could speak. "This technology delivers high-value jobs, in very high numbers, not just for out-of-towners, not temporary, not what we've seen in the last twelve months. Jobs that stay. And they'll get better as the technology advances. And advance it does, very rapidly. It's not a done deal but—"

"Talk is cheap, Miss Jenkins," Sanders scoffed. "Let's go back to where—"

"Mr. Anderson will have a share in the new company."

Applause erupted.

Mary put her hand up. "I'll have one too. Skin in the game. I'll—"

"You?" Sanders barked.

"Me. This woman." She tapped her chest.

"You'll be putting money—"

"Yes, sir. Me and Joe Bertolo."

"What money?" Sanders mocked.

Murmurs in the audience, then jeering.

Mary smiled. "I think you can figure that out for yourself, but I know what I'm saying. We'll have the money. The deal's not done yet, but we're very close. And the exact location in the city hasn't been chosen. Mr. Anderson, Frank Anderson, is working with the State and the investor, who doubles as technology provider. As mayor I will move heaven and earth to bring this new industry to our town."

She stood up and stretched her hands out to the crowd. "That's my promise!"

A standing ovation ensued. Whistles and wows. Lively discussions in the crowd.

Sanders shrugged. "And who's this beneficent Manitou, this genius with all the dough? We should at least know his name so we can thank him," he said, his tone dripping scorn.

"This gentleman wants to be unnamed for now, for good legal and tactical reasons, but he's an honorable person and firm in his commitment to Frank. And to me, along with Joe. We really hit it off."

"And we citizens have to take your word for it? What tune do you plan to sing once the election is over? That it all was a misunderstanding? That Mr. Unnamed has reneged on the deal? That you're very sorry? That the good folks here will unfortunately be stuck with you?" He gave Mary an angry stare and pointed at her. "That smooth-talking, empty-headed broad, that harebrain will get us all in trouble!" He shook his head, disgust all over his face. "You and your Mr. Unnamed," he sneered, waving it all off with his hand. "You're in over your head, girl."

Joe jumped up from his chair. "Sir," he said, his tone pure indignation, "I demand respect for my wife! She's—"

"Did you get married?"

Sanders's sarcasm didn't play well.

"She's my partner, sir," Joe asserted. "Let me tell you something straight: you don't like 'Unnamed'. Who does? I don't. Mary Jenkins will get you the name of that gentleman in due time. Soon. She's no idle talker. Neither is Mr. Anderson, who's doing this community a great service. Tell me, when my wife does deliver that name, will you then tell us *your* names, the names of the crooks who transferred their bribes into your bank accounts? The Doornaert and Supren bribes? I hate 'unnamed' too." He looked at Mary and sat down.

She flinched, taken aback. Then she smiled.

Frank grinned and patted Joe on the back.

Perkins sat open-mouthed.

Sanders, face crimson red, took off his mic and stormed off the stage.

Great speed for a potbelly. Mary chuckled.

The audience looked and sounded dumbfounded. Loud discussions ensued. Applause began to swell and rolled wave after wave through the crowd. Mary got another standing ovation. A long one this time.

***

On Tuesday, it didn't take long for the election officials to declare Mary Jenkins the new mayor of Noredge for the next four years. By nine she and Joe were back home, with Frank and Joanna.

"Dan Clark is on his way with Lydia," Joe advised.

The celebration was in full swing when Frank received a call. "From Bakersfield, California. Cisneros,' he said, looking at Mary. He clicked. "Alejandro? Good evening... yes, all good! Mary will be the new mayor! Let me switch to speakerphone. I have Joanna here, and Mary and Joe with the kids and some friends."

Sleep-starved Jimmy and Andy had their eyes wide open, looking impressed.

"Wow! Good! Hello my friends! Hello Mrs. Mayor! Congratulations! Great job all of you there," the Californian roared, his tone exuberant, his accent slight. "Let's forge ahead. Rosita and I look forward to seeing Noredge with our own eyes."

Joe winked at Joanna and Mary and raised his glass.

Frank's face radiated pride. "Yes. Welcome! We want to have you and the lovely Mrs. Cisneros here soon."

"Thank you!"

Mary moved closer to the phone. "Mr. Cisneros, Mary Jenkins speaking. I want to thank you so much."

"You're very welcome, Mayor Mary." The man laughed. "Congratulations again to...my newest partner, I hope!"

"Oh. Yes. Absolutely. I look forward to that. Joe sends his best."

"Thank you! Nice to get to know you, Joe. Partner. *Y Joanna? Qué tal mi amor?*"

"*Todo bien. Gracias, Alejandro.*"

Mary took over again. "Mr. Cisneros, do you know what they call you here?"

"Already? Something nice, I hope," he joked.

"Manitou!"

"Wow! Alejandro Manitou Cisneros! Rosita will like that!" he laughed.

"They mean it, sir. Noredge welcomes you!" She teared up and fell into Joe's arms.

Printed in the United States
By Bookmasters